White Sands, Black Heart

by Serenity McLean

COPYRIGHT

DOME TREE
Publishing

Published by Dome Tree Publishing

ISBN eBook: 978-1-989447-00-0

CHAPTER 1

"I must have a word with you."

Her heart seized. She heard this same thing a few months ago and it ripped her heart out. She heard it again a few weeks ago and what followed shattered her world. *What does life have its cadaverous hands on this time? What's left to take?*

"Yes Mr. Johnson. As soon as I'm finished with a couple of appointments."

Against her will the memory of the children's hospital pressed in. "Your son has a brain tumour." She took a breath and focused on her work.

When she finished with her clients she knocked on the salon's office door. She could smell stale coffee on Johnson's breath.

He said, "You must handle the manicurist appointments. I had to let her go." She'd heard this extra duties speech before.

Although she looked at him, thoughts of her daily struggle swirled in her head. That morning the empty half of the double bed held her blank attention for countless minutes. Skipping a shower, she picked up a pair of jeans and sweater from the floor then walked through the minefield of clothes to the hall.

The single closed door halted her progress down the dark hall. She rested her hand on the knob and wondered how people survived this kind of thing. Unable to resist, she looked in. Another empty bed – a little crib with a stuffed horse. Painful memories threatened.

She quietly pulled the door closed and continued to the kitchen.

Stopping at the fridge, she pulled the battered door open – a quart of milk, two brown bananas, and a bag of green fuzzy mush that was once beans. Thinking she could make a cup of tea she looked in the milk carton, but the rancid odour and lumpy liquid dissuaded her. She returned it to the fridge and closed the door.

Glancing at the retro sunburst clock – 20 minutes before she needed to catch the bus. She slumped down on a kitchen chair and stared at the floor – absent of feeling, absent of hope.

How much more will life dish out?

The sound of Mr. Johnson clearing his throat jolted her from her reverie as she refocused on the man sitting across from her – this man who had taken over the business while the owner recovered from surgery. "Good team players do all it takes for the success of the team."

I'm not a team player? What about the late nights? All the extra shifts? What about handling extra appointments when the new girl quit? What about washing the laundry when this man cancelled the service? He is a bully and will ruin the business before the owner returns.

She drew a deep breath. "Mr. Johnston, I am a team player. I think I've done plenty around here to prove that. But I'm a massage therapist. I know nothing about doing nails."

"You're a woman. You have nails. So what's the problem? You believe you're above this work? Let me pour you a tall glass of get over it."

You have nails too. How about you handle the appointments? "You can't keep pushing people out the door and expect me to pick up the slack."

He shook his head. "I fail to see what Kathleen sees in you. I'm really beginning to doubt her judgment. It's a good thing I'm here to clean up this mess." He sat back in his chair, full of arrogance. "Now, if you don't want this job –"

Looking down at her hands, she clenched her teeth and silently counted. *One, two, three...*

A dead husband. A dead child. A dead heart. And now a dead job. I don't think I can handle any more crap. I'm done. I no longer care. Karma or fate or whatever is in charge – you win. I give up.

She scraped her chair back and stood up. "I quit." She turned and walked away.

He yelled at her as she made her way through the salon. "When science discovers the centre of the universe, you will be disappointed to find you are not it."

Grabbing her purse and coat, she stepped out into the cold November rain. The door snapped shut behind her.

In the entry of her apartment she dropped her purse. She let her coat land on the floor in a damp heap. Slumped on the couch, the hours ticked by. Unaware of life slipping away she found herself in the dark when the phone rang. Ignoring the call she stood at the balcony window looking down on the street below.

What's the point in living? All life ended when little Lucas died. Cam is the lucky one. They thought he had a heart attack while driving, taking out both he and the truck driver. He left me to deal with all of this alone. I wonder if he couldn't handle it and ended it all.

Life sucks.

She looked at the traffic stopped at the intersection.

All those people with places to go and friends to meet – all the text messages making plans, all the busy bars. I'm no longer a part of this world. Oh Cam, where are you? Is your life better now? Do you miss me? What waits on the other side of death? How could you leave me? All of our plans now vapourized. This is so unfair.

She looked at the lights reflecting off the wet road then above the dark leafless branches into the black sky.

I was part of this busy world, but everything that meant anything got ripped away. All life violently sucked from my heart. Now I exist separate and distant. The inky cold of this dark sky is who I am.

She assessed her emotions thinking she should weep for her loss. She wept until a few weeks ago. But now she felt empty – empty and alone.

I need to focus on surviving one hour at a time.

The phone rang again.

She let her forehead rest on the cool glass of the slider. *Why couldn't I have been the one to die?*

The phone continued to ring.

Maybe I should answer it. I'm in just the right mood to tell Angeline to leave me alone. I'm not looking for a vacation right now. I'm not good company for anyone. I want the world to leave me alone.

In a terse tone she answered. "Hello Angeline."

"Hi Jenny Jaye. I finally got you. I tried earlier."

There's no point to dragging out this conversation. "Listen, if you are calling again about coming for a vacation, the answer is no."

"Hmm. Sounds like one of those days where everything went wrong. What's up?"

"I'm alone. Isn't that enough? But no, life decided that I should lose my job."

"Oh JJ. I'm sorry. But listen. I have a favour to ask. And maybe this is perfect timing. All your great ideas for the business were wasted on Johnston. So how about taking over the spa here? The gal managing it eloped and I need someone right away. You would be perfect. Besides, you need to get out of Dodge."

The corner of her mouth twitched at her friend's description of Sioux City.

"So? What do you think? Can you be here tomorrow?"

"I don't know."

"Oh come on. How many times have you complained about the snow? I worry about you up there alone. Just come down. You'll love the winter here." Angeline could hear JJ breathing. "I think you need to stop punishing yourself. It's time to heal."

"I don't think I'll ever get over this."

"So why not be miserable in sunshine and warmth? With all these happy vacationers I could really use you to balance things out."

A slight smile flickered.

"So you'll come? Like, tomorrow?"

After a long pause she said, "I doubt I can manage tomorrow."

"But you will come? You'll take this job? Oh JJ, what a relief that is. It'll be like college, only better. And the weather is way better. When can you get here?"

She sighed.

What's here for me? I doubt I could drum up any desire to find another job. And I'm miserable alone. "Okay. Give me a few days to sort things out."

"What's to sort? Throw your stuff in some suitcases, give your notice for the apartment and catch a flight. I can pick you up in Miami."

"It's at least three days driving time, and I must do something with the furniture in the apartment."

"Oh right. I guess you can't fly your car down. Okay, so one week from today?"

"I'll try."

"Great! We are coming into our busy season and the spa urgently needs a manager. Oh hang on." JJ's phone pinged with a new text. "I just sent you a picture I took today. The ocean was still and reflecting huge clouds. It's beautiful here. I know you'll love it."

She looked at the warm summer blues of sky and sea and thought about her minor in art. The professor wanted her to switch it to a major, but she stuck with business. "It is beautiful."

"More spectacular than the barren winter landscape up there. Bring your paints. I think you'll love the Keys."

It had been a long time since she'd painted – since she married. She sighed.

Ang is probably right. My healing won't be found in the dead of winter on the lifeless prairie. It's been too long without colour, without warm skies, and without the sound of waves rolling ashore. Maybe penetrating the blackness with tropical blues would bring relief.

Angeline snapped her out of her wandering thoughts. "Do you remember that quirky professor you loved, you know, the one that always dressed like that science fiction guy?"

She smiled. "Dr. Who?"

"Yeah, that's him. I think you'll find the locals here are just like him, either whimsical or plain offbeat. You'll fall in love with them all. There's one who wears a different pair of sneakers every day of the month. Another talks about his collection of palm trees like they're people, each named after someone famous."

JJ paced by the window. "Okay, okay. I'm coming."

When she hung up she said, "Whimsical." Rummaging through her closet, she pulled out a dusty sketchbook with curling corners and a box of watercolour pencils. She flipped through the pages, stopping at the first blank one and wrote down the date, her friend's name and the word whimsical. With quick strokes she rough-sketched the image that popped into her mind – a window full of multi-coloured, stained glass wind chimes – the first image in five years.

Colours. In a desolate life, whimsical is a window letting in the sunshine and bright colour. Whimsical lets in light? Where did that bizarre thought come from? I think I might be losing my mind here in Dodge.

Turning back one page she looked at the last sketch she drew a month after her wedding – a panoramic landscape of grey greens and yellows, a lonely section of the Camino trail, and the back of a young woman laden with the cares of the world walking alone towards the distant dark mountains and heavy grey sky. And written at the top was, "modern-day bindlestiff." She traced the trail as it disappeared into the cold heart of the mountains. An urge welled up to draw an alternate path leading away from the dark lands ahead. *Too late. I've travelled far into those forsaken depths and the burden is unbearable.* Her eyes searched for a passage out of the bleak, rocky prison.

She closed the book and rested her hand on the cover.

It's been a long time. Somewhere on that road I've lost much of me.

She hoped to find the way out of the abyss. But many wander the labyrinths of desolation never finding an escape.

CHAPTER 2

The dried patchwork of brown fields passed by as the packed Jeep rolled south to Kansas City, then east to St. Louis where she stopped for dinner. She planned on finding a motel, but decided to press on toward Nashville. About an hour out of St. Louis she took an exit south, but once on the road she realized it was not the right highway. She looked behind in her rearview mirror. With no cars on the desolate road she pulled onto the shoulder. Flipping on the interior light she looked ahead at the highway sign and glanced down at the map.

A knock on the window startled her. A man stood beside the car. She glanced in her rearview mirror to see a car behind her. She hadn't noticed the bright headlights pull in behind her. Nervous, she dropped the window only an inch.

He stood back a few feet from the car and smiled at her.

Yeah, I'm not fooled by your harmless-grandpa-in-overalls look. You won't be using my skin for some party dress.

He said, "Do you need help?"

"Oh it's okay. I'm just checking the map."

He looked up and down the road. "You've taken the wrong exit. You need to get back on the highway and head east another 10 or 15 miles to Interstate 57. That will take you Interstate 24 which goes to Nashville. This is highway 51."

"Oh okay. Thanks. I guess I saw the exit sign and thought this was right."

"Turn around and take the first ramp to the interstate and you'll be on your way."

She glanced in the direction he pointed and nodded. He tipped his baseball cap and headed back to his car. She immediately noted her mistake on the map. She glanced in her rearview mirror to give the man a wave before he pulled out, but the car was no longer behind her. Nothing passed by and she couldn't see any tail lights in her mirror. She spun around. There were no vehicles in sight – not ahead, not behind, not on the ramp, nowhere.

Her brows knit. He'd been at her window only seconds ago. Then she realized *he knew where she was going.* She didn't tell him, he just knew. She paled. Something quite unusual just happened. Looking around again, she remained alone on the road.

He appeared out of nowhere. He knew I'm on the wrong road. And he disappeared without a trace. Oh God, did you just send me an angel?

She blew out a deep breath, put the Jeep in gear and headed back onto the interstate as the man, or rather angel, instructed. Her adrenaline kept her going to Nashville where she found a motel with a vacancy.

The next day she enjoyed the green trees along the gentle rolling highway toward Atlanta. She shed her winter coat, tossing it in the back. It felt a relief to leave behind the cold bleak winter of Iowa. She stopped overnight in Gainesville, glad to be in Florida on her second day.

She walked to a nearby upscale restaurant and the waitress seated her in a four-person booth, lighting the candle as she settled in. The hostess showed a man, his wife, nanny and infant in a carrier to a six-seat booth, but the woman demanded the four-seat one behind JJ. The waitress suggested placing the baby carrier on a chair, but the woman insisted the floor would be better. They argued over the hazards of leaving the baby on the floor in the aisle. They settled on squeezing the carrier in beside the nanny.

A few minutes later the husband ordered a pitcher of beer. After the waitress left, the woman raised her voice to accuse him of flirting. She dumped her glass of water on him, some of it striking JJ on the back. She turned to complain, but the couple were in a heated argument so she moved to the other side of her booth.

Now with a clear view, she couldn't take her eyes off the live reality show. It quietened down for a few minutes then escalated. The woman was spitting angry about something that occurred earlier. Amidst wild gesturing, she tried to make her point. The man laughed, setting off a hysterical tirade.

JJ smelled a sharp odour of acrid smoke and looked around to trace the source. She spotted the telltale vapour rising from the woman's hair. *That silly woman set herself on fire!* JJ stood up to alert the woman. Before she could say anything, the man threw his glass of water at his wife, leaving her sputtering.

This is like Big Kahuna's Water Adventure.

JJ noticed the woman lost a couple of inches of hair on the one side.

The woman stormed out, followed by the nanny carrying the baby and chuckling man. The entire restaurant cheered.

JJ sat back down.

Well now. I've never seen such a lively floor show in Sioux City. An angel yesterday, a woman lighting her hair on fire today – I can't imagine what tomorrow will bring.

She smiled then furrowed her brows. She swallowed hard then looked out the window at nothing. Tears rimmed her eyes, one escaping down her cheek. Muttering, she grabbed a napkin and wiped it and the brimming moisture from her eyes.

Oh blackness, you wait for the first sign of life then roll in like an invasion force. You overwhelm. You crush and consume until there's nothing left.

On the third day, she drove across the everglades without event. She stopped for gas on the outskirts of Miami. While setting up the pump, a taxi pulled up to the station and a middle-aged woman with flaming orange hair, neon-green lipstick, an all-pink outfit, sparkly purple gel flats and a blue and yellow striped bag got out. It was hard not to notice the vibrant clashing ensemble. The rainbow woman opened the door to the convenience store, then paused, shouting at the cabbie, "I will be right back. Now, don't you go anywhere."

JJ muttered, "These are the slowest pumps in the world."

A minute later Rainbow came out of the store with a package of Twinkies. Smiling, she opened one and glanced at the people pumping gas. Clutching the dessert like a microphone she walked up to JJ.

Not knowing what Rainbow wanted, JJ smiled at her then focused her attention on the pump.

In a deep, gravelly voice Rainbow said, "Oh honey, you have no idea, do you?"

"What?"

Rainbow dropped her bag, cleared her throat and sang *Leaving on a Jet Plane.* Launching on too high a note she had to restart. JJ glanced around to confirm, *Yup everyone in a three-block radius was staring.* She nodded to Rainbow and tried to stop her by thanking her. Undeterred, the woman continued to the end. Feeling the final chorus needed a little extra pizzazz, with surprising agility, Rainbow hopped up on the concrete stand at the end of the pump island and leaned back like she was on a grand piano. She held the last note for what seemed like minutes. When she finished, everyone applauded.

She jumped down and bowed. After acknowledging her fans she approached JJ, flipped her hair back and said, "I'm flying to Spain today. When I came out and saw the taxi waiting I couldn't help myself." She produced a business card and handed it to JJ. "I do a regular show at the Palace. Come and see me sometime."

She walked back to the taxi with a wiggle that would shame Mae West, and ate the Twinkie.

JJ looked at the card. "Peaches N. Sunshine, drag queen artist." She looked at Peaches pulling away in the cab.

I think Peaches can count as my weird incident of the day. It's kind of going downhill from the angel on the road. But the rest of the day should be uneventful.

She tucked the card in her pocket.

Ang is not going to believe this story without proof.

Five minutes south of Homestead she got her first whiff of salt water. She opened her window and drew in several deep breaths. The first glimpse of water came at the marina on the edge of the mainland. On the bridge to Cross Key, the first of the islands, a small sign announced she was now on the scenic Overseas Highway. With little fanfare, she left the continent behind.

She pulled off to the white sand shoulder, walked down to the water's edge and let her hands glide through the warm channel water. A large yacht navigated the waterway. With a lull in traffic the sweet notes of a songbird danced on the air. On a branch outstretched over the water a colourful painted bunting sang his song one final time then flew off into the scrub.

The sunshine and tropical colours around her pressed on the black heaviness of loss that clung to her. A shiver ran down her back. Sensing one of her picture ideas was about to take birth, she grabbed her sketchbook and returned to the water's edge. Lost in thought she wrote, *bridge from desolate*.

Looking across to the mainland, she scanned the horizon and above. A few fluffy clouds scattered across the big blue sky. While enjoying the lightness of the day her mind envisioned black ominous clouds filling the sky over the mainland. She still saw the blue sky, but she also saw the menacing storm overlaid. It was like a double exposure. With her visions, she could choose to focus on the image or reality, both in equal detail. She closed her eyes and still saw the tumultuous sky. But to study the detail of her mental picture she opened her eyes.

While looking at the envisioned dark clouds, a bird burst out of the tempest then froze in place. Interested by the particularly detailed vision, she ran her eyes over the bird, studying the feathers and form. She sketched dark ominous clouds filling much of the page and the bird flying out of the mist. Using several grey watercolour pencils, she painted the clouds, allowing its darkness to flow into the bird's tail. Although the back end of the bird was caught in the muted grey of the storm, sunlight lit up the rest of the bird.

Replicating what she saw, she chose several rich deep reds to fill in the back. The red blended into a mid blue for the belly then morphed into an iridescent green chest. Increased sunlight on the head brought out lighter, brighter colours. From the cooler colours of the chest and belly, sunshine orange tinted the neck and shoulders. The fullness of light flushed the head with a lemon yellow. As with many birds, midnight black formed a long band around the eyes and spilled onto the beak.

There's something about those colours – some deeper meaning. She furrowed her brows.

There's something about storm over the mainland and the bird flying out of the colourless maelstrom and into vivid light. I think this contains a significant message.

She let out a long breath. "I don't know what it all means, but I think you represent me. You are one colourful bird aren't you? I don't think I'm a colourful person. Actually, I'm mostly black inside." She stroked the bird's head. "Dear me. Find your way back into the light. Maybe the mainland won't be the only thing I escape."

Touching the clouds, she thought of the Camino Trail Mountains.

"My Abyss. You have me firmly in your grip. But maybe there's a way out. Maybe in time, maybe in this land of white sand I can free myself from your bleak mountains.

"Is it as simple as flying out of the desolation? Is that the hidden escape I've been looking for?"

CHAPTER 3

Plantation House Resort spanned the entire west point of Pirate's Cove Drive on Stirrup Key, a little isle off the north side of Marathon. The resort's impressive entry spoke of understated luxury. Impressed that her friend rose to manager of such an upscale hotel, she briefly wondered if she had the skill and experience for this job.

While Angeline talked with a guest she wandered the massive concourse lined in dark wood and filled with tropical plants and fountains. When the guest left, Angeline hurried to her friend with as much decorum as her excitement allowed.

"Jennifer Jaye! It's so good to see you. How was the drive down? Would you like a glass of iced tea or something? I've cleared my schedule for the rest of the day so I can show you around."

JJ smiled. "Good to see you too. Interesting. And yes, please."

Ang paused a moment to match up JJ's answers with her questions, then said, "Let's go to the outdoor lounge and you can tell me about the interesting bits."

After hearing about the spontaneous gas station concert, Ang thought JJ should frame Peaches' card as a memento. They chatted for half an hour before Angeline took her to the spa at the north end of the resort. They toured the facilities both indoor and outdoor, the hot tubs and saunas.

JJ said, "It's quite extensive – not like the ones in Sioux City. This is beautiful. I'll enjoy working while listening to the ocean." She turned to her friend. "Maybe you are right. Maybe I'll find healing here." She looked out into the distance. "I think I've lost me. I feel hollow, like all that makes me who I am was scraped out and thrown away. It's black inside. Grief leaves me a poor friend, but I'm glad I came. And I'm grateful for the job. Thank you."

"You've been through a lot, but you still have all your smarts and skills. You're perfect for the position. The owner is looking for us to expand the business and I know you will have lots of great ideas. It's amazing how island life restores people."

Angeline showed her around the rest of the facilities – the pools, multiple long docks for boats to tie up, a long palm-lined beach filled with lounge chairs, and a line up of barbecue grills. Ang said, "Every Thursday evening we have a beach barbecue for the guests."

Inside the main building were a coffee shop and a long restaurant with a spectacular view of the ocean. There were two floors of guest rooms above in the main building, then a long line of guesthouses, with up to six units in each.

They spent a couple hours setting JJ up then Ang left her to familiarize herself with the spa operations.

By seven p.m. many of the staff gathered around the outdoor lounge to celebrate the lounge barman's birthday. He was a classic Greek with a smile that left a trail of broken hearts. JJ wished him a happy birthday. In a rich accent he said, "It is made happier with you. Welcome to the Plantation." He held her hand and bowed.

She laughed. "I can see why they keep you around. You're a charmer. Thank you for a warm welcome, Nicolas."

"My good friends call me Nic. You call me Nic, yes?"

She laughed. "Yes." *My first new friend here and he's a Greek god of intoxicating words.*

As an annual toast to a successful winter season, the bartenders brought out champagne and stood among the crowd to open them. One of the young bartenders struggled to remove the cork. Finally it rocketed out hitting JJ in the neck. She lurched back in surprise, propelling the man behind her backwards. In a desperate attempt to get his footing, his flailing arm smashed one of the therapists in the face shattering her glasses.

She spun around hitting her head on the post of the bar and knocked herself unconscious.

The ambulance attendants insisted that JJ go to the hospital along with the injured woman. After being checked for a blood clot and released, she stopped to examine herself in the bathroom mirror.

Fantastic. My first night with my new colleagues and I'm involved in an incident with a champagne cork. Well why not? It seems my life is on a trend of weird encounters. I think getting a hickey from a champagne cork qualifies. Today is a twofer. For decades they'll talk about the day of Peaches and the cork.

Ang drove her home, settled her friend in her spare room and reminded her she could stay as long as she wanted. JJ crawled into bed grateful to be with someone who cared. She thought about the evening with the warm friendly staff and realized how lonely her life had become. In the dark, on her side clutching the pillow she thought about her life.

Foolishly I thought it couldn't happen twice in one lifetime and I took a chance. Yet again, here I am engulfed by this darkness of loss – this void of loneliness unconstrained by time and stretching beyond comprehension. I hate that it rolls in over and over again. It constricts until you are empty of hope. This time I'm also empty of myself, like tube of toothpaste, squeezed out and discarded. Grief stealthily encircles and crushes until nothing remains. Yes, the grief anaconda coils around and around. It extinguishes all life within and without.

If I'm honest, my life had become – narrow – shallow – a small footprint. I gave up my friends, my painting, my passions and dreams to marry and move to a place I didn't like. Sure, I loved Cam, and I loved little Lucas, but they were all I had in life. And now they're gone. And so am I. The abyss finally swallowed me, engulfed me. There is nothing left. How many times can a person survive this dark place?

Without a moon, the darkness cloaked a stranger outside her window – a brewing malicious intent studied her.

CHAPTER 4

On her lunch break from a morning of appointments, she found packing slips from a morning delivery and a beautifully wrapped gift on her desk. Ignoring the gift she took the papers to the stockroom and unpacked the delivery, discovering several discrepancies. She checked her watch and headed to her office to call the supplier.

A 12-year-old girl appeared at the door behind her. "Hi. Are you the new manager?"

JJ looked up and smiled at the beautiful girl. She always had a weakness for African American girls with a wide white smile and wonderfully curly hair. "Yes I am. My name is JJ. What's yours?"

"Most people call me Pen."

"Well, hello Pen. Is that short for Penelope?"

She shook her head. "No." She eased into the office. "Is your name really just two letters?"

She motioned for the girl to sit down and offered her a candy from the well-stocked bowl she found on her desk. Pen, already familiar with the candy options, fingered the candies until she found the kind she liked.

"My name is Jennifer Jaye, but all my friends call me JJ. So you can call me that too. Are you a guest here?"

"No. My mom lives in town. Karen – that was the lady here before you – she used to let me hang out with her. Sometimes she gave me work too. Maybe I could work for you too?"

"What did you do?"

"Well, Karen would pay me to come after school and clean up the treatment rooms – like gather up the dirty towels and stuff for the laundry and take them down to Miss Eulah. And I sometimes bus the tables."

"What's your last name, Pen?"

"Noble."

She nodded and picked up the phone. "Hi Ang. Tell me about Pen Noble. Does she work for us?"

"Yes. Karen took a real shine to her and we pay her for two or three hours of work after school. She's a very hard worker. Anything you need done, she's your gal."

"Okay, thanks."

"So you work after school?"

With a bright smile Pen said, "Yes, ma'am."

JJ motioned to the door. "How about you show me all that you do."

She and Pen rolled the linen carts to the laundry facilities, the territory of Eulah, an older African American woman. Eulah greeted the young girl with a warm hug. "Pearl! Where you been girl? I haven't seen you in three days."

"Been busy at home. I wondered if I still had a job after Karen left."

"My little chickadee, you're employed here now. It doesn't matter if one boss leaves and another comes."

JJ watched as the young girl helped sort the dirty linens for the old woman. The blackness threatened. She felt the cold grip of loneliness squeeze her heart. She let out a quiet sigh, trying to push back on the darkness.

With hands on her hips Eulah said, "Now what do you need? Sheets? Towels?"

Pen glanced back at JJ, then pointed at the various stacks and put in her order. "I can take what you have ready and if it's not folded or rolled, I can do that."

Eulah collected, JJ stacked the cart and Pen folded. As they rolled back to the spa JJ asked, "How did you know what we needed?"

"I saw the schedule and who's working. Some therapists use a lot of towels and stuff and others use not as many." She shrugged her narrow shoulders. "I don't know how I know. I just know."

JJ noted the time and excused herself for another appointment.

Finally when able to return to her office, Pen dropped in. "Miss JJ?"

"Hi Pen."

"I've stocked all the linens and cleaned all the rooms. I can't come in tomorrow. Momma says we have to go to Miami and visit my uncle. But I can come in Saturday morning."

"Okay. Thanks for telling me. I'll see you Saturday."

Pen stood by her desk looking at the candy dish.

JJ smiled. "You want another one?" Pen replied with a big smile. "Help yourself then."

While Pen fished out the one she wanted she said "Um, the azure room supply cupboard is low on aromatics and I took the last from the stock room. Karen said they were the items missing on the previous order."

"Okay. Thanks Pen. Just for that, take another red one." Pen took a third candy, smiled and left. She watched the young girl disappear.

Her heart squeezed. She shook her head.

She sighed at the thought of Pen's endearing smile. She stood up and watched a couple holding hands and walking along the shallow surf on the beach.

Why did I lose everyone – again? Why me? Why can't I live a normal life? Is there a target on me that says, sure take everything. My life is like a bowling alley. I get all the pins of life set up, friends, family then along comes fate and knocks it all down. I've had so many strikes, I just don't want to bother setting up again. What's the point? That big old 14-pound black ball will come rolling down the alley and knock it all over again.

Everything that means anything is gone. No one else loses everything over and over again. Nope. Just me. Everywhere I look I see people, whole people, people surrounded by friends, family and dreams. But not me – I am extra special. I'm without hope, and I doubt I can love anyone ever again.

The turmoil of anger and fear wrestling with her true nature left no clear winner. She sat back down, looked in the bowl and sighed.

I'd better keep this well stocked – with red ones.

She picked up the gift left on her desk, turning it over to look for a card or tag, but found nothing. Inside she found an empty clear plastic ball. The packaging described it as nothing, absolutely nothing, noting that nothing is precious, simple and sacred. And it promised an enthralling experience when she opens it up and nothing happens.

I best remove the packaging later. After the cork hickey, I don't know if I'm ready for enthralling. Day four and strange comes for another visit. Who would give me this? Is this some kind of beatnik islander thing? Here newbie, have a great big ball of nothing. She turned it over a couple of times. I don't know about precious or sacred, but it's right about one thing – nothing is simple.

In the parking lot the driver of an old Land Rover stared at the resort. "It's time. It is finally time." A giddy laugh erupted then faded. "Ah, but you must learn a few things first."

CHAPTER 5

The jingle of the bell announced her entry into the cool of the store. Her eyes took a moment to adjust from the bright morning sunshine reflecting off white sand. She picked out staples from the small grocery mart.

A man stood talking to the grey-haired cashier. He wore his sunglasses hooked on the neck of his shirt, a black coral necklace, several leather and metal bracelets, windblown sandy brown hair with sun bleached highlights, and a day's growth with a little grey mixed in. JJ thought he looked like ocean mingled with wind.

He stepped aside to let her check out. In a deep, mellow voice with a hint of a southern drawl he said, "You wouldn't be the new spa manager at the Plantation House?"

"Yes, I am."

"Angeline mentioned you were coming – from Iowa, I think she said."

She nodded.

"How do you like island life?"

She thought for a moment. "There are better colours here."

He tilted his head and looked at her more closely. "That's an unusual answer."

She smiled. "I used to paint a lot a few years ago – before I moved to Iowa. The vivid colours are more inspiring than the browns of the prairies."

"So you're an artist. Well you'll love this place. Almost everyone who lives here pursues their creative side."

Angeline's total lack of artistic ability sprang to mind. She smiled. "So what is your artistic specialty?"

"I dabble in photography and pottery."

The cashier cleared her throat. "He doesn't *dabble* in photography. He's a National Geographic photographer."

Intrigued, JJ turned to the man with more than his fair share of dashing.

National Geographic? When other girls talked of becoming a nurse, I wanted to be a National Geographic photographer. And now I meet someone living my childhood dream?

Without thinking she said, "I'd be interested in seeing your work. Do you have a gallery?"

"There's a workshop where I and my guests work on our clay creations. I have several items for sale there. It's a gallery of sorts. I don't have a photography gallery, but I have several photographs around my house. You are welcome to look."

Before it occurred to her to think it might be creepy to wander a stranger's house, the cashier said, "Don't let Jason put you off. His house is a stunning gallery. There are beautiful images and collectibles from all over the world – including several great photos from around the keys. You should go see them."

He handed her a card. "If you're interested, here's my address and contact information. There's pottery classes on Wednesdays. You're welcome to join us."

She took his card and tucked it into her cutoffs pocket – same place as Peach's card. "Thanks. I'll think about the class."

He smiled, interpreting her coolness as a little too much mainlander, and expected it would wear off in time.

She thanked the cashier, took her groceries and said, "Nice to meet you, Jason."

"I didn't catch your name."

"Everyone calls me JJ."

He offered her his hand. "JJ. I'm sure we'll run into each other again. It's a small island."

"I'm sure we will."

She started her Jeep as Jason left the store. He waved to her and continued on his way. She surreptitiously watched him. *Jason, National Geographic world- travelling man of wind, ocean and freedom.* She thought about all the NatGeo magazines she bought in Sioux City as an escape from the lonely prairies.

I wonder if I've seen any of his photos.

She stopped at the post office to pick up a package. She looked at the return address. It was from Big Pine Key. Her eyebrows furrowed. She shrugged and tossed it on the seat beside her.

She spent her first day off in the warm sunshine at a local's beach. It felt good to let the sun warm her bones. She wandered the shallows, watching the lines of light ebb and flow across the sandy bottom. The tide caused the sand to form in ripples. She studied the light and shadow colours of sand and the rippling dancing lines of sunlight playing over the sand ridges. Their mesmerizing motion intrigued her. She tried to capture their elusive movement in her mind.

As the sun dipped low in the sky she walked back to her Jeep. A bench overlooking the beach invited her to stop and watch the blue sky morph into reds and oranges. A few minutes later an older African American man with pure white hair and a face etched in character lines asked if he could join her. He sat resting both hands on his cane and scanned the horizon. "Looks like a beauty tonight."

She looked at him and nodded.

"My Esmeralda loved a good sunset. We'd come and sit right here almost every night to watch the sun leave her stage, letting the moon have a moment of glory. Then we'd walk along the beach and Esme would laugh at the way the moon wake followed her."

A wonderful image popped into her mind. She looked down at the beach, the vision overlaid reality.

He sat for a moment. "It's been six months since cancer stole her life. I still try to come and watch the sun disappear. But I don't like sitting here alone." He looked at her. "Thank you for letting me enjoy this celestial spectacle with you."

She looked out to sea. "I lost my baby boy to cancer a few months ago and my husband to a heart attack."

"Oh I'm sorry. Then you know the sweet reprieve of sharing

this moment with a fellow traveller."

"I'm JJ." She offered her hand.

"Nice to meet you JJ. I'm Jedediah Carter."

Together they watched the day pass into night.

When she stood up to leave she said, "Thank you for telling me about your wife."

He nodded. "I hope to meet you here again. It's been good to have a sunset friend again."

"I'll be back Jedediah. Goodnight."

"Goodnight JJ."

That evening she took out her sketchbook and wrote, "Moon wake. Jedediah and Esmeralda Carter." She sketched a beautiful young African American woman dancing on the beach under moonlight with sparkling diamonds of reflection riding the gentle waves following her like a spotlight.

Moon wake.

She turned back a page and pondered.

It's been so long since I've had an artistic vision and now I've seen three since deciding to come here. Maybe this is a place of inspiration.

Flipping to the next page, her pencil poised with an idea for another sketch. She thought a long moment then closed her book.

It's not your time yet, ocean and wind man.

Before she turned out the light, she remembered the package left unopened in the Jeep. She dashed out in her night T-shirt relying on the cloak of darkness to prevent her from being seen. Sitting cross-legged on her bed, she ripped the brown paper wrapping off the box. Inside she found an old stuffed pink bunny, a photo of a young girl and a baby, and an newspaper clipping about a fire in a family home killing both parents. They were survived by their two daughters, one seven years old, and the other an infant.

Confused, she looked at the address again.

I know no one on Big Pine Key. And why send me these items?

She studied the photo taken on the front porch of a house.

She didn't recognize the house or the kids. The young girl's clothes suggested early 90s. She reread the newspaper article. The couple were Brande and Robbie Bodine. She looked out the window into the darkness trying to recall anyone by that name, but drew a blank. She read on. The authorities suspected arson.

She picked up the teddy. It was a cute little pink bunny with long floppy ears, one crusty and damaged. The eyes, nose and mouth were stitched thread, with one eye unravelling. She examined it for a tag to show where it was from, but found nothing.

She looked in the box for a letter or something to explain the strange collection. Nothing explained these items or why someone would send it to her. She looked at the return address. There was no name, just a post office box number.

Unable to figure it out, she put them all back in the box and left it on her dresser.

But some things cannot be ignored. Once exposed, they must reach their inevitable conclusion.

When JJ's bedroom light went out, a shadow headed for a mustard yellow Land Rover. "You almost forgot about my gift. Sweet dreams."

CHAPTER 6

Her phone rang interrupting her work on the budget for the next month.

"JJ? It's Olivia on the front desk. Mr. Ryan Miller is here to see you."

She heard a man speaking to Olivia. "He says he doesn't have an appointment, but hopes you can make time to see him. He's with –" She could hear more talking. "Green Earth Biologicals."

"Okay. Would you mind directing him to the outdoor lounge? I'll be out in a few minutes. Thanks Olivia."

He was easy to spot among the sea of bathing suits. She offered her hand. "Mr. Miller?"

"Yes. Thank you for seeing me. Call me Ryan please."

"Okay, Ryan. I'm going to get an iced tea. Can I get you something?"

"The same would be great, thank you."

At the bar she ordered their drinks. As he placed them on the counter Nic winked. "I added a squeeze of lime to yours. You are the pink umbrella one."

"Why are you not married?"

"I'm waiting for you, beautiful lady JJ."

"You're blowing some sunshine there, but I love you anyway."

He grinned.

She returned to the table with the drinks. Ryan stood to hold the chair for her.

"You're with Green Earth Biologicals?"

"Yes. I'm a managing partner." He handed her his card. "You spoke with my partner late last week about getting information on our products." She nodded. "I work out of Miami and thought rather than calling, I'd pop down to meet you and give you some samples."

Somehow he made a well-rehearsed sales pitch sound authentic. He had a charming sense of humour and she enjoyed their conversation. Their products had a solid reputation, so she didn't need the sales pitch, but she enjoyed his banter so let him go through the entire spiel.

When they finished their business, she walked him to the front lobby. "Thank you for coming by. I'll email our order by end of day."

He held her hand a little longer than is customary in business. "I've enjoyed meeting you JJ. Thank you for your business. On a more personal note, could I take you out for dinner sometime?"

Dinner? No, no, no. I was not expecting this. I can't. I just – I'm so not ready for getting tangled up with anyone. I can barely live with myself.

She extracted her hand and drew in a breath. "I've been through some difficult things and I'm not dating right now. But thank you."

"No pressure. Just dinner and a few laughs." He looked at her resolute expression. "How about I ask again next month?"

"You can ask, but really I need – I'm just not dating."

"Fair enough. But I'm not easily discouraged."

"Goodbye, Ryan."

He laughed. "Goodbye, JJ."

For lunch, she picked up a sandwich from the bar. Looking for time alone, she wandered down the beach to a quiet bench she'd seen earlier. She felt a twinge of disappointment to see Eulah already there. "May I join you?"

The older woman smiled, nodded, and said, "Please," indicating the other half of the bench seat.

"How are you today, Eulah?"

Rheumy eyes glanced across the endless ocean and sky. "The good Lord has seen fit to put me in paradise, and it's a beautiful day. I couldn't be better. And you? How are you enjoying your new job?"

She thought for a moment – of the obnoxious man she worked for in Sioux City, of the cold, brown prairies, of the Key's bright colours, warm sand and water, and of the welcome party. "It's the best job I've had and I like the people who work here. It's a good place."

JJ unwrapped her sandwich and took a few bites. Eulah nodded and made a little humming noise. "Tell me, what is Iowa like?"

"Hmm. If you like it here – the warmth, the blues and greens, the ocean, you wouldn't like Sioux City, I think. It's a dusty, flat, brown, agriculture town."

"It doesn't sound like you were too happy there."

"No."

Eulah waited.

JJ sighed. "I was married and we had a little boy, Lucas. He became very sick. The doctors found advanced brain cancer. There was nothing they could do. He drew his last breath in my arms. Then my husband died in a car accident – they think he had a heart attack. Happiness left me long ago. So no, I was not happy there."

"And Angeline offered you this job."

"Yes."

"Do you believe in God?"

She shrugged. "I did once. But why would a loving God continually take people before their time? I want nothing to do with that kind of God."

"Mmm hmm. That's an overwhelming amount of loss. Yes, a lot of loss. And the pain is still fresh, isn't my dear?"

She nodded, feeling the heat of anger at the injustice of her losses. They sat quietly for several minutes.

The old woman shook her head. "My, my, my." She laughed, patted her leg twice and said, "Yes, I understand."

"Are you talking to me?"

"I was just asking God about you and all you have lost. He

answered me."

She hardly knew how to respond.

Is Eulah one of those crazy women you read about? She seems so sweet and kind. Maybe she's just a harmless nutter and the Plantation House keeps her around as a character. Is this going to be my weird encounter of the day? Oh great. Now I'm expecting weird visitations.

"Can't you see how blessed you are?"

Blessed? Is she kidding?

"Blessed is not the word that comes to mind, no."

"Oh child. You are one blessed woman. One of the most blessed I've ever met."

"I don't mean to contradict you, but for me blessings are about as rare as an everyone-wins lottery."

"You're looking with the wrong eyes, child."

The wrong eyes? What is she talking about? Can she really hear from God? "What do you mean?"

"You are a chosen one. You must be one strong woman for God to set you on this journey. Oh yes, you have a remarkable destiny ahead for you."

"God just said this to you? About me?" *I think He's confused and talking about the wrong person – or she's confused. Somebody's got it wrong.*

"God is a giver. This fallen world takes from us, not God. But He will turn the sorrows of this world into a bright future. With the world stealing so much from you, the Lord will turn it around to something amazing. That is my God – and your God too, I think."

JJ shook her head. "No. There's death everywhere – cancer, deadly viruses, murderers, animals that rip each other to shreds and eat them, there's tsunamis that wipe out thousands of people, wars and fires that destroy peoples' lives. If God is in charge, if God is the creator, then He stinks at it. This is a horrible world He made. You can keep your God. I want nothing to do with Him." She set her sandwich aside.

"Oh honey, this is not the world God created. God placed

Adam and Eve in the garden. He looked over His creation and said it was very good. There was no death or sickness. But there was a tree of the knowledge of good and evil. God warned them not to eat of that fruit as their disobedience would open the door for evil to invade this world, and it would open their eyes to the concepts of good and evil. No, when Adam and Eve sinned, they turned the keys for this world over to Satan and along with Satan came two nasty characters, death and the grave. This fallen world results from mankind's sin, not God's creation."

"But then why doesn't He stop Satan? Why let this evil go on? Why allow cancer to take an innocent baby boy? Why a constant stream of death in my life?"

"As soon as they sinned, God told Adam and Eve He would provide a redeemer who would crush Satan. His name is Jesus Christ. God squeezed Himself into a little baby who gave His life, and shed His blood, to save all of creation. Why did it take 4000 years for that part of His plan? Who can know and understand an infinite God? But He came, and He provides a way to lift us out of this sin-infested world.

"You ask why God lets evil go on? He is God. He has His reasons. I think He wants many, many people to join Him in eternity, so He's allowing this fallen world to carry on a little longer to bring in more people to His kingdom. Jesus said it's like growing a garden. He planted the most glorious flowers you can imagine, but there are vile weeds springing up everywhere. And they cling to the good plants, choking them and pulling them down. But if the gardener pulled out all the weeds, it would uproot the good plants and they wouldn't bloom and produce seeds for more flowers. I think God wants heaven filled with these exquisite flowers and is using the weeds to build character in each of us for now.

"That doesn't mean He isn't in control of the garden. Never get the idea He's not in control. He is so big and so powerful that He uses the weeds to build strength and character in the flowers. Each flower is unique in its beauty because of the weeds.

"And when a Christian dies, they are in a far better place. Heaven is so wonderful. Their happiness is greater than we can imagine, and they wouldn't choose this fallen world if given the chance to return. You can cry for the hole in your heart, but in time God will mend it and fill it again with His goodness.

"I don't know about that. It's a monstrous hole and I see no sign of it getting any better. But there's every indication that my life will continue in death's black vortex. I'm still not seeing a good God in this. Why take my family and leave me here alone again? It's not fair."

Eulah thought for a moment. "Mmm hmm. Yes." she drew in a breath. "I have a friend, Jason. And he makes pottery things."

Crazy how everyone knows everyone here. "I've met Jason."

"Now he's one of the good ones. Imagine all Jason crafted was small little vases – hundreds, thousands even. After awhile, the vases complain. Some desire to be tall, others round, and still others long to be flat. In unison they say, 'It's not fair.' But what is fair? He is the potter, and he creates what he wants, not what the clay wants. Now let's say when he's finished making all those little vases, he puts them through the kiln to dry, paints each one in beautiful vivid designs and fills them with the sweetest fragrances ever. When the vases see their destiny, they no longer complain of neither of the heat nor of the fairness.

"When you see your destiny and all that God has for you, you will not think it unfair."

"So I have to accept whatever comes my way. I have no say in the matter? And you call this fair?"

"You have a choice."

She stared at Eulah. "What choice? My family – *all my family* is dead and gone."

"Your response to the weeds pulling you down is the choice you have. You can choose to live and stand tall, or you can let those weeds choke the life out of you. Choose life."

"But how do I *choose life*? From where I'm standing, death is all around me. I didn't choose it. But it's here anyway."

"When I look at you and your life, I see the fingerprints of

God on you. He sees something of great value in you. And He knows the bloom you will become if you walk with Him. He will give you the strength you need to walk through this difficult time. He will mend your broken heart. You just need to ask Him to walk with you."

"I don't think you or God have any idea how hard it is to loose everything that meant anything."

"God knows the dear cost to you. Now when I look ahead for you I can see what God is doing. Your life feels empty, but He turns circumstances around despite the destructive forces of this world. He will fill your life with things your eyes have never seen, your ears have never heard, nor has your glorious future entered your heart as a possibility. He knows the deep desires of your heart because He planted them there. So He wants to bring those to fulfilment in your life in a way bigger than you can imagine. God says He will provide an abundant life for those who love Him. He loves you, JJ. And He offers an abundant life to you."

JJ stood up. "Thank you, Eulah. I appreciate you sharing your thoughts on God. Really I do, but I don't know if I buy it. While I like the thought there's hope ahead, considering I'm in the blackest of places. I don't see it the way you do. Have a good afternoon."

"Remember little lotus, you are the bud of a beautiful flower of God emerging from murky depths to rise above the bog. You carry in you the promise of a most glorious bloom. And yet you are a bud underwater. Don't let the weeds keep you down."

She looked out to the horizon, blinked back the hot stinging tears and returned to her office.

The ball of nothing, the weird package, pretty boy Ryan and crazy Eulah – these strange encounters danced on the periphery of her mind.

I'm a weirdness magnet. I walk out the door and whoosh, bang – anyone with an idiosyncrasy comes flying toward me.

She felt irritable all afternoon. Before heading home she

took a walk along the beach to work off some of the negative energy. The beach gave way to the tangled roots of a mangrove thicket. The trees pushed her journey into the shallow waters as she followed the edge of the forest.

I'm a lotus flower bud? And God didn't send death into my life, but He's using it to strengthen me? What if I don't want to become this strong person God has in mind? No one asked me if this is what I want. What good can come of two deaths? Scratch that. Six if you count the dog. It's too much to expect of me to stand tall amid a shattered life – again.

She heard something drop in the water and spun to check it out. "I can see the headlines now. Leftovers of a woman found beside a belching gator." She looked under the branches and spotted a rotting canoe. Hearing another splash she returned to the safety of the resort. She wondered if gators hang out in the keys.

She turned her thoughts back to the things Eulah said. *What if she's right and God is interested in me?*

She stopped to watch a low flying pelican glide by. She drew in a deep breath of salt air.

My only hope is something positive will come from the overwhelming losses. What did she say? He will fill my life with things I can't dream of. Yeah, I could use a bit of that. And yet, life sees fit to send me the ball of nothing.

Yet the ball of nothing is the perfect parody of my life. I don't see how I can ever get past the huge holes in my life. It's hard to have hope when you're deep in the black abyss and any effort to escape is rewarded with a deeper plunge.

Hearing the faint noises of the guests, she looked up the beach and thought of Nic flirting with all the ladies.

The Plantation House, a place of life – human interaction in all its richness. And I walk around in my own separate death bubble. They could make a movie of that – the girl in the bubble of nothingness.

She sighed and sat down on the warm sand to watch the sun, now low in the sky. She thought of Jedediah who loved and lost his wife, and how he still seeks the spaces they shared.

He treasures his memories, and I want to escape all this death – I wish I could just forget it all. The memories aren't worth this pain.

She hugged her knees. Tears rolled down her cheeks.

Why me, God? Can you fix a person emptied of life? Can you take away this blackness that's filled my soul? Eulah's right about one thing – I'm drowning in deep murky water – an empty black void.

She closed her eyes and listened a long time to the steady wash of water rolling in. Finally, she stood up and brushed the sand off and the tears from her face.

God, if you're about helping and not harming, then maybe we should talk sometime. But my heart boils when I think about losing everything for the second time. Before I buy into all this hope and future stuff I will need a real answer for all the loss in my life. And a promise it won't happen again. I can't fall for hope and life, only to have it all ripped from me again. I can't face carnage a third time. I can't handle a third strike, all pins down.

Sitting alone on the back deck after dinner, the barrenness of her life brought fresh tears – the lonely teen years, the friendless marriage years, all the dead loved ones. Sorrow washed over her, filling all the empty crevices. She let the pain of loss stain her face.

The image of the bird flying out of the colourless world into vivid life sprang to mind.

Out of the darkness, out of the mainland and into the bright sunshine and the vividness of life.

She brought out her sketchbook to look at the image.

I wonder. When I drew you, I felt there's a bigger meaning, like I too am coming out of the storm, the black abyss. Perhaps Eulah's right, this dark emotional place is a storm and it will pass.

She stroked the sketch as though it were a frail delicate creature.

But then there was something significant about the colours. What was first? The back of the bird was first, wasn't it? The deep red back.

Her eyebrows popped up.

Yes, this vision is really symbolic of me. I think the colours are the story of my journey from this desolate place. My current anger weighs heavy on my back. I cannot fly out of the storm with this load. Anger. The millstone of grief.

She closed the book.

When I've dealt with my anger I'll be back.

A person stepped out of the shadows and walked down the street. "Getting back into art? How precious. I'll put an end to the delight of expressing yourself. And tears? Get a grip, my pet. I'm a long way from finished with you."

CHAPTER 7

One warm Saturday morning, she arrived early to work and took her laptop to the lounge. A few sailboats anchored in the bay, bobbing in the gentle waves. She watched a couple move about the deck then dive in the water. With a sigh she bent to her work, letting it absorb her thoughts for an hour.

The scraping of a deck chair across the concrete caught her attention. She spotted Pen gathering up towels and dishes from the previous evening and wiping down the loungers. Resort guests emerged to stake out their spot around the pools. One new guest asked Pen where he could get fresh towels. Pen's bright, sweet smile caused JJ's heart to ache.

Imagine being her age again. A fresh chance. Not marred by pain or loss. For her, life still holds hope. Imagine just being happy in yourself that a smile comes so easily. I wonder what nasty things this world has in store for her that will steal that sweet smile. Oh God, let her go as long as possible before the wrecking ball shatters her life.

At lunch she headed for the bench and found Eulah already there. She settled in, unwrapping her sandwich. "There's been something I've been meaning to ask you."

"Mmm hmm."

"Why do you call Pen Pearl?"

"Well, that's her name, honey."

"She said her name is Pen."

"Her full name is Pearl Evette Noble. Her half brother saw her initials and called her Pen from the beginning. I guess it caught on. I like Pearl because the Bible talks about a man who found a pearl of great value and sold everything he had to own it. I tell her she is a treasure of great value, and Pearl is a name to be proud of."

"I like Pearl. It's a beautiful name. I think it suits her. But I've called her Pen for a few weeks now. It would be hard to change."

"Mmm hmm."

She sighed. *Sometimes the effort to be sociable seems too difficult.* She almost gave up trying to make conversation, but she felt Eulah's presence beside her. With little interest she asked, "Tell me about yourself, Eulah. Did you always live here?"

She laughed and rocked back and forth. "No one's asked about my story in many years. Well, let's see now. I'm 68 years old. I come from Raleigh, North Carolina. I went to Chapel Hill University back in the '70s and received an undergrad and masters degree in psychology. I earned my doctorate from Harvard. I worked as a clinical counsellor for a few years. Then I went through some rough waters and found Jesus. I decided I wanted to work in a job I could spend the day praying and speaking with Him."

"Wow. I doubt many people with doctorates work in a laundry room. Are you still happy with your decision? Any regrets?"

"It's the best decision I ever made. Like the man in the Bible, I too found a treasure of great value in my relationship with Jesus and I gave everything I had to pursue it. Nothing in this world means as much."

"But you must be smart to earn a doctorate from Harvard. And now you're in a job that doesn't tap your potential at all."

"Oh I don't know about that. God sends me people all the time that need my help. He tells me what I need to know about them, and I have lots of time to pray for them. Then He gives me the opportunities to connect and help."

She looked a long moment at Eulah. She wore an easy smile on her face as she looked out to sea.

Amazing. I think she lives in genuine happiness. I don't understand this woman at all. She has smarts and a prestigious degree to go with it and she works in the laundry. It makes little sense. Maybe circumstances left her stuck here and she made the best of it. That's kind of sad.

Eulah turned and looked at JJ with a focused intensity. Her gentle demeanour dissolved like the wax of a hot candle. "Don't you go thinking I've wasted my life, or wasted God's gift of education. God has sent me clients that would never have received His wisdom and direction if I called myself a counsellor. Over my lifetime, I've counselled a long list of clients. So many broken lives that God has healed and restored. No, don't you ever think mine is a fruitless life." Eulah's gaze softened and she looked away.

JJ continued to stare.

Did she read my mind? Who is this odd woman? If she knows what I'm thinking, she might be the best counsellor on the face of the earth.

"I'm sorry if I offended you."

"No offence taken. Generally when people go quiet, they pity me. What they are thinking is that I'm a wasted life. You misplace your pity. You must learn to see things from God's perspective. When I arrive to heaven, I know the record will show I lived a successful life by God's measure. I know He will say 'Well done, good and faithful servant.' Now that is a life well lived. How could I have any regrets? God has touched and changed many lives through me. I am exactly where I need to be to make a difference in people's lives. Never pity something so wonderful. I use that God-given education just about every day."

"Eulah, you are a most unique woman. You don't live by the normal rules."

"Thank you, honey. I'll take that as a compliment to God's beautiful work in me. A beautiful destiny awaits you, if you'll let Him take you there. He is a God of joy, laughter, and peace and He wants you to bear the fruit of His Spirit too. I know you're hurting, but He can bring healing and restoration."

"The only thing that will heal my broken heart is for my family to come back. And that's not going to happen."

"No. That will not happen." She thought a moment then shook her head. "Mmm, mmm, mmm. Lordy that's a story from the long past." She took a deep breath. "My dear, let me tell you about my son Jonah. He was 15 when some bad folks killed him. It doesn't matter the circumstances, but like you, I lost my son, my only child. I understand the heartache and anguish. I know what it's like to live out each day with a massive gaping wound in your heart and huge holes in your life. Every day you fall into one of the holes, into a dark, terrible place." She looked at JJ, head down with tears streaming down her face.

"Oh Eulah, I know death and loss are hard, but the depth and breadth of the darkness is astounding. I didn't understand what grief is. Death steals not only the life of your loved one, it plunders your life and leaves you in a pile of wreckage. And there's nothing you can do to stop it. You can't talk about it. People don't understand."

"That's true. Most don't understand until they've walked through that grief themselves."

JJ sniffed. "When things don't seem like they can get any worse, some new level of horrible barrels in and crushes me. How did you get through? This seems impossible. It's too much."

"Yes, this fallen world sometimes asks too much of us. But you and I have God. Jesus died on the cross so we could live an abundant life. Not that there won't be challenges, not that there won't be pain and loss, but we could turn to Him and let Him do the amazing, even impossible, work of taking all the bad things the world dumps on you and turn it to good. What is the price tag for His goodness? He wants a relationship with you. He wants to talk with you and walk this journey with you. When you invest in your relationship with the Father, Jesus and Holy Spirit, then He heals the terrible hurts of this world and brings you to a place of rest. He told us to make Him the priority and He'll take care of everything else in our lives. Jesus himself said so in Matthew."

JJ rocked forward, cupping her hands over her eyes. "The anger, the frustration – it's overwhelming. It rolls in without invitation. I don't know that I see anything good ahead. It's just all so black. I say nothing to people because no one would understand this dark, bleak abyss I live in. No one would understand the emptiness. In Iowa, emotionally I was a wasteland, but coming here seems to have awakened a deep anger. And when I'm not raging angry I feel hopeless – like life offers nothing good for me. And I feel so alone in this black, icy void. And when I'm not dealing with anger, hopelessness or loneliness, it's the numbness. It's like I'm a zombie making my way through the day, talking to people and getting my work done, but I don't feel connected to reality. I feel – lost. I feel like I've lost me."

Eulah rubbed her back. "Oh honey, I know that dark place. I stumbled through that abyss for many, many months. And I know there are no shortcuts through grief. But I also know there is an end to that chasm. I know you will find yourself again. And I know the God who created you now walks beside you. He longs to make this journey lighter for you. He promises that to walk with Him is a light load. You can continue to stumble your way through, or you can grab a hold of His hand and lean on Him. I promise you, it's a far easier journey through grief when you give Him your burdens to carry."

She shifted to look directly at Eulah. "I don't know how to do what you're talking about. How do I lean on something I can't even see? And before you get going on some lengthy complicated thing, I don't have the strength to figure out God."

"He's easy to get to know. Let's start with what you are doing. Tell me about what things you do to maintain your relationship with Him."

"I used to read my Bible a bit. And I used to go to church. I've abandoned both."

"Well girl, how do you expect to have much of a relationship, one that will take you through these dark days, if you spend no time with Him? Reading His word is important, but if you're reading it out of obligation and not getting any insight from it, then you're not growing your relationship. Church is good too, if you are worshiping God, praising Him and building your relationship. Aside from all that, I'm talking about the time you spend talking with God – just you and Him, enjoying a conversation, letting Him speak to you."

"I'm not super spiritual like you. I don't hear God talking. He doesn't talk to me. I guess I'm not special that way."

"Jesus said His sheep know His voice and follow Him. If you are His child, then you are one of His and every one can hear His voice if they listen. When Jesus went to heaven He sent His Spirit to come inside us to guide us, instruct us and help us in our weakness. Those led by the Spirit of God are His children. God talks to me through His Spirit, just like He did to Peter, Paul, John and all the others. And He speaks to you all the time. The problem is you don't know how to hear Him."

She shrugged. "I don't know. I believe in what the Bible says, but I don't know about this stuff with being led by the Spirit. What do you *do* that you hear God talking? Is it like an audible voice?"

"Some people hear an audible voice like Samuel did, but most don't. When I read my Bible I take my time. It's not a race. You want to get to know God and that is an unhurried process. Sometimes I read a verse that touches my heart and I close my eyes and repeat the verse, then I still my mind and wait for Holy Spirit to teach me more. And He does. Those thoughts that pop into your head out of nowhere, those thoughts that seem too insightful to be your own, that is Holy Spirit talking to you. And you can ask questions. He will answer, His Spirit directly to your mind. You need to be still – to quieten your thoughts to hear Him. I also have a journal I write in. That's important. You want to go back through the things He tells you. Again, I quieten myself. I thank God for all He has done for me. Then I ask Him what He wants to show me today. I always write what He tells me."

"How do you know it's God talking and not just some crazy thing that popped into your head?"

She laughed. "Now that is a wise question. First, I write everything down. Later, I evaluate what I hear against the character and nature of God to be sure it's not just me, but it's from

Holy Spirit. And if it's something I should act on, I look for confirmations outside the idea popping in my head. Sometimes that confirmation will come as a verse. Sometimes it will be something someone says who knows nothing of my conversation with God. Sometimes I'll have a dream. And sometimes I go to trusted Christians that have a deep relationship with God so I can ask for their wisdom. I'm a sheep that's been hearing God's voice for so long now I recognize Him." She paused.

JJ stared at the ground trying to process what Eulah said.

"Would you like me to pray with you that the Lord opens your ears to His voice?"

"I can't live this way. So, yeah."

Eulah held both of her hands. "Lord, you know your little lamb JJ. You know her journey, and you know the dark place of her spirit and mind. She is your child, your beloved one. Still her mind to allow her to hear your voice. Make thin the veil between her mind and your Spirit. Press into her heart your love and care for her. Give her courage and strength for this walk through the valley of the shadow of death. Be her shield of protection against the hopelessness. Let her feel your closeness as a refuge from the loneliness. Right now, Holy Spirit, we invite You to help JJ hear You. We look for your comforting presence."

Eulah continued to pray quietly.

JJ took a deep breath, held it then released it slowly.

Eulah said, "What did you hear from Holy Spirit?"

"I don't know. A warmth. Maybe feeling lighter. I kept thinking – hearing in my head the words, "Out of the mud and into the sun.""

Eulah rocked back and laughed. "Well, well. That is definitely Holy Spirit. He's confirming what I said the other day. I see you as a lotus flower. That's what He showed me about you. And those are flowers that have their feet in the mud, and yet they reach up through the murky depths to the sun then burst forth in an extravagant, unblemished blossom. That is your journey and destiny – to one day burst out of the darkness and display your amazing beauty that formed in the mud of this abyss.

That's a promise directly from the heart of God. Now that's one for your journal!"

JJ looked out over the ocean and thought about actually hearing God speak to her. She wrapped up her uneaten sandwich. "Thank you, Eulah. I should probably head back. I'm expecting a call. Sorry I took all your lunch time, but you've given me a lot to think about."

"This is the first day of a deep, meaningful and real relationship with Jesus who loves you beyond your wildest imagination. Any time you want to talk, you know where to find me."

She squeezed Eulah's hand. "Thank you. I think I'll take you up on that offer. You've made the abyss a little less dark."

"Not me, that's all God. And may you feel His presence for the rest of the day. Peace and rest, little lotus."

She sauntered along the water's edge.

The darkness, the emptiness, the holes in my heart still exist. And yet there is something different. A quietness. The gnawing anguish is silent. And there's a hint of strength. Oh God, is this really you? Did you show up? Am I for the first time in my life hearing you? After breathing putrid air of death, grief and loss, this is like a breath of fresh air. Lotus flower. Right. I hope I hit the surface soon.

Everyone knows it's darkest before the dawn. JJ glimpsed the first hints of her dawn from grief.

But she couldn't anticipate an ominous evil would hurl her into an oppressive blackness few survive.

CHAPTER 8

Angeline dropped by mid afternoon to invite her to try out stand up paddle boarding. "It's a beautiful day, the water is still and there's a couple boards available."

Still on her high from her encounter with God, she agreed.

Are you making a way for me to step into life again?

The board rocked almost knocking JJ off, but she quickly caught on. They circled Shands Key, and headed back to the point on the south end of the resort bay. Angeline pulled into the private dock of a sprawling mansion.

JJ looked at the *Cool Change*, a new 30 ft. powerboat then an old Adirondack chair missing half its red paint on the beach.

Who lives here? A sprawling mansion. A huge power boat. And an old chair out front in desperate need of attention. What a contrast!

She watched Angeline dismount on the dock and tried to do the same, but her board shot away as she stepped off. She barely avoided falling in, leaving her board happily bobbing untethered in the waves and drifting out to sea. Laughing, Ang hopped back on hers and rescued the stray.

"Hey, ladies."

I know that deep smooth voice.

JJ turned around to see Jason coming down the dock. Angeline skipped up the dock and wrapped her arm around him. He hugged her back. "Long time, no see."

Ang responded with her usual bright smile. "You too. It's been a few weeks I guess. I spotted you up at the workshop and thought it's a good time to introduce you to my friend JJ. She's the gal I told you about."

He smiled. "We've met at the grocery store. How are you?"

"Good. Although I think I might be sore tomorrow. It's my first time on one of these things."

"They are a good workout. Would you two care for a cool drink?"

Ang said, "I'd love a tall, cool water."

"C'mon up. There's lots of bottled water in the workshop fridge. Help yourselves. By the way, Indigo's here. We were chatting about maybe organizing a class for the local kids."

Angeline nodded. "That would be a huge opportunity." She handed JJ a water bottle and looked in the workshop. "Hi, Indigo. How are you?"

The woman captured JJ's attention.

Her hair is stunning. It's white, but then it's not white. It's blue, like the blue of denim, but then it's not blue. I've never seen hair this colour, and it's so becoming. Despite the colour, the woman appeared about 50 years old.

"Hi Tangerine. I haven't seen you in awhile. How've you been?"

Ang reached to shake Indigo's hand. She introduced JJ to "one of the most talented sculptors in North America."

JJ offered her hand. "Indigo – nice to meet you."

She took JJ's hand and looked at her from various angles. "I will call you Cerise. You're almost a fuchsia – you are very vivid pink, but –" Her hand gestured circles about JJ's body. "You have too much blue for fuchsia. Yes, you are cerise. The sweetness of pink cooled off with the right amount of blue."

JJ didn't know what to say. "Um, okay." She smiled to herself. *Wha-zing. Weirdness transported me to Toontown and I'm a cerise-coloured lotus flower.*

Indigo took her arm and turned her to face Jason. She leaned in close as though to share a secret, but spoke at normal volume. "I see people in colour. I'm not too good with names, but I remember your colour. See? Look at this man," she said gesturing toward Jason. "He's cognac – almost leather, but much, much warmer. It's this wonderful velvety smooth colour, so rich in flavour. There's spice and heat in there too. Like an fine cognac, age, experience, life developed his flavour and complexity." She drew in a deep breath and looked expectantly at JJ. "Can't you see it? There is no other word for him."

Velvety smooth, complex and spicy?

Before she could answer Angeline said, "I'm Tangerine."

Indigo said, "Yes, yes! You radiate sunshine and this wonderful depth of pure colour. You have saucy tang too. One of these days I must do a piece in your colour."

Angeline nodded toward the table. "What are you working on today?"

"I came down to the Keys to rest. But you know, I have a show coming up in a few months and I decided I need another piece. So here I am in Cognac's workshop working on this sculpture of a ballerina. I thought she would represent tranquility, but she seems to have different ideas. My friend's word eyewater keeps coming to mind." She took them to the bench where her new work stood.

JJ thought, *Eyewater*? *That is a great word.* "She's beautiful, Indigo, so – real." She pointed to the dancer's back. "You can see her strength under her skin. The movement's so graceful. I love the draping of her skirt. It's exquisite."

"Thank you. I call her Rain. She's misty blue-green-grey. The colour of gossamer film, yet laden with – with tears." She tenderly touched the ballerina's face. "She's lived a difficult life – a lot of loss, a lot of pain. Yes, a complex human mix of composure and eyewater, of strength and vulnerability. Despite her fortitude – perhaps because of it – she is a quiet rain."

JJ could feel tears threatening.

Now what? Tears? Really? I think I prefer angry to crying in public. At least I can keep my anger to myself.

While others commented, she looked around the workshop to pull her thoughts away from her own burden of tears.

I think I'm like Rain, a lot of loss and laden with tears.

She drew in a fresh breath and smiled at Indigo. "I like that name. It suits her."

Ang looked at her watch then turned to Jason. "We should

be on our way. I wanted to pop in and say hi."

Jason walked them back to the dock. "I hope you ladies can come to dinner tomorrow night. It'll be the regular folks, including Mike."

Ang said, "Oh thanks for reminding me." She looked at JJ. "Would you like to come?"

"Sure. I'd like to see your gallery that's not a gallery."

"Drinks and photo tour at 6 p.m. if you can swing it."

They set off on the 20-minute paddle back to the resort. JJ pushed off the dock and waved goodbye to Jason.

No tears since Cam's death, then I come to the Keys and the dam seems ready to burst. Just not now –

She focused on the pattern of water swirling around the paddle. Glancing back at the weathered chair she thought, *maybe you do belong here with the mansion, the boat and the man of smooth and spicy contrasts.*

She turned her thoughts to the dinner invitation. She called to Ang, "Who is Mike? Jason said, 'including Mike.' So?"

Ang stopped paddling, letting JJ catch up. "Mike Boland. He's a local policeman."

"And?"

"And nothing." Ang started paddling again.

JJ hustled to keep up. "Okay. If you don't want to tell me I'll ask Mike when I meet him."

She called back over her shoulder. "We've been out a couple of times."

"And?"

She shrugged. "And I like him." She stopped and looked at her friend. "It's just been a couple of movies. It's pretty casual."

Catching up JJ said, "Is that the entire story? Jason seems to believe there's something going on."

"I've never dated a policeman. It's interesting."

"You two haven't been out since I've been here."

"Our shifts haven't worked out too well. We have plans for the weekend."

"Okay." She stopped paddling. "Ang, don't let me and my

grief stop you from moving ahead with your life."

Ang rested her paddle on the board, leaning on the handle. "I won't. Don't worry. I think you'll enjoy tomorrow. Jason and the gang are a lot of fun. What do you think of Indigo? She's one of the quirky people that seem to congregate here."

"I will need a decoder ring to know who she's is talking about."

Angeline laughed. "You can pick up who she's talking about because either someone else uses their real name or you can tell from what's said about them. She's talented, don't you think?"

"I'm not familiar with the world of sculpture, but she's fantastic."

"So you already met Jason? You didn't mention it."

"Yeah. I stopped at the grocery store to pick up a few things and he was talking with the cashier. She mentioned he's a National Geographic photographer. He invited me to see his photos sometime."

"I think you'll like his work. All his images have a lot of feeling. He's another interesting person."

"*So rich in flavour*, I understand."

"And a bit of spice." Ang laughed. "Indigo is eccentric, but she's accurate in her assessment of people. Jason looks like still water, but he runs deep."

The red chair – that's the red to his white wind-capped waves and blue sea. I think there's a painting of freedom somewhere in there.

She thought about Indigo's assessment of her colour – the sweetness of pink, and cooled off with just the right amount of blue. *Maybe she's right, but it feels like a lot of blue and not much pink these days. Oh God, don't let the blues overcome my sweetness. Please keep the gnawing anguish silent. Please allow a little warmth of life in.*

Late afternoon JJ popped in to see if Ang was ready to go home, but she had two evening conference calls. JJ stopped by the local dive shop to look for a new bathing suit to leave at the office. The huge selection made choosing difficult. She decided on a couple two-piecers, a pink and purple number to leave at the office, and a beautiful blue Body Glove one – just because she loved the colour. At the cash she added a leather anklet in shades of blue. She fingered the woven leather.

May as well go full-on native. Maybe if I blend in, crazy won't find me so attractive.

After eating dinner alone JJ sat on the back deck. She put on her new anklet and held out her leg.

Okay, do your magic. Keep the fruitcakes at bay.

She watched a little lizard scurry across the deck, missing her toes by inches. Rustling through the underbrush, one of the local roosters appeared, a fine looking fellow with flowing orange feathers, rusty chest and an iridescent black tail. "So you're the one who wakes us up every morning. I think I will call you Chanticleer, the gullible and proud creature of fable." He stood a moment considering her then continued on with his quest for bugs. Absently, she watched him move about the yard.

She turned her thoughts inward checking on her state in the abyss. She closed her eyes and drew the scent of the potted flowers into her lungs and held it there.

Marathon is a spectacular place. Thank you God for bringing me here.

She let out her breath slowly.

Thank you for the reprieve from the constant grinding of sorrow. I am deeply grateful for the break.

A little smile tweaked at the corner of her mouth.

Was that you? Did you say you love me? Is this you? Is it this easy to hear you? Why haven't I heard you before? If your sheep are supposed to know your voice, how come I never heard you before?

She listened and so began their first conversation.

Darkness crept across the sky. JJ stood up, stretched then remembered the unusual word Indigo used. An image of Indigo fondly touching the cheek of her sculpture sprang to her mind. She pulled out her collection-of-words sketchbook and quickly drew the image then settled in to capture just the right sense of tranquility and tears. When finished, Rain expressed her nature in blue-greens with a trail of tears down her cheek, Indigo, like her name, wore pure mid-blues for her peace. She wrote Eyewater at the bottom.

Oh to be so at ease with myself, so filled with tranquility that my art could express both the peace and pain of the human existence.

I wonder. Does pouring that pain out in your art act as a release of that pain? Does Indigo find a place of tranquility because *she allows her art to be her anguish, her sorrow? Maybe great art is the outcome of the artist creating the piece to express their deep emotions, and that's what reaches across the divide between people. Maybe that is the intangible that resonates.*

She thought about her near life-long relationship with death. Memories of past losses flared, swirled and mingled with those of the past year. Crushing sorrow rolled in. She fell into bed on her side hugging her pillow. Eyewater blurred her vision.

Loss is loss – so much loss. My grief extends so far back. It's the second time You've asked me to go through death stripping my life of everyone I love. My five-times-broken heart is irreparable. This time nothing of me remains. How can I put the pieces together again?

What happened to that peace from the gnawing anguish, the bit of fortitude and the quietness? Grief rolls in and crushes any sign of survival. It's all gone, and the indescribable sorrow sits on heavy my chest. God, I need You to show up in a big way.

Racking sobs welled up. Pain and anguish poured out. For the first time, her deepest pain expressed itself in long mournful wails. The floodgates opened and she let the sorrow of a life too familiar with death to dominate unchecked. When the emotional wave passed she fell asleep on her damp pillow.

Outside her window a low chuckle faded into the night unheard.

CHAPTER 9

The next day the resort buzzed with anticipation of a visit from the owner, Jerry Kipling. It took JJ by surprise when he knocked on her office door. "You must be JJ. I like to know all my managers. Do you have a few minutes to talk?"

"I do. Please have a seat, Mr. Kipling."

"Jerry, please. Would you mind if we took a walk. There's a bench a ways down the beach I enjoy."

She smiled. "I know the one. It's becoming a favourite lunch spot for me."

He looked at her a moment. "Indeed."

He stopped at the bar to pick up a Coke. They chatted about her education and experience.

He shared some of his story. "I was a young man when my father died in a car accident. He just bought this resort. It fell to me to make something of it. I struggled in those early days." His gaze rested on the distant horizon, the vague line separating sky from sea.

He drew a breath. "And then I met someone who put things into perspective." He broke his gaze. "And now, let's get to business. I told Angeline I was looking to develop the spa portion of the operation. You've been on the job for a few weeks now. I'm sure you've formulated some ideas."

"I have a few thoughts. They aren't fully developed, so I've said nothing to Angeline yet."

"I'm very interested to hear what you're thinking. Ideas are the birthplace of great business."

"I've noticed several sailboats anchor in the bay at night. What if we market our services to the boat set? We could accept reservations for all of our services including the restaurant and sport equipment, not just the spa. Maybe offer a day pass for mooring at the dock and use of the showers, pool and access to the bar." She paused, realizing she spilled out her thoughts without taking care to present them properly. "If you're okay with opening the resort to non-guests."

"Interesting idea. Many of the sailboats here are charters of local operations."

Her heart sank. *He thinks it's a stupid idea.*

"But that doesn't matter. Whether local operators or visitors from up the coast, they don't have a restaurant or spa facilities. We could partner with the local guys. They are often out several days to weeks at a time. Use of our spa would add a touch of luxury to their guests' vacations. The ladies might enjoy an afternoon at the spa while the men go fishing. Yes, I like the idea. We should encourage reservations, not just drop-ins, to ensure we still provide a great experience for all of our guests. And we'd need to keep our eye on the growth. I think the idea is worth developing.

"Don't worry about Angeline feeling like you've gone over her head. She knows I like to hear ideas directly from my managers. Work with her to put together a proposal with costs and the three of us can talk about it again. Do you have any other ideas?"

"There's a local guy that has a pottery workshop. He offers classes. I thought it might be fun for the kids of our guests if we arranged a morning workshop where they could make a little pottery lamp. Then they could use their lamps at the beach barbecue and take them home as a memento of their time with us."

"Hmm. I like it except I don't want the liability of children running around with open flames in their lamps."

"There are little electronic flameless tea lights. They aren't expensive and we could buy in bulk. They would be safe."

"Does Jason know of this idea?"

It surprised her he knew Jason. *Then again, everyone seems to know him.*

"Not specifically, but I think he would be open to the idea."

"Talk to him. If he's interested, work out the details and let me know. We could add the cost of the tea lights to the workshop. Other than promotional material, it doesn't sound like much expense to us. Now, any other ideas about the spa, other than opening it up to the sailing set?"

A new idea popped in her head. "Maybe one. I've looked at the bookings and budgets over the past couple of years. Obviously we are busier in the winter season, and business dies off in the summer. What do you think about opening to the locals during the off-season? It might allow us to keep some of the seasonal staff employed over the summer and tighten our connection to the local community."

"So you see the spa operation as it's own entity. It's always been tied to the hotel and our guests, but you're thinking of the hotel guests as just one of many sources of clients." He scratched his chin. "Yes, I think that is a good approach. As long as we keep our high standards, I see no reason to limit you to hotel guests."

"We could also market to some of the B&B's in the area."

He laughed. "Angeline was right. You are full of good ideas. Work things out with her and send me your proposals. Let's get moving on these." They chatted about his travels and other hotels as they walked back. He thanked her for her time before settling down at the bar with the restaurant manager.

On her way back to her office she remembered Eulah's words, "If an idea or thought pops in your head and it's more insightful than you are, then it's Holy Spirit talking." She thought about the idea for the B&B's and opening to the community just appearing right when she needed them. She thanked God for the ideas. A bright spot of joy in impressing Jerry passed through her heart. Then the old familiar pain of her losses welled up. *Why must sorrow crush joy and hope?*

To keep her skills, JJ scheduled herself to treat several clients per week. That afternoon, she and another therapist treated two older ladies in one of the outdoor rooms. These ladies came every year with their husbands. She listened to their chatter about the latest news on friends, kids and grandkids. She thought about the long full life of each of the ladies and how that wonderful life encircled them with the richness of friends and family.

Cam was a loner. We didn't have friends. I never realized how lonely my life had become even before he and Lucas died. Maybe I've been without joy longer than I realized.

When finished their treatment, JJ walked down to the beach.

I should have sought out friendships even though he wasn't interested. Maybe I wouldn't be in such a black place today if I surrounded myself with people who shared a longterm closeness and affection. But then, everyone around me dies. Maybe it's best we were loners – limit the devastation. Those ladies are more blessed than they realize.

She turned back and noticed Jerry sitting on the bench with Eulah. He leaned forward, his elbows on his knees, his head turned to look back at Eulah. She nodded at something he said, and they both laughed. In her head she heard his words, "Then I met someone who put things into perspective." She watched them together for a moment.

Eulah is that someone. He's one person in her long list of people she's helped. Even the boss goes to her for advice. Now that says something about her.

Their conversation turned serious. Eulah said something. Jerry tapped his fingers then sat up and rubbed his face, drew in a breath and nodded in agreement. They talked for a few moments then he wrapped his arm around her, hugging her. He kissed her cheek causing her to laugh.

JJ looked away.

Friends – everywhere, deep friendships. And I'm alone in the black abyss. Oh God, please don't leave me here. I don't want to do this alone again.

In bed, she turned to her island bird sketch.

I promised to visit you again when I'm past my anger. Yes, the load of anger I carried weighed me down. In my heart I've let go of my anger and I'm clinging to the hope that God will show me the way through and bring life. So where am I now?

Her finger moved from the red back to the blue belly.

Ah, a gut full of sorrow. Well God, I bring my sorrow and anguish to You. Show me the way through this visceral pain.

She felt warmth and peace fill her heart. It poured in like an ointment, soothing the wounded parts of her heart.

Thank you. Please let the healing continue. Lead me to life again.

She rubbed the bird's green chest. "And what are you? And after you my journey takes me to an orange neck, a black beak and eye band, and finally a yellow head. If you really are me, then I hope the rest of the colours are good things. Please, let them be good things."

CHAPTER 10

After stopping to pick up another package at the post office, JJ and Angeline arrived fashionably late to dinner at Jason's home. While Jason poured two white wines, Ang introduced her to everyone.

"Excuse me everyone. I want to introduce you to my friend and talented artist, Jennifer Jaye McCurdy. I know I don't exactly fit in with all you artist types, but she's my contribution to the creative. Now let me introduce you starting with Deon King. He cuts steal drums and paints these gorgeous tropical sea creatures. He makes a fine living selling them to tourists and on-line. Deon, JJ."

He held up his beer to her. "Nice to meet a fellow artist. What is your specialty, JJ?"

"I paint both watercolour and acrylic. It's just a hobby."

"The Keys are an inspirational place. You may find it becomes more than a hobby here. That's what happened to me. Anyway, welcome."

"Thank you, Deon. I would love to see your work sometime."

Ang pointed to a large, colourful angelfish hanging on the wall. "Here's one of his pieces."

JJ loved the vivid enamel colour painted in an abstract style. "It has a real native feel to it. Quite lovely."

"Thank you. I'm half Seminole and half African American. I think it's the Seminole in me."

Ang said, "You know Indigo already."

"Good to see you again, Cerise." JJ nodded and greeted her.

"And next to Indigo is Sydney Jamison. She owns the local grocery store, the one where you met Jason."

She stood up and shook JJ's hand. "Nice to meet you again. JJ
–" She looked around at the others. "I should be able to remember that." Everyone laughed. She leaned forward. "I'm terrible
with names, especially new names. Can't remember them at all.
I remember the first letter, then just make something up. Yours
is just letters. I should have no problem at all with it."

JJ smiled. "Nice to meet you, Sydney."

"And next to Sydney is Mike Boland. He's our local police
detective."

She noted his rugged good looks and smiled.

He stood and extended his hand. "I'm new to the area too.
Hope you enjoy it as much as I do. Welcome."

"Thanks, Mike."

"And next to Mike is Theo Pample. Theo is the minister of
the Baptist church here in Marathon."

"Welcome to our slice of paradise. Most of these reprobates
don't come to church, but you are more than welcome to join
us on Sundays. We're a laid back group. It's a good way to get to
know people in town."

*Not a chance of that happening. I'm not sure I'm ready for full
on God just yet.*

"Thank you. I'll think about it."

"And this is Gunner Lewis, our local dive master. He's the go
to guy if you want to be certified to dive."

The well-muscled, dirty blond Adonis, wore a most unusual pair of orange and purple canvas tennis shoes in bare feet.
"Nice to meet you JJ. Yes, if you're interested in diving, I'd be
happy to get you set up."

"I haven't thought about it, but I guess the diving around
here is good?"

"They call Key Largo the diving capital of the world. Here
in the Keys we have a nice selection of marine life, lots of coral
and artificial reefs – some great shipwrecks. Thunderbolt is a
military ship that sunk nearby, and Sombrero reef off the south
side is a fantastic dive. I gather you're not certified to dive?"

"No, but I've done snorkelling."

"I can provide you with lessons and the certification dive. Just let me know if you're interested."

"Okay, thanks. I will." Glancing at his canvas shoes as he sat down she wondered if he is the quirky one who wears a different pair every day.

"And last, but certainly not least. This is our local DJ." She gestured toward the person on her right, a tall, dark-haired, handsome man. "This is Catamaran Dan Banyan, the morning DJ on our local station. Dan, this is JJ."

He stood and offered her his hand. "JJ is it? I once knew a woman called BB. Well, at least that's what we boys called her."

Handing a glass of wine to each of the newcomers, Jason said, "Careful now Dan. Mixed company."

"Ah you fret too soon, my friend. We called her BB because she shot at us boys with her bb gun every time we climbed her apple tree."

Laughter erupted. One person said, "Do you still have buckshot in your behind?"

His right dimple appeared. "I set off the metal detector every time." Dan turned back to JJ. He looked at her a long time saying nothing. The room went quiet.

JJ, feeling a little uncomfortable, said, "Is there something stuck on my face?"

Jason said, "Danny boy does this when he's considering what you're song is. Not everyone gets a song, so count yourself special."

She looked back at Dan and shrugged. "Make it a good one."

He looked into her eyes, nodded then tapped his hand in the air mouthing words. "Yes, that's the one." He sang the first verse to her. She hadn't heard the song in a long time. It was about being confused in life, looking for light in the rain, and about getting lost in the music and drifting away.

Someone said, "That's the Doobie Brothers! Nice."

Dan shook his head. "Actually, it's *Drift Away*, originally done by Dobie Gray. Uncle Kracker did a new release of it featuring Dobie. JJ, I think the soothing rhythm and harmony of the

Florida keys will get into your soul, bring you joy and maybe bring your creative out. Yes, that's your song."

Ang said, "And now you'll catch him humming it when he sees you."

"I must download it to my phone. Does everyone here have a song?"

Jason said, "Mine is *Cool Change* by the Little River Band. It's about the exceptional feeling of sailing on the blue waters. Moving here was definitely a cool change."

Ang said, "Mine is *Pretty Woman* by Roy Orbison. Instead of singing it to me, Dan does the little growl thing. Makes me laugh every time."

Theo piped up. "Dan nailed it for me. Mine is *Dance* by Petra. It's the perfect song for a minister with a spotty past."

Gunner smiled. "Me too. Mine is *I Can See Clearly Now* by Jimmy Cliff – my life is bright sunny day indeed."

Deon said, "Mine is *Simple Man* by Lynyrd Skynyrd. I don't know how Dan knew, but it's been a favourite since I was young. My dad sang it all the time." He nodded at Dan. "Good choice."

Jason said, "Indigo?"

She stood up. "Dan chose one of my favourite songs for me." She flung her arms in the air, whirled about, circling the coffee table, singing *Dancing Queen* by Abba. She completed the entire song in her unique interpretive style. Everyone sang the parts they knew.

Swept away in the moment, JJ heard the music in her head, and let the rhythm fill her body. For a brief time, joy filled her heart. For a moment she drifted away.

Dan said, "And that's why it's the perfect song for Indigo."

JJ said, "Your dancing reminds me of your sculpture *Rain*. You are as expressive as she is."

Indigo nodded a thank you. "She has more stamina for dance than me, I think."

JJ laughed and turned back to Dan. "Thank you for giving me a song and letting me be a part of the in crowd. Good to meet you, Dan."

Jason said, "And you're back to me. Now that you've met everyone, you said you'd like to see my photography work?"

"Yes, I would."

He led her around his home, talking of his exotic travels in India, China, Malaysia, Chile and places she'd never heard of. Many of his images expressed mood, some haunting, some achingly lonely, some mysterious and some quiet. Several she recognized from the magazine. As she slowly moved around the rooms her reactions spilled out – "I like this one," "oh my, I didn't even see the shark at first," and " such desolate beauty." His work mesmerized her. When finished the tour she said, "You are quite talented. You have a wonderful eye for composition, but you also capture deep emotions. You make me want to see everything you have seen. Are you still travelling and working for the National Geographic?"

"I guess you could say I'm semi-retired."

Her eyebrows shot up. "But you're too young to be any kind of retired. When I was young I dreamt of being a National Geographic photographer and travelling the world. I can't imagine ever quitting such a great job. Looking at your work, you are exceptional. Why would you quit – or semi-quit?"

He took a sip of his drink. "Ah, now there is a story. At least the way I would like to tell it, it's a story."

"I'm intrigued."

"Way cooler to tell people that a rhino ran me over, but the truth is I was in a bad car collision in Nairobi. I was in the wrong place at the wrong time – a victim of an underworld clash. Speeding down a highway, a vehicle pulled along side and they executed my driver. Needless to say, the car careened out of control and crashed. It fractured my thigh in several places and took three surgeries to repair. After deciding to retire, I moved here. I took up diving and it changed my mind about retirement. I decided to focus my work with NatGeo on underwater photography, because diving is therapeutic, and because I avoid a lot of exposure to locations with a high level of criminal activity.

As they walked along the hall to the great room she said,

"The photos underwater – are they here in the Keys?"

"Many are. I didn't do underwater photography until I moved here. Gunner talked me into taking up diving and it's been fantastic. It's a whole different world down there. So – peaceful. I've done several overseas photo shoots and have many more in the planning and development stages."

He watched her study the photos, ambling along the hall. "You must come out with us sometime. I think you would enjoy it."

"I'll need lessons first. But yeah –" She stopped at one of dark waters, with beams of light shining down through the depths and a two upright manatees, looking like two women sharing a secret. She stared at it a long time. The light breaking through the dark and the intimacy of the two creatures captured her attention. She felt a tug at her heart. "I'd love to see this." Pointing back to all his work she said, "I'd love paint these kinds of things."

"Now that you've seen my work, you must show me your paintings."

"Ang exaggerates. I paint for me. I have a minor in art from college, but I haven't done anything with it. So now it's my way of letting out some of my thoughts and feelings. I'm not in the same class as you, Indigo and Deon."

"You have the soul of an artist. There are a lot of artist souls living here. Many soon come to make a living from their art. The Keys are an inspiration – the light and life here just reaches into your soul."

JJ nodded. "Oh that reminds me. I want to ask you something. You mentioned talking with Indigo about doing classes for the community kids. I don't know if you're aware, but every Thursday evening we have a beach barbecue for our guests. I was wondering if you'd be interested in running a pottery workshop for the children of the guests, where they could make a simple pottery lamp that fits those miniature electronic tea lights. Then they could use their lamps at the barbecue and take them home with them afterward. Reservations would provide you with expected numbers. What do you think?"

"Let me think on that. There's a young mother in town that would be an excellent teacher for such a group. If she's interested, then I don't see why not."

"How much would you charge?"

He did quick calculations in his head and gave her a reasonable number.

When they returned to the great room Jason said, "Everyone ready to eat? It's a simple meal tonight. I have foil-wrapped potatoes cooking on the barbie. They should be close to done. There's salad. And Mike, could I get you to do the steaks?"

Indigo linked arms with JJ and headed for the kitchen. Sydney followed. "We'll get the table set." As they worked JJ noticed Ang and Dan in what appeared to be a deep conversation. She laughed at something he said then rested her hand on his arm while she answered. Dan smiled. When she dropped her hand, he stretched his arm to rest on the back of the couch behind her.

JJ grabbed the napkins and headed for the table.

Ang could never read men's interest. There is always one buzzing around her and she's blind to them. And what happened to her and Mike? I thought they were an item. How come she's sitting with Dan and not out with Mike?

Then she looked at Indigo.

I wonder if she knows Dan's interested and that's why she grabbed me to give him time with her. And then Sydney left. Perhaps everyone sees it but Ang. I hope Dan doesn't end up with a broken heart.

She looked at Dan.

Then again, I hope that Mike doesn't end up with a broken heart either.

After dinner they sat on the back deck watching the sky darken and the first stars make their appearance. The discussion moved to what they found hardest about their job. Indigo talked of her heavy travel schedule. Dan talked about the deeply weird callers that try to get airtime to tell the world they are dating a telephone pole. Mike said the hardest thing was seeing the kids of drug addicts, knowing they didn't have much of a shot at life. Theo talked about counselling parents of a dying child. Sensing the direction of the conversation, JJ quickly headed for the bathroom. She made it into the house when the tears started.

Jason slipped away as well, to spend several minutes in the kitchen under the pretence of getting more wine.

I'm going to have to explain to Theo about JJ's past. Poor girl. That one blindsided her.

He knocked on the bathroom door. "JJ, you okay? Sorry about Theo. He's unaware of what you've been through. He wouldn't hurt anyone."

"I'm okay. Thanks Jason."

He thought for a moment. "Can I show you something? I haven't shared it with anyone, but I think you would understand."

She blew her nose, wiped her eyes and opened the door. "Sure."

He led her to his bedroom. She noticed a stunning photograph of an old woman's hands held by a young man. From the top drawer of a dresser that looked like it came from a Malaysian plantation he pulled an intricately carved wood box. He sat down on the bed and invited her to sit beside him.

"It's beautiful," she said, running her finger along the top.

"It's from India." He set it on his knee, and stared at it without seeing it. "I was in Mumbai working on a story about the trains. There was this kid, a street urchin, who took a liking to me – followed me everywhere. After a few days of trying to get rid of him I gave in and offered to share my dinner with him. He ate like he hadn't seen food in weeks. He was a great kid who stole my heart. I can still hear his laugh.

"For a week, I'd come out of my hotel in the morning and he'd appear out of nowhere and spend the day with me. He was a cute kid – funny, bright smile. Every day he gave me a crayon drawing of the two of us doing something from our previous day. Even with a crayon, he showed real talent.

"One day I scheduled meetings with important city offi-cials and I told him he couldn't come. We argued. I got mad and we parted ways. When I got back to my hotel that evening he did not show up. I shrugged it off, expecting to see him in the morning. When he didn't show up the next morning, I looked for him. After bribing multiple kids, I found the place he called home – a couple pieces of cardboard on the edge of the city dump. He was there – his face bloodied, his body broken and bruised." Jason's voice cracked. He paused, absently rubbing the box with his thumb.

"He often begged on street corners. While I was in my *im-portant* meetings, a man pulled him into a back alley and raped him, then beat him and left him for dead. He crawled back to his home. When I found him, there wasn't much life left – no time for medical help. I held him in my arms. I kept telling him I was sorry. If only I let him come with me, none of it would have hap-pened. This little life snuffed out because of me."

He opened the box. "Before he died he reached under the cardboard, in a crack in the ground, and pressed into my hand his only treasures on this earth." He handed her the box.

She wiped her eyes and to look at the treasures – a plastic dinosaur missing one leg, an elastic band, a little bracelet made of colourful string, several folded sheets of paper, and the nub of a blue crayon.

Pointing to the paper she said, "Are these his drawings?"

He nodded. "Open them. Tell me what you think. Was he talented?"

Carefully she unfolded the stack. The first one was a sketch of Jason, younger, but identifiable as him. "It's amazing the de-tail and shading he captured with just a crayon." She looked at the other sketches – sitting together on the train, eating to-gether, looking at a map, and the last one of the two of them walking away with Jason resting his arm on the young boy's shoulder. "Oh Jason. He loved you." She pressed her hand to her heart, unable to say anymore.

"Yes, he did. And I loved him too." He let out a shaky breath. "He died in my arms. As per the Hindu practice of burying children, I arranged for his burial and a marker for his grave.

"For weeks I lived under a heavy cloud of guilt and remorse. If only I hadn't insisted that he leave me alone. When I left India I booked three weeks of holidays in search of a way to shove all this emotion into a closet and lock the door. I ended up here in the Keys at the Plantation House and within a day or two I stumbled upon Eulah. We talked every day. She straightened out my thinking. She helped me work through my guilt, remorse and my if-only thinking. From there I moved to blaming God. And Eulah showed me how God is good. It's this fallen world that brings death in it's many variations. When I placed the blame where it should be, with the man that had done this, anger and hatred burned within me. And she helped me deal with those feelings before they took root as bitterness. She is a very skilled counsellor, and I got through those difficult emotions with her help.

"JJ, there's no easy way through grief. You can't tuck those feelings away and ignore them. If you do, they linger waiting for a life event to erupt and force you to address them. You have the hard work of dealing with painful thoughts and emotions. And that hole in your heart will always remain with you. But in time, if you deal with all the other thoughts and feelings, you find a way of living a full rich life, despite those holes.

"I showed you all this to tell you I understand the pain of loss and grief, and I survived. You will too. You are in the dark place of grief now, but you won't stay there. Talk to Eulah. She's an educated counsellor, despite what her current work looks like."

"I know. We've found each other already."

"Don't feel bad that talk of children dying sends you to the bathroom in tears. It sent me to the kitchen. My Scottish Grandma used to say, "Gardyloo" when she saw hard things coming across your path. Theo's conversation was worth a gardyloo warning. But I didn't think you'd know what it meant."

She shrugged and shook her head.

He laughed. "Nana was a character. Back before there were flush toilets in Scotland they used to dump the contents of the chamber pot out the window. They'd yell gardyloo to warn people below of what was soon to follow. My nana adopted the word to announce when life was about to dump a load of nasty on you."

JJ smiled. "Nana sounds interesting." She slowly nodded her head. "Gardyloo. I think it's a keeper word."

"It's a great word, but the impact is far less when you have to explain it. Anyway, I'm sorry Theo stepped into it."

"It's not his fault. It's just so hard. Do people ever get over the sorrow?"

"It still sneaks up on me, but that's okay. A little sorrow remembered honours the love I felt. But now it comes for a short visit then passes. I'm no longer a prisoner to it. It's now a welcome but occasional visitor."

"I can't even imagine getting to that place. I see no light, nor the end of the tunnel. It feels like I'm facing years, decades, a lifetime without hope. There are days I wonder if I can do it."

"Those who have walked the path of grief understand, yet it remains a journey of one. You walk through those dark places alone and that is how it has to be. Those dark places are in your soul and spirit, where only you and God operate." He put the box back in the drawer. "Let's take a walk down to the water. It'll give us both the chance to clear thoughts before we join the others."

They walked past the old red chair. She couldn't help running her hand along its weathered surface. They boarded the boat and stretched out on the padded benches at the back, listening to the water lap against the hull. JJ leaned back and looked at the stars. "The thing about gardyloo is that hopefully you avoid getting hit by the nastiness. Unfortunately, no amount of warning can help you avoid the anguish of loss."

"Yeah, I didn't understand the agony someone's death brings. I had no idea of the long list of emotions I'd have to deal with. I just didn't see any of it coming. I didn't expect a street urchin in a strange land stealing my heart, and I certainly didn't expect his violent death. Grief is not easy. By far, it's the most difficult thing I've dealt with because of the turmoil of emotions and thoughts that grip your life. I know the lure of slamming the door on all the pain, but that just traps you there. You've got to embrace that pain and deal with all the emotions. I can tell you there is a way through it all. I've walked grief's deep valley twice and I can tell you, there is a way to come back to life and hope despite the deep wounds."

Fresh tears rolled down her cheeks. "For months I couldn't cry. I felt nothing – just numbness. Now Indigo talks about her sculpture or you talk about your grief and I tear up."

He laughed. "Yeah, that too will pass – eventually. It took awhile before the tears showed up for me. They appeared somewhere between numbness and blaming God. And it's worse for a guy. You know, boys don't cry."

"Neither do big girls, apparently."

"Well aren't we a pair of rebels, or perhaps bohemians is a better word."

She nodded. "I must get myself a suede fringe vest." Her smile faded. "At least tears are a sign my heart still functions. How long did the whole grief journey thing take? How long before things get better?"

"No one can answer that for you. How long is the sky? It's just not something we can measure out. Your journey is uniquely yours. It is a mental and spiritual journey and where you have to travel depends on your personal circumstances. I can tell you two things made a big difference for me. One was Eulah. She is very wise and a skilled counsellor in dealing with the mind. And the other was inner healing for my spirit. Your mental and your spiritual being are involved in grief's journey and the path out requires healing in both."

On the way home, Angeline asked her how she enjoyed the evening. JJ watched the passing houses, the palm trees catching light from the front porch lamps. "It was good. They are an interesting group." She thought about the various personalities and the laughter-filled evening, losing herself in Indigo's song, the little box from India and Jason's offer to talk whenever she wanted.

"Sorry about Theo. He doesn't know what you're going through."

"It's okay. I didn't want to hear an example, when I am that person."

"Yeah, I understand. What do you think of everyone? Quirky! Didn't I tell you? Everyone here is quirky."

"Yeah, in a good way though. Not weird. Just interesting." She thought of Dan and his assignment of songs. And Indigo's dance brought a smile. "By the way, is Gunner the person who wears a different pair of tennis shoes every day?"

"You remembered. Yes, he's the one. He buys them white and paints them himself. That is his artistic thing. I knew you would like it here. It's perfect for you. You being an artist, you'll fit in with the locals better than me, and I fit in just fine." She paused. "I hope you can find happiness again."

JJ cleared her throat. "It's been a long time since I had any friends. It was just and Cam, little Lucas and me. Then everyone died."

"I imagine it's difficult starting over again. I'm sorry all this has happened, but I'm glad to have my best friend here with me. I've missed you. And I love sharing my place with you – it's our place now."

JJ reached over and squeezed Ang's arm. "Thank you."

Ang grabbed and held her hand.

They finished the short drive in silence. Ang sensed tears threatened to flood out if she said more. And she didn't think JJ needed the burden of any more tears.

At home JJ took the second mystery package to her bedroom. She turned the brown envelope over looking for an indication of who sent it. *Same address as the first package.*

Inside she found three photos and another newspaper clipping. The first photo was of her dressed up as a princess for Halloween. The photo captured her and her dad walking toward the camera. Trick or treating with her dad was a fond memory, but she'd never seen this image before.

The next photo was of her and her mom at the art museum. They stood close together looking at a painting. Again, she had no recollection of this photo being taken. The third was of her and her parents coming out of church together. She'd never seen these photos before. She didn't know who would have taken them.

Looking for some meaning, she read the newspaper clipping of her father's obituary. Memories flashed through her mind of sitting in the garage drawing and painting while he worked. Her heart ached for him. She remembered standing at his graveside watching the coffin lower into the ground. At 13, she knew life had just snuffed out her carefree existence. The pain of that loss and the ones that followed rolled in – again.

Jason is right. If I don't deal with the thoughts and emotions of a loss, it lurks, waiting for a vulnerable time to pour back in.

Looking at the items, she felt uneasy. She sensed a foreboding – like these packages tell a story she may not want to hear. She dropped them in the box with the stuffed bunny and other items from the first package. The box then went to the back of the closet.

I don't have the steam to deal with anything more right now. Whoever is sending this and whatever it means, I can't deal with you now. I've got five deaths to grieve. I've got a hurting mind and spirit in desperate need of help.

But every child knows monsters lurk in the back of the closet.

CHAPTER 11

While JJ fought with the toaster the next morning Angeline took a brief call on her cell phone then asked if JJ would like to join a few of the gang going scuba diving. "Gunner had a last minute cancellation. He and Jason are organizing a dive. Gunner said he could begin your lessons if you are interested in coming. He'll have you out diving today. It's called a resort certification when you dive right away and you'll only be able to go out with Gunner until you're certified. I learned with Gunner this way and quickly moved on to open water certification."

It only took the memory of Jason's photographs to convince her to agree.

Sitting on the deck of Jason's boat, Gunner began her lesson as soon as the boat left dock. When they arrived at their dive location, Jason, Dan, Mike and Angeline did their safety checks, rolled off the side of the boat and disappeared under water. While the others did their morning dive, Gunner continued with the dry land lessons.

After an hour, the divers emerged brimming with happy chatter. They enjoyed lunch, laughs and a little relaxation while Jason took them to a shallow dive location. Everyone geared up, including Gunner and JJ, and plunged into the water. Gunner and JJ practiced basic skills, but soon she was underwater and swimming down to the coral reef and colourful fish. In the distance she spotted the others exploring the reef and Jason busy with his camera.

After a thrilling hour, Gunner checked his gear and signalled there was 10 minutes left. As they made their way back to the boat, the others caught up. Jason tapped her shoulder, gave the signal for manta ray and pointed. Out of the blue distance, a large sea creature gently glided by. Stunned by its size JJ watched until it disappeared into the ocean depths. When on the boat, they told JJ how unusual it was to see one of those majestic creatures swimming during the day.

With the gear put away and the empty tanks back in Gunner's truck, everyone gathered on Jason's back deck. While Mike barbecued the burgers, Jason disappeared for a few minutes. When he returned he handed JJ an envelope. Inside was a signed photograph of the manta ray. "Your first day of many in the new world, Jason."

She traced the lines of the creature.

This is going on my dresser mirror until I can get it framed.

"It's beautiful – both the animal and your photo. Thank you."

"So what do you think of scuba diving?"

"I can see why you love it. It is like entering another world, one that is very pristine and peaceful." She turned to Gunner. "If you're game to get me through to certification, I'm interested."

Gunner smiled. "Hooked another one. You bet. You'll bring us back up to six divers. Sydney used to come, but she has health issues that keep her from diving."

Two days later, JJ and Ang spent the morning in the outdoor lounge putting together all her ideas into a plan. She stopped by the bar to get a coffee for Ang and a tea for herself. She chatted with Mark, the barman. As she waited for their drinks she realized she missed Nic's charming grin and their usual banter. Aside from Ang, he was her first friend at the resort and he'd become her favourite.

The two women worked steady until they had a budget for each idea, a timeline and a plan for staged implementation. JJ stood up and stretched. Ang said, "This is a solid plan. Jerry will be pleased. I think we'll get a quick approval. He mentioned how impressed he was with your conversation. And I agree. These are great ideas, and will be good for Plantation House."

JJ sat back down and squeezed her friend's hand. "Thank

you for all your help. It wouldn't be as good without all the work you've done to pull it together into a real plan. You make me look good."

"You're welcome, but it's you that's making me look good."

JJ picked up her tea mug. "To our success."

They clinked their mugs and drank the last of their long-forgotten beverages.

Back in her office another gift awaited, like the ball of nothing, this one had no tag. *Who is doing this?*

She opened the box to find over two-dozen small lumps of coal.

Right. It's nearly Christmas and someone thinks I'm not nice. Seriously?

Then she noticed writing on the inside of the box. "You've fooled everyone. But not me. I know who you really are."

Throwing the whole thing in the trash she said, "I'm not much for this secret Santa garbage."

The next two days she visited the outdoor lounge to grab a tea and chat up Nic, but he wasn't in. On the fourth day with no Nic, she asked Ang if something had happened to him.

"Yes, it is the third day he hasn't shown up for a shift and it's not like him to miss work. He's not answering his phone. I've got a call into Mike and asked him to stop by Nic's home to check if he's okay. I'll let you know when I hear anything."

A few hours later, Ang came to JJ's office. One look at Ang's watery eyes and JJ knew this was not good news.

"Mike called. He stopped by Nic's house and found him dead. He says it's not foul play and it doesn't look like suicide. They'll do an autopsy to determine the cause. I've called his parents. They're devastated."

JJ's heart seized. In a moment, all the pain and heartache of losing little Lucas washed over her. She ached for herself and for Nic's parents as only a grieving parent can do.

The rest of the day, the heaviness of the news mired her in the darkest places of grief. She wanted to talk with Eulah, but couldn't find her. She walked down the beach to where it ends at the mangroves and sat in the warm sand. Hugging her knees, she let the pain have its voice.

Why God? Why? Why is it so many people around me die? I befriend Nic. He dies. When is it going to stop? When I think there's a glimmer of improvement, I'm hit with more crap to deal with. I am not this kind of strong. I can't do this. I can't take any more. Where are You in all of this?

She wept, letting the anguish run its course. Emptied of emotion, she watched the waves tumble in and withdraw, wave after wave. In the quiet of nature's rhythm, she felt the relentless ache dissipate.

She drew in a deep breath and let it out.

I think I get it. When my internal storm rages, I can't hear you so well. But I can find you in my stillness of being. Here I am Lord, broken inside and hurting.

As she listened to the waves' gurgling laughter rolling in, and their receding quiet whispers, a vision of two little girls playing together in the sand sprang to mind. She watched the two toddlers squatting in the wet sand, bare feet washed by last push of the wave. With heads almost touching, they looked for shells. She heard the whispers of their young girl discoveries followed by their bubbling laughter.

"Why would this image pop into my mind? Is this from You, God? Do You speak in these images I see? If this is from You, please tell me what it means."

Look at the two girls closely. You call them Broken and Hurting. But I see two innocent toddlers. I see them together discovering the world around them. JJ, they are indeed you. I see you discovering your life again through the beauty of nature. I have brought you to this place so it can whisper life and laughter to you. You will learn that Broken and Hurting are really Wonder and Delight.

"I think I need a pair of your glasses, because what you see is vastly different from my reality. I'm still broken and hurting – even more with Nic's death."

Why do you seek out the quiet spaces of nature? Why are you sitting where you are now? Why do you love the smell of salt water and the sound of waves rolling and crashing? I planted in you a love of nature. It draws you because in it you find peace, calm, contentment – in it you find Me. Wonder and Delight are still young toddlers, but give them time. They will grow and become foundational in your new life.

"Thank you for talking to me. Thank you for giving me this quiet place where we can meet. Thank you for giving me some peace. Thank you for this image of two happy girls, of Wonder and Delight. But I still want answers, like why is the grim reaper stocking me? Why me? Am I some kind of cosmic death magnet? And when will it end? When will I get to the wonder and delight part?"

After a minute of silence she thought, *Well, okay. No answer today. Thanks for the promise of wonder and delight. Thank you for the infusion of peace. I am more than grateful for that.*

As she stood up and dusted off she said, "I hope You can meet in other places too. It will be difficult to get here when we need to talk."

A moment later she laughed out loud.

Yeah. Fair enough. You are everywhere.

That evening she got a call from Jason. "I remember how you liked that photograph of the two manatees. I know where several hang out. I thought you might be interested in visiting it. We could go snorkelling."

"Oh I'd love to go swimming with manatees."

The next afternoon, Jason gave her a boat tour of the islands in the area. He wove between a maze of small atolls and stopped in a spot a million miles from civilization. While he anchored the boat, she drank in the peace and solitude of the area.

Solitude, is that the right word? It is indeed solitude from people, but it is an abundance of creation, of beauty, of life. Yes, solitude in the meditative, not the lonely sense. I can breathe here.

"This is an amazing place." She smiled. *Wonder and Delight.*

"Yeah, I've never run into anyone here. And there are lots of manatees. So I suspect few know about it."

They geared up, sat on the side of the boat and rolled

backwards. She loved that plunge into the other world. In the warm waters of the Keys, she felt like this underworld wrapped its arms around her in a loving embrace. They swam for several minutes through the mangroves. It opened into a sheltered pool of water. Jason stopped her and pointed. In the distance she could see several manatees grazing on the vegetation. One stopped grazing and looked their way, then continued its meal.

She surfaced and pulled out her snorkel. "How close can we go?"

"We don't want to disturb them, but they are mellow creatures. They can be curious and sometimes they approach. It's awesome when that happens. Follow me. We'll swim around the bay and see what happens."

They watched a mom and her baby. She was grazing while the youngster rested. When it awoke, it fed for a few minutes then spotted the two observers. As is the way with many wild youngsters, this curious one swam over for a greeting. JJ reached her hand out and the moppet edged closer for a rub. Mom came over to supervise. They spent several minutes with the two creatures. Losing interest the two moved on.

She popped her head out of the water. "That was awesome! I had no idea they are so big. You just don't get the sense of their size from photos. But so amazing to have them swim right up."

He smiled at her excitement. "Let's continue around the pool. Other manatees might welcome a visit. When we're done there's a shallow reef awaiting exploration if you're interested."

"Absolutely."

They saw a few more manatees grazing and sleeping, but no more curious ones. Swimming past the boat and mangroves, they headed out into open water. They made their way along the inner side of a reef watching the abundance of fish. On the way back they swam along the outer edge. A bunch of nurse sharks rested together at the bottom of the reef. Fear gripped JJ, but Jason said they are bottom feeders and wouldn't be interested in humans. The sharks didn't move at all, undisturbed by the two visitors.

Back on the boat, JJ raved about all she'd seen. Jason smiled while he listened, remembering his enthusiasm when he first started diving.

"I thought sharks had to keep moving for oxygen, but those ones just rested on the bottom."

"They're nurse sharks. They can remain motionless on the sea floor and pump water through their gills."

She joined him in the wheelhouse as he piloted out of the maze of islands.

Once clear of the reefs he opened the engines to cruising speed. Enjoying the wind and salt air, she rocked with the steady rhythm of waves. "It's kind of like dancing. The ocean is a good partner. I can anticipate her moves."

"You like dancing?"

"Love it."

He nodded. "I know a good bar in town. People often dance there. We can go sometime, if you like."

"I'd like that. Do you dance?"

"It's not pretty, but I enjoy a good turn around the floor."

Something floating on the water caught her attention. "Hey, what's that?"

He slowed the boat and turned to approach. "I think it's a dead animal."

He threw it into idle and coasted in close. It was a manatee mangled by a propeller. The damage was shocking. JJ couldn't look. It was too heartbreaking. Jason noted her determined stare ahead and slipped the boat into gear. She left the wheelhouse to watch the wake from the engines and let the tears flow.

So much death. I'm so sorry little manatee. I'm sorry for your pain. And I hope your death was not prolonged. God be with you now.

Jason gave her a few minutes, then shut off the engines, grabbed two bottles of water and joined her in the back. He handed her one. "I'm sorry you saw that."

"It's such a cruel death for such a sweet, harmless creature. It's so pointless." She tried opening the bottle then gave up.

He took the bottle, cracked it open and handed it back.

"Nature *is* beautiful. I love connecting with the animals, but sometimes that connection brings you face-to-face with the hard fact that life always ends in death. I've watched the birth of a young zebra, a new life kicking up its heels with joy in the liberating experience of running. And I've seen a leopard snatch that life away, leaving nothing but a pile of bones. The fall of humanity brought a dear cost to God's creation. This stunning beauty of life is no longer free. But between birth and death is the exquisiteness of life, in its infinite variety, naturally doing what seems impossible. It's the mystery of the vividness of the tiger's orange, black and white astonishingly melting into a jungle. It's creation's flawless concert in the key of unbounded joy." He nodded toward the ocean. "It's the enigma of something with unimaginable weight inviting you to visit its weightless world. There are countless expressions of beauty through which creation beckons humanity to engage every day. Don't forego that rich experience because of the cost of sin. Yes, death and pain are heartbreakingly hard to see, but God's creation is still there in all its beauty. Life and nature – they're like the most interesting person in the world. Sure, there's an ugly stain on their shirt, but they make you laugh. They make you think. They make you feel connected. And they make you a better person."

"I guess so. It seems that for me, death is ever present, always lurking, and marauding. I find something to care about, and death swoops in and kills it. I care about the manatees and boom, here's a dead one for ya."

He studied her face. "I guess I should have said gardyloo as we approached."

She laughed. "Yeah, I'm not sure that would have helped."

Jason lifted one of the bench seats and found a tissue box.

She grabbed a couple and said, "It's not just the manatee. My favourite barman at the Plantation was found dead in his home yesterday." *You like your colleagues? Boom. Here's a dead one for ya.*

His brows furrowed. "I'm so sorry to hear that. Who was

it?"

"Nicolas Galanos."

"Ah yes, I know Nic. Great guy. I *am* sorry. I met his parents last year at one of the barbecues. Good family. They'll be devastated."

She nodded, mopping her eyes.

He looked out to sea. "I have an idea. Let's grab something to eat, then there's an evening show I think you'd enjoy."

"A show? Here on the island?"

He nodded.

"What kind of show?"

"Ah, a little mystery in life is like chicken soup for the soul."

"Uh-huh."

He stood up and held out his hand. "Trust me?"

She squinted her eyes and looked him up and down. She took his hand. "I suppose, Austin Powers."

He laughed. "Why Austin Powers?"

"He's the international man—"

They finished the sentence together.

"Okay suspicious. C'mon. How about I teach you to pilot the *Cool Change* as a distraction for your curiosity."

He took her to the Sunset Grill. *I haven't had sushi since college. This is going to be awesome.* They talked of African plains and college days, of childhood dreams and working realities, and where to discover joy.

With the sun sinking below the horizon, he paid the bill and grabbed her hand. "Show time." He drove to the Crane Point Hammocks Museums and Nature Centre. He bought two tickets, and they settled in to enjoy the night sky program.

Afterward, he took her back to his place. He opened her door and walked with her to her car. "Feeling better?"

"Yeah, I'm okay. Thank you for a good afternoon, an awesome meal, and a great night show."

With a warm smile he said, "You're welcome. I enjoyed today too. Thank you for your company."

She flipped through her keys then lifted her eyes to meet his. "I –" *Cognac. Warmer than leather. Velvet smooth. Rich in flavour.*

"I'd better go."

He held the car door until she was in. "Good night, JJ."

"Good night, Jason. And thanks again."

He closed the door, tapped it and stepped back. He stayed to watch her back up. They waved at each other. He turned into the house.

The mustard yellow Land Rover followed a few minutes behind.

The next day she ate lunch with Eulah. After the usual pleasantries she said, "I need help. I can't live this way."

"What's on your heart today?"

"Every time life takes a positive turn, death rips someone from my life. Now I'm afraid to let people into my life. It's like a death knell sounds at the first sign of happiness and I glance around to see who will die this time. I'm really struggling with seeing anything good ahead. I now anticipate the next death. Death is all around me. Soon, everyone dies."

"You've mentioned that before. Who do you mean by everyone?"

"It started with our dog. When I was 13, I came home from school and found her dead on the porch. A week later it was my dad. Mom couldn't get over it. She died six months later. My grandmother took me in, and she died a year later. Then they sent me to a distant cousin two states away.

I hardened my heart for many years vowing I would not let life break me like it did Mom. Thinking I'd overcome my fears I got married, but that ended with a dead husband and child. And here I am, broken like Mom. Only worse. Mom lost her husband. If I add it all up I've lost my dog, my dad, my mom, my grandmother, my child and my husband. I have no family left. Life won. It broke me. I feel like my presence is the grim reaper and someone will pay the price for knowing me. Now it's Nic, and a propeller-shredded manatee. I don't want to consider who is next."

"That's some pretty powerful thinking. Do you believe you carry the power of death?"

"No – I guess I mean I'm bad luck – or bad karma. Everyone was okay down here until I come, and wham, someone dies."

"People die all the time. It will happen to everyone. Isn't that so?"

"I know this sounds crazy, but there *is* a lot of death around me. I'm afraid to let anyone into my heart in case they're next. And you'd better watch yourself."

"I'll check with the Lord, but I'm sure He will say what you speak is not truth, and it's not life."

"Still, hard to deny the overwhelming numbers. Things appeared to be improving, and next thing, Nic dies. It's like I'm Peppy Le Pew, you know, the skunk on Bugs Bunny. I'm walking through life and behind me people are falling down and dying in droves.

"I can't handle all this death. I need a break. When I was out with Jason on his boat to swim with manatees we came across this dead one and I fell apart. I discover a fondness for manatees and life immediately gives me a dead one. I can't stop this death trend, and I see no evidence that God is stopping it either. And if that's true, I cannot face a lifetime of death."

"Are you thinking to end your life?"

Shocked, she looked at Eulah. "No, nothing like that. Just that I see no point in making any effort in living. Best I avoid any meaningful relationships."

"Oh, beautiful lotus. This is not of God. None of this is what God wants for you. He *is* love. Walking in His presence is walking in love. And love is an exchange between people. Avoiding relationships is not living in His abundance. Tell me, what you think when you ponder the word hope."

She drew in a deep breath and let it out. "I see a world filled with people living in hope and moving toward their dreams. They expect good things ahead. But for me, I've seen a steady stream of death and think there's only more death ahead. When I make a step toward something good, a friendship, a marriage, a family, here comes the grim reaper. When I think about hope, I think it's for everyone but me."

Eulah thought for a moment. "You are suffering in both your soul and spirit. We will direct our efforts to healing both. You mentioned being out with Jason?"

She nodded.

"I'm glad you're establishing friendships. That is a good positive step."

"I'm afraid to let anyone get too close. It's not that I don't want friends. I'm quite aware of my loneliness in this dark place and I want to move away from it, but I can't face another death of someone I let get close."

"Mm-hmm. Consider new friendships as homework, and that's an ongoing assignment. Here is another exercise. I want you to get a pad of paper. Every time you have a helpless, hopeless thought, I want you to write it out. Visualize your feelings draining out onto the paper. For every negative thing, write an I-am statement on a sticky note that is the opposite. For example, when you think 'I am the grim reaper,' the opposite would be?"

"I am not the grim reaper?"

Eulah smiled at the small sign of spunk. "Yes. Can you expand on that?"

"I'm not the grim reaper. I'm not responsible for life and death. And death is not my companion." *And standing in the vortex of death is not permanent.*

"That's a good start. Stick these notes where you'll see them every day. Read them aloud to yourself. Now, that piece of paper with all your negative thoughts poured out on it – crumple it up and toss it into a paper bag. Let those negative feelings separate from you. Seal the bag and throw it out or burn it. You are done with these thoughts.

"And I have one more piece of homework. What hobby or activity do you love? Something that brings you joy. Something that maybe you haven't done in a long time."

"I used to paint. It's been several years though."

"How do you feel when you're painting?"

The corners of her mouth quivered up. "I feel – transported to – no, enveloped in the world of the painting. It's like getting absorbed in a great movie and leaving your present circumstances behind, if only for a little while. I feel whole."

"This is the first time I've seen life bubble up from within you. So, make time to paint. Your full homework is to continue to build new friendships, paint, toss out the negative and reaffirm the positive."

On her way home that evening she listened to the radio and heard Eric Church's song *Those I've Loved* for the first time. She parked in the driveway listening to the final verse. Tears streamed down her face as she thought about all who she'd loved and how that love moulded her into the person she'd become. She thought about her old life, her new friends, her losses and the good things that have come into her life since moving to Florida. She thought about how Jason finds abundant life in connecting with nature. She thought about how Indigo pours her sorrow into her art.

After dinner, she pulled out her sketchbook to look for inspiration for her first homework assignment. She stopped at *moon wake* and got an idea. The painting absorbed her soul for a few hours. She looked at the results of her efforts and smiled.

I know just what to do with this.

CHAPTER 12

After working in one of the outdoor rooms, she found a message waiting on her desk. "Ryan Miller called and asked you to please call back."

"Hi, Ryan. I got your message."

"JJ. Thanks for calling back. I have some new product lines I'd like to discuss over a meal. I'll be in your area tomorrow. Can I meet you for dinner?"

Eulah's words sprang to mind – build new friendships.

This is a real stretch, Eulah, but okay.

"Sure. When and where?"

"When are you done work?"

"Oh around six I guess."

"How about I pick you up at Plantation House at six tomorrow?"

"Okay, see you then."

Ang dropped by in the afternoon to let her know she'd heard from Jerry about their proposal. "He green-lighted stage one and wants you to provide an update every couple weeks. Congratulations, JJ. I think this calls for a celebration. How about we invite the gang over on Friday evening, maybe do Mexican?"

"Yes!" JJ did a little hand pump. "A party? Mexican sounds great. Thanks for all your help." She dropped her hands to the desk, paused then pushed up to stand. She looked at Ang, then out her window then back to Ang. "Do you remember?"

"What's that?"

She broke into her happy dance.

Ang laughed.

JJ held her hands to her heart. "I almost expected him to say no."

"I told you he loved your ideas."

"Now I need to make it work."

"They are good ideas, and *we* need to make it work."

"Thank you, Ang."

When alone she said, "Thank you, God. You gave me the ideas, now I will rely on you to help me make it a success. And thank you for a glimmer of hope."

That evening she worked on her *Moon Wake* painting. By bedtime, she sat back and looked at her progress. Pleased, she decided it needed a few minor touches and it would be done. Considering she had done no acrylic painting in years, she was thrilled with the results.

Six o'clock the next evening her office phone rang. "Hi JJ. It's the front desk. You have a Mr. Ryan Miller here who says he has a meeting with you?"

"Thanks, Sara. Please tell him I'll be right out."

She locked her computer, stood and with a deep breath said, "I can do this."

She entered the lobby. "Ryan."

He set the pamphlet down and stood up. "JJ. Thanks for meeting with me."

He had a mainlander-Miami look – trim beard, manicured nails, a white silk button-down shirt with sleeves rolled up tucked into mid-blue knee length shorts with a white belt. She considered how comfortable she was in her bright flowered shorts, cotton shirt and leather anklet and smiled. *Mainlander meets islander.*

He led her to his car, a white convertible Mercedes Benz. As he held the door for her he said, "I thought we could go to the Island Fish Company. I don't know if you've been yet. It's a waterside Tiki bar."

"Not yet. It sounds great."

After they ordered, and Ryan unfolded and placed the napkin on his lap and steered conversation to business. They discussed the spa and her plans for growth.

He said, "I've read about Jerry in several financial and entrepreneur magazines. He has a solid history of making winning moves. If he's supporting this, it's good for business. You couldn't ask for a better endorsement."

"Thanks." Thinking of the Mercedes in the parking lot she said, "You and your partner seem pretty solid. Your business is going well?"

"It's exploding. We've tripled our staff in 18 months. I moved into an upscale neighbourhood and now my fashionista neighbour has me looking like I'm fresh off the set of Miami Vice."

She laughed. "Are you comfortable in that look?"

He scratched his beard. "Yeah. I guess so. I fit in with the Miami crowd. And you? You look like a comfortable member of the Conch Republic."

"What's the Conch Republic?"

"Ah. Well, it's the tongue-in-cheek secession of Key West from the U.S. in the early '80s to protest a police checkpoint. They called it the Conch Republic. Since then they've kept it alive as a tourist thing, and expanded to include all the Keys. It goes from the Last Chance Saloon at the tip of the mainland right down to Key West. Adherents say it exists as a sovereign state of mind. They advocate a life of humour, warmth and respect."

"Sounds good." She raised her glass and clinked with his. "Here's to me, the latest citizen of the Conch Republic."

"So have you heard what we, up in the U.S. are doing with blending oils?"

"No. Do tell. It's good to keep on top of what you foreigners are up to."

They discussed the latest trends. They talked about his childhood home in Nebraska. And they laughed.

A raucous bridal party celebrated at the bar. The young women were playing a treasure hunt of sorts. One of them approached the table, pulled Ryan's chair back and sat on his lap. She planted a big kiss and asked why he never called. While he stumbled over an answer, she turned to JJ and said, "Oh honey, you are so lucky. This one's spectacular." She ran her hand through his hair.

Blushing, Ryan said to JJ, "I – I've never met her." He grabbed at her hands to stop her. "I think you've got the wrong guy."

JJ watched, half laughing, half shocked. She glanced around the bar. *Yup, half of Marathon is watching.*

The woman said, "Well, how about you buy an Amanda." JJ burst out laughing.

He shrugged.

She caressed his cheek. "It's a new drink. That gorgeous barman over there –" The barman smiled and nodded. "He designed a new drink for my friend Amanda who is getting married. You must have one."

Ryan took a quick look around and wanting to hurry her on her way, he said, "I'd love an Amanda. Thank you."

She signalled one to the barman. "Okay you have to sign my bingo card."

"Where am I signing?"

"There." She pointed to a square under the G. "This square – flirt with a handsome stranger." He handed her back the pen and she said, "Oh and you need to sign there for buying Amanda."

The drink arrived and she moved on to the next table.

He pulled his chair back to the table and cleared his throat. "Well that's a first. Way more fresh than Nebraska bridesmaids."

JJ laughed. "Your hair, it's –"

He smoothed it down, adjusted his napkin and peeked at the nearby tables.

He took a sip of Amanda. "Do you like coconut?"

She nodded.

"Would you like an Amanda. I'm not a big fan." She smiled to herself. *You can't take the meat and taters out of the farm boy.*

After dinner, a DJ played music. Several couples joined the partiers on the dance floor. The bingo gal returned and asked Ryan for a dance. He glanced at JJ and she shrugged. He let her pull him to the floor.

JJ thought, *Cam wanted nothing to do with dancing.* She watched Ryan chatting with all the girls. *But there's nothing like a country boy for charm.* She laughed when he resisted an alcohol-fuelled kiss. *And there's that mainlander stiff. No, stiff isn't right.* She watched him for half a song.

I don't think he's comfortable in his shoes. The city-successful trappings don't fit right. There's a lost country boy feeling about him.

A Kenny Chesney song come on that got the whole bar singing. He asked JJ if she'd like to dance. She learned the chorus and sang it out with the crowd, "No shoes, no shirt, no problem." The DJ followed with another Chesney song. She struggled more to learn all the parts of the chorus, but enjoyed the camaraderie of entire bar dancing and singing together. Many clinked their beers and a few guys leaned in to sing to her. For a few hours the blackness receded.

I really enjoyed myself this evening – the fun with a large group of people. Happy people. Living people. And dancing, oh it's been so long since I've danced.

When Ryan dropped her off at the Plantation House he said, "I had a great time. You're easy to be with. I hope we can do this again." He leaned in and kissed her cheek.

"Thanks Ryan. I had fun too. But I'm not dating. We can be friends and I'd love going for dinner when you're in the area. But let's keep it as friends, hey?"

"Friends? That's not the word I would choose for you. But I'll respect that for now."

In bed she relived the evening, the happy people, feeling connected through singing and dancing together.

It's been so long since I've tasted the sweetness of life. Eulah is right. It's good to build friendships. I never want to drift into the abyss of alone again.

Hot tears flowed down her face.

Great, now I'm crying when I'm happy.

Ang, Dan, Jason, and gang, even Ryan – you're my start. Tonight, I commit to my friendship with you all. I won't hide and I won't run. Conch Republic, the land of humour, warmth and respect, we will enjoy a lifelong friendship. Thank you, God, for planting this little lotus flower here.

Thursday after dinner she wrapped the finished Moon Wake painting and headed to the locals' beach. As she rounded the corner, she was glad to see Jedediah sitting on the bench.

"Hey Jedediah."

"Well, hello JJ. Did you come to enjoy the sunset?"

"Partly. I wanted to see you. Do you remember the first time we met? You told me about your wife Esmeralda and how she loved to dance in the moonlight on the beach because the light of the moon would follow her."

He nodded.

"Well I have something for you. I hope you like it." She handed him the wrapped painting. "It's been awhile since I've done any painting, but your story stayed with me."

He unwrapped it, handing the paper to JJ.

Holding the painting up he looked a long time, tracing the woman with his crooked finger. His lower lip quivered. "Esme." He reached for JJ's hand.

He stared at the painting whispering the words to a long forgotten song.

"It's just like I remember." His moist eyes looked at her. He patted her hand. "Thank you. You've given me back a piece of my Esme. I think this is the most precious gift anyone has ever given me."

They watched the sun go down, she thinking about the power of love to bring life, and he lost in memories. As the moon rose, she watched him shuffle down the path, cane in one hand and painting in the other.

CHAPTER 13

Friday night arrived. Both Ang and JJ left work a little early to get ready for their celebration party. Ang was a little disappointed that work prevented Mike from coming, but soon their place filled with chatter and laughter, and her disappointment slipped away.

Once everyone arrived they toasted to JJ's success. Dan brought a playlist he prepared for the evening. It included several Jimmy Buffet songs, McGraw, Keith, Brooks, Nichols and Paisley and Chesney – the music played throughout the Keys. She knew a few of the tunes, but it amazed her how everyone knew all the words and sang along to certain songs. She leaned over to Gunner who was standing beside her. "What's the deal with everyone singing?"

"We're a part of the no shoes nation."

"What?"

No shoes nation? Here I thought it was the Conch Republic. Hard to keep up with where I'm living.

"The no shoes nation. It started with a Chesney song, *No Shoes, No Shirt, No Problems*. Now there's T-shirts, hats, tanks, boat flags, beach towels and even license plates. His music captures the feeling of summertime, friends, and causal living. People love what he embodies. He's got a big fan base. He's popular here because his music expresses what island life is all about. And that is the no shoes nation."

"I'd heard his name, but I've not seen anything like this before coming here. It's kind of amazing."

Cam wasn't into music, or dancing, or parties – or friends for that matter. He was happiest out on the prairie working the land alone. This is a very different life. I like being a citizen of both the Conch Republic and the no shoes nation. I'm starting to feel the heartbeat of the life around me.

The meal was a make-your-own fajitas and quesadillas. Dan seemed to have no clue about how to roll a fajita and soon engaged Ang in helping him. Amidst a lot of laughter, the fajita became oversized and impossible to fold. Stray food littered the table. JJ smiled at his attempt to eat the monster fajita and wondered if he was as helpless as he appeared.

She took her plate and sat beside Theo on the couch. They exchanged some pleasantries, then he said, "A celebration of work success isn't the time for this, but I want to apologize. I didn't realize all you've been through when at Jason's the other week. I'm so sorry to have caused you any pain. Will you forgive me?"

"Oh Theo, you did nothing wrong. It's all good. But thank you for your apology."

As conversation moved to island life, JJ glimpsed Dan pointing out stray salsa on Ang's mouth. She tried to wipe it away, but missed it. Using his napkin, he got it for her lingering a moment on the final wipe. *Dan two. Mike none.*

Later in the evening JJ, Jason, Ang and Dan were on the deck sharing funny stories. They had been laughing so hard JJ's stomach ached. Dan told a story that crossed his desk that morning. "In Australia, the cops arrived on the scene of a three car pile up – " His laughter interrupted the story.

"A pile up between –" He laughed so hard everyone laughed with him.

He sniffed and started again. "There was a three car pile up between Giggles and –" The fits started again.

As is the way with laughter, everyone joined in without knowing why they were laughing. Jason wiped tears from his eyes.

Dan barely squeaked out, "Giggles and BooBoo the clowns –"

Jason smacked the arms of the chair. "BooBoo. In a car accident?"

In a high pitched voice Dan said, "No, no. I'm not finished. It was Giggles, BooBoo and Chick Jagger, a man dressed as a parrot."

The two guys collapsed, rocking in their chairs and gasping for breath. They gathered themselves then Dan said something that only Jason heard and that sent them into snorting fits. They tried to straighten up, but couldn't. Dan got up and left, laughing uncontrollably.

JJ couldn't help but get caught up in the laughter.

When Dan thought he had it under control he tried returning, but one look at Jason and the two of them started up again – jokes, thigh slapping and feet stomping.

He made one final attempt to join the group. Still snickering, he looked at Jason. "Don't start, man." Making an effort to straighten up, Jason focused on the conversation on his other side.

JJ said to Dan, "Some day you must tell us the end of the story."

"I don't know if I can get through it. We lost it at work and couldn't talk about it on air." He sat down beside Ang, his knee bumping up against hers. She pushed back, their legs rocking back and forth together. *Dan three, Mike zero.*

As the evening wound down, Jason leaned over and whispered in JJ's ear. "Come with me. I have something for you." He took her outside and pulled a large package out of his vehicle. "This is for you – to remember this moment, this place where the good begins."

The sat down on a bench. "Oh Jason. You will make me cry."

"I'm not sure that's as impressive a feat as it sounds."

She laughed. "Okay, I promise I won't cry ever again with you."

"Uh-huh. How about you open it and see what it is before you go making promises you and I both know you can't keep. Here let me get you started." He pulled one corner of the wrapping loose.

She pushed him away. He leaned back, and stretched his

arm out on the bench behind her. She picked off the wrapping paper, opened the box inside, and pulled out three metal stars to hang on a wall.

"Deon made them for me."

"They're beautiful. I love the design of all the little abstract stars inside. It's so beautiful. I've never seen anything like this." She read the line along the edges. "In the darkness she sees the beauty in the stars, and their twinkling hope touches her soul."

Tears brimmed her eyes. "They are perfect. I love it." She rested her hand on his leg. "Thank you so much."

"You're welcome." He gestured toward her moist eyes. "So much for promises."

"I'm a Bohemian rebel." She sat back. "I asked Eulah to help me. She gave me homework."

He laughed. "Ah yes, I remember the homework."

"You're part of my homework."

"I hope I'm a term project and not just a short answer question."

She laughed and leaned her head on his arm. "The stars are out."

He glanced up then looked at her.

"You're definitely not a short answer. Eulah says I need to build friendships. And I think it's time I build long lasting ones. I see people everywhere surrounded by friends and family. Well, I don't have family, but I can have friends."

"Sounds like you're sinking down your roots in this island sand."

"I like it here. I hope things turn around for me."

The front door opened. The party broke up and people were leaving. They joined the others in saying their goodbyes. She and Ang stood in the driveway waving as people left. Jason said, "Congratulations JJ, and let me know when you want help with your homework."

She nodded.

He turned to Ang. "Thanks for a great party. See you ladies."

JJ said, "Bye Jason, see you."

JJ showed Ang Jason's stars and they started a quick clean up. Ang said, "So, what's up with you and Jason, stars and homework?"

She shrugged. "What's up with you and Dan?"

"He's kind of cute, don't you think? And funny. I didn't realize how much he makes me laugh."

JJ smiled. *Ang was always easy to distract.* "Yes, he's handsome. You two were inseparable. He likes you."

"You think? Huh. Who knew?"

"Ang, everyone knows he likes you – except you."

She wrinkled her nose. "I might kind of like him."

"Try to figure that out before anyone gets hurt."

"You mean Mike?"

"Well, everyone. Mike and Dan, for sure. But this is a close group. Everyone will hurt if one of those guys gets hurt. You have the looks men fall over. They buzz around you and you've just never seen it. But these are great guys. They are worth you figuring out what you want before hearts break."

Ang loaded the dishwasher then stopped halfway through the glasses. "You're right. When I think about it, I'm comfortable with Dan. He makes me feel good about me, not like I'm just a dumb blond. Not that Mike makes me feel stupid, but it's just different with Dan. I kind of feel special."

"I once heard you should be with the one who makes you a better person."

Fluffing up her hair and throwing out her hip Ang said, "So it's not all about me feeling good?"

Her antics made JJ smile. She thought of her relationship with Cam. "I think if the basis of the relationship is you feeling special, that will wear thin. A day will come when people tire of continually pouring into their partner with little in return. On the other hand, if being with him makes you a better person, then the joy in the relationship comes from who he is and who you are, not what performance he has to give to make you feel special."

"Wow, that's deep. I never looked at it that way. When you say it that way, I sound selfish, like kiss my toes and treat me like a queen, you nobody."

"Oh Ang, I'm not saying you're selfish and it's not wrong to feel special around a man. All I'm saying is don't measure the success or health of a relationship based on one of you making the other person feel special. That's too much to expect of anyone long term and relationships are hard enough without that kind of pressure. Now if he makes you feel special and you do the same for him, well then that's good."

Ang hugged JJ. "Thank you for being honest with me. This is why I need you around. You make me think." She stepped back. "Now tell me about Jason. Is he the guy that makes you a better person?"

JJ's eyebrows flashed up. "I haven't gone there in my thinking. We're just friends. I need to get the ground under my feet before I think about anything serious."

"He likes you – everyone around you sees it."

She looked at Ang and saw her barely containing a laugh. She threw the wet dishcloth at her friend. "You're a brat."

"Maybe, but I speak the truth."

In her room she thought about Ang and Dan. She felt happy about her friend finding someone she might make a life with and hoped things would all work out for everyone.

Then she thought about what Ang said about Jason and fear seized her heart.

What if Jason is next on death's hit list? No, no, no, I couldn't live with that. I like the person I am around him. With him, I feel connected to life again. But I couldn't bear to see anything happen to him. I need this friendship. It's pulling me out of the abyss. But I can't imagine the bottomless pit I'd plunge into if something happened to him. I don't think I'd find my way out of that hole.

A familiar ache filled her heart. She pressed her hands to her chest with the intense pain. When she realized she was grieving a non-existent event, she grabbed her pad of paper and poured out her heart. She wrote about every nuance of her fear. She let tears stain the paper and run into the ink. Then she took her pad of sticky notes. Pen posed to write, she thought for a long time. She read through her fears a few times.

She wrote, "Death is not my companion. I live in the light and love of God." She peeled it off the pad and put it on her dresser mirror beside Jason's photograph of the manta ray. On the second note she wrote, "I am a good friend. Nothing bad will happen to people I care about." And on the third note, "I am committed to letting the brightness of life into my world." She stood looking at the three notes beside the manta ray. She read his note on the photo. "Your first day of many in the new world." She nodded her approval and read all three out loud.

I don't know if I believe these yet, I will keep saying them until they get into my heart.

She looked at the three stars leaning against the wall. "In the darkness she sees the beauty in the stars, and their twinkling hope touches her soul."

This is maybe the best room I've ever lived in. Here in the Conch Republic I've found my place of healing. Jason, your sparkling hope touches my soul. Thank you for showing me the beauty in the world around me.

The next morning Jason called. "You up yet?"

She smiled. "I'm sitting on the back deck with a tea."

"Oh good. Listen, I promised a friend I would take photos for her and I'm wondering if you'd like to come along. She runs a turtle rescue and rehab centre. I know the manatee bothered you and thought you might like to see people giving nature a helping hand."

"Okay, when should I come over?"

"How about I pick you up in two hours. We can grab lunch before we go over."

When she hung up Ang looked at her.

JJ laughed. "What?"

Ang smiled and dropped her gaze to the newspaper. "Nothing."

JJ expected Jason any moment. She dumped out her purse

for the second time searching for her sunglasses when the doorbell rang. She tossed the stuff back in and left without the glasses. Jason was in the kitchen talking with Ang. In a glance she took in his blue T-shirt and board shorts, and his tousled hair still damp from a shower. The bluest of eyes and a warm smile greeted her. *There's that man of ocean and wind I met at the grocery store.*

"JJ. You ready?"

"Yes. Sorry I was looking for my sunglasses, but couldn't find them."

"I've got a spare in the Land Rover you can have."

"Then I'm ready."

They went to the Brutus Restaurant and Seafood Market for a seafood salad lunch then headed over to the Turtle Hospital. Jason introduced her to Betty Zirkelbach, the manager of the rescue centre. She took them through the entire facility and showed them all the turtles in rehab. It surprised JJ how massive these turtles become.

These are not the little painted turtle pets we had as a kid. These are like – Turtlezilla.

She helped carry Jason's gear, handing him cameras and lenses. She didn't think he needed her, but watching Jason immersed in his work fascinated her. He took a lot of shots of the different aspects of the operation and of their public educational programs.

At the door Betty said, "Thanks again for donating your work and the photographs. I'll let you know when we plan our next release. JJ, please join us. People find it an amazing experience to see them swim back out to sea."

Jason said, "You're welcome, and for sure let us know about the release."

"Hey, are you going to the radio station's fund raiser? What about printing photos for a display?"

"Yes, I'm going. And printed photos are no problem. I'll pop by tomorrow with some contact sheets and we can pick out which ones."

"Sounds good. Nice to meet you JJ."

"You too, Betty."

They packed up his gear in the back of the Land Rover and hopped in. He started up the engine. "Thanks for coming with me."

She moved the borrowed sunglasses from the top of her head to cover her eyes. "You take me to the best places – the manatee pool, the sleeping shark reef, the stars night program, sushi and the turtle hospital. You really know how to show a girl a good time."

He slid the truck into gear. "It's a gift."

In a low voice she said, "It's a gift to me." She felt tears sting her eyes. She looked out her side window to compose herself, grateful for the reflective pilot's sunglasses. "You'll never know how these things bring light into my darkness. Just want you to know, it means a lot."

He pulled up to the highway. Glancing at her, he tapped the wheel with his thumbs. "I know how dark that road can be. I'm glad I can help you find your way."

He turned on the signal and waited for a clearing in traffic. An old, yellow Land Rover pulled in behind them.

Jason said, "That charity event that Betty mentioned, it's next weekend. Dan's radio station is hosting it, so he'll be there. They are raising funds for the Turtle Hospital. It's a dinner, dance and auction. Jimmy Buffet will be singing a set. Would you come as my guest?"

She cleared her throat. "A dance? I'm in."

He smiled. "I will limber up."

CHAPTER 14

Next day at work, JJ headed to the counseling bench for lunch. "Hi Eulah. Got time for a chat?"

Eulah patted the bench beside her. "How has your week been?"

JJ sat down and unwrapped her sandwich. "I think things are better. I've written several pages of negative stuff, and had three trash ceremonies. And there are several sticky notes on my mirror I read every day. I finished one painting and gave it to a friend. I think it meant a lot to him and that made me feel good. And I'm accepting invitations with friends. My life feels fuller, richer – and that's good."

"I sense a but coming."

"There is one thing I struggle with almost every night – a fear that all this investment in life will come crashing down. Someone will die, and I'll find myself in a deeper darker place than I am now – a place I won't be able to get out of. I repeat the positive affirmations, but this fear is gripping."

"Yes, that is the spiritual side of things. I think we need to spend a few hours going through an inner healing."

"What is that exactly?"

"There are patterns of thinking and behaviour that can trap us in this negative stuff like fear. Things happen in our lives, and we form judgments against people, and make vows we have no business making. All of this can open the door for a spiritual battle we cannot win on a human level. Inner healing addresses all those things so you can take a spiritual stand against things like fear."

"Okay, I'm game to try it. I don't want this fear anymore."

They met the following evening and through the tears,

Eulah led JJ through the process of identifying the origin of her fear, asking for forgiveness, then addressing the fear. As they prayed together afterward, God gave Eulah a vision.

"I saw a young girl journeying down a difficult path. There was a female tiger secretly following behind, often knocking her down. Despite the many falls, she never realized the tiger stalked her. But Jesus walked in between, limiting the power of the tiger. Then I saw Him turn around and deal with it permanently. The she-tiger disappeared. Now, the tiger wasn't the usual colours. It was a dark yellowy green instead of black and a muddy pink rather than orange.

"I feel this vision has a double meaning for you. One is tied to your fears of loving and losing again, and Jesus is your shield and protection. I feel what we've done tonight is the beginning of no more fear. But there is another perhaps more significant meaning. I think circumstances will bring this deeper meaning to light and explain the unusual colours."

The paradox of lightness of being while feeling a warm fullness intrigued her. On her sticky notepad she wrote, "I live in the place where my soul is weightless in freedom and my spirit is weighty in the fullness of joy." Lying in bed, no fear gripped her heart – for the first time since she was 13. Over the years, she failed to notice the darkness creeping up on her, until the fear became unbearable. She now felt the lightness of freedom in its absence. In her soul's quiet, she slept.

Several days later after work, JJ stopped at the bank to withdraw some cash from the ABM before picking up something for dinner. She put in her card and heard unusual scraping noises from inside the machine. "Great, you're probably going to eat my card, aren't you?"

From the ABM she heard, "Hello? Can you hear me?"

She glanced behind her. *Right. Where are the hidden cameras?*

"Hello? I'm stuck in the machine. Please, I need help."

A talking bank machine? Weee-ooo-eee-ooo-eee-ooo. Sargent, we got a 10-96 here. Send backup.

Knocking started. "Hello? Are you still there? Can you call

the police?"

Oh excellent idea. Now, let me think how would that go. "Yes, please send an officer to the bank. The machine is talking to me." *I do that and it's straight to the booby hatch.*

"Please, they accidentally locked me in here when they locked up the bank."

Welcome to Crazyville, where it's always March and there are mad hares everywhere.

She sighed as she pulled out her cell phone. "Hello, Mike? You are not going to believe this, but I'm at the bank and I think there is someone stuck inside the ABM. Can you or one of your guys come and help?"

She didn't notice the man lined up behind her as she finished the call. She bent down to the machine and loudly said, "I've called the police. They should be here shortly to deal with you. Can I have my card back?"

Gratefully she took her card as soon as it ejected. "Thanks."

As she stood up she noticed the guy behind her. "There's someone stuck inside the machine."

He noted the size of the ABM. "Uh-huh." He looked at her a long moment then said, "If you're done chatting up the machine, do you mind if I do my banking?"

She stood back and gestured for him to go ahead.

He put in his card.

The guy inside the machine said, "I can't give you any money, sorry."

The man jumped back and glared at JJ.

"It's not my fault the machine's not working."

He hit the cancel button, grabbed his card and stormed off.

A police car pulled up and a uniformed officer got out. "You called the police?"

I wonder if he carries a straitjacket in the trunk.

"Yes. It seems there's a guy trapped inside the ABM."

"Uh-huh.

Yeah, I wouldn't believe me either.

And what makes you think there's someone inside?"

Because the machine told me and I believe it? Let's just get the straitjacket now.

"I know this sounds crazy, but I heard a voice say that they got locked in by mistake when the bank closed."

Oh, here it comes.

"You heard a voice?" The officer smirked and knocked on the machine. "Hello, talking ABM. Are you really a man trapped inside the body of a machine?"

"Hello? Is that the police?"

Perhaps you should grab a straitjacket for yourself.

The officer's smirk quickly faded. He bent down to talk through the money door. "This is the police. Who are you?"

When he realized the ABM repairman was accidentally locked in, he let JJ go on her way.

That should cover my quota of nuts for the entire week.

The day of the fundraiser, Dan arrived early to pick up Ang. He took her to the pre-party to meet Jimmy Buffet. Alone, JJ connected her phone to the speakers in the living room, found a rockin' playlist and cranked the volume. It boomed through the house. She danced her way through the shower, hair, makeup, and dressing, letting the words and rhythm wash over her. The deep joy bubbled up demanding her physical expression.

Noting the time, she opened her jewellery box.

Over the music she barely heard, "Hey JJ! It's Jason!"

She yelled back. "Oh, Jason! Hang on! I'll turn the music down!" She hurried to the living room to adjust the volume. Already there, Jason held up her phone and she nodded. With a couple of taps, he adjusted it to a conversation level.

Sheepishly she said, "Just getting into the mood. I guess I lost track of time. Sorry about that."

He looked at her, eyes twinkling. "No worries. You look spectacular."

She twirled. "Thank you, kind sir. You're not too shabby yourself. Blue becomes you."

Grinning he said, "Thank you, fair maid."

"Give me two minutes. I need to get my earrings on."

She searched through her collection of earrings and found the long, dangly faux diamond ones. Giving herself a once over in the mirror, she took a lipstick out of her clutch purse and touched up her lips. Another check. *About as good as it's going to get.*

"Okay, I'm ready."

He looked up from his phone. "I'll be the envy of all the men tonight."

"Thank you. There will be dancing, right?"

"Most folks ask about Jimmy Buffet or the meal. But not you – you want to know about the dancing. I guarantee dancing tonight."

"Just checking. I'm all pumped. I don't want you to back out."

"I'm a man of my word." He reached for her hand. "I promise we will cut the rug tonight."

"I haven't heard that one in a long time."

"That's my nana's saying."

They wandered through the gallery of articles for auction. When she saw Jason's framed and signed photograph of a storm on the sea's horizon, she stopped and grabbed his arm. "I *knew* this was your work. It's gorgeous. You captured the stunning beauty of that dark, brewing monster."

"There's always beauty found in a storm, no matter how threatening."

She looked him in the eyes. For a long moment, they exchanged a silent communication only survivors of deep grief share.

After dinner they went to the beer garden. They chose a table at the edge of the tent. Jason assumed his usual kickback, islander position – one arm resting on the back of her chair, legs stretched out, and sipping his beer. They watched a senior couple for several minutes.

Over the speakers, *Southern Voice* played. With the beer resting in his lap and his other hand tapping the back of her chair, Jason sang the first verse to her.

That deep resonant voice gets me every time.

She said, "Where were you raised? I hear a drawl in there."

"I'm a South Carolina boy, from a small coastal town. Grew up on the ocean. I can't imagine living anywhere I couldn't smell the salt water and feel the soft breezes."

A picture of a young lad sitting on a surfboard, looking back to a low golden sun, the wind ruffling his long wet wavy hair popped in her mind.

"I thought I lost my Carolina accent, or so my family likes to tell me. Where are you from?"

"The other side of the country. For the first 14 years I lived in California, then inland to Colorado."

A rock tune played over the speakers. "I think it's time." He stood up, offering his hand. She happily accepted. They headed for the dance floor.

It surprised her how he knew the words to most of the songs. It seemed to flow from him. But his natural rhythm and easy dance moves surprised her the most. She enjoyed his strength and grace in leading her. They even tried a merengue, where the dancers hold each other close while moving around the dance floor. That one earned them applause from the other couples. By far, he was the best partner she'd ever danced with.

The music paused for the auction. People bid on donated fishing trips, overnights in hotels, scuba lessons, a wreck dive and several art pieces from local artisans.

"And the next item is a stunning photograph donated by Jason Williams, one of National Geographic's finest photographers. He now lives here in the Keys. And we're proud to call him one of our own."

JJ held her breath while they auctioned his photograph, and she cheered when it brought in several thousand dollars. After the auction, they announced they had raised nearly $80,000. Several people approached Jason afterward, wanting to talk about his photographs and his life as a NatGeo photographer. He gave his card to those interested in hiring him for their special projects.

They announced Jimmy Buffet's set. The crowd acted like a bunch of teens at a concert. Jimmy came off the stage and moved among them. He held the mic for several people to sing along, had the crowd sing parts of his songs, and all-round gave everyone a great time. When Jimmy finished, the DJ returned for another few hours.

After several fast dances came a few slow ones. Earlier in the evening they danced the slow ones as casual friends, but with the thinning crowd and the late hour, he held her close.

They stayed to the last song, another slow one. At the end, JJ whispered in his ear. "Thank you for the best night of my life."

He hugged her tight then pulled back to look at her. "You're welcome. It was a pretty good evening for me too."

She broke away and punched him in the arm. "When I asked if you danced you said –" She imitated him with a deep southern drawl. "'It's not pretty, but I enjoy a good turn around the floor.' That's what you told me."

Holding his shoulder and protecting himself against another hit he laughingly said, "So?"

"No guy with limited ability would think about attempting a merengue, let alone pulling it off to the applause of everyone. You lied when you said you're not pretty."

Still laughing, "I didn't lie. I'm not pretty. I like to think I lean more toward handsome."

In exasperation she sighed, then considered him a long moment. "I know the truth now. And I wouldn't say no any time you feel like keeping your skills up."

He turned, putting his hand on her back and led her to his car. "I'll keep that in mind."

When he dropped her at her house, he walked her to the door. She turned to him. They stood close for a long moment. She rested her hand on his chest. "I had a great time. Thank you. You're a good friend."

He hesitated, then stepped back. "I had a good time too. Have a good night's sleep, JJ." He squeezed her hand, turned and headed to his car. As he got in he waved to her, then pulled out of the drive.

A low chuckle. "Jason, man up buddy. You should have moved in quick. Instead you got a 'You're a good friend.' Sorry dude, but that's code for not interested." A few minutes later, the old Land Rover turned on it's lights and left, unseen.

CHAPTER 15

Over the next several weeks JJ finished her scuba lessons with Gunner and earned her open water certification. Her first couple reports went into Jerry, and his email back said, "Keep up the great work!"

Jason had a photoshoot on the coast of Oregon for a couple of weeks. She missed him, but filled her time by completing several paintings. One, she entitled *Wonder and Delight*, was of two giggling, whispering girls playing in the bubbling wash of waves along the shoreline. Her favourite one she entitled *Argonaut*. It captured the vision she'd had of Jason as a teen. Her homework with Eulah progressed, making a significant impact on the darkness inside.

The police released the autopsy report on Nicolas' death. A blood vessel ruptured in his head and he died quickly – a congenital defect, they said. Before taking his body back home, his parents arranged an island service for all of Nic's friends. Dark ominous clouds dumped their burden on Jason and JJ as they hurried into the funeral home. She couldn't help but think, *he died too young and alone, just like Cam.*

This thought sent her on another trek through the blackest places in the abyss.

When they left the service Jason glanced at the sky. "It promises to be a spectacular sunset. Interested in joining me on the boat to grab some shots?"

"Sure." She drew in a deep breath. "I love the smell after a storm."

He held the door for her. "It's God's reminder that after the storms of our life, there is peace and a wonderful fragrance of life."

She slowly nodded.

Yes, I'm gradually seeing that peace, and life is getting better.

When he started the engine she said, "Thanks for coming with me."

"I remember my first funeral after India just shattered me. It's not something you should do alone."

Once in the open waters past the islands, Jason turned the wheel over to JJ. He let her know where he wanted to be then snapped off a bunch of shots. After three or four locations, she positioned the boat without his input. Looking at the sky brought her a profound realization.

This brief return into the abyss makes me see with clarity the increasing light that has come in my life. I can stand in my current place and take a backward glance and see the deepest valley of grief behind me. The blackness recedes like the back end of a passing summer storm. I'm coming into sunlight again. Thank you, God.

He took over a hundred shots. As the colours in the sky faded, he packed up his camera. "I might need to hire you when I go on assignment. You got me some great shots. Thank you."

"You're welcome."

He stepped below and grabbed a bag of chips, turned on some quiet music then joined JJ in the wheelhouse. With the engines slightly above idle, she spun the wheel putting the boat in a slow turn. "Where to now?"

He tossed her the bag and shut off the engines. "Come on. Let's watch the night sky dress herself in stars."

He tossed her a pillow and watched her get comfortable. "How's your grief doing now?"

She leaned her head against the bulkhead. "I'm good. The funeral boiled up all the deepest darkest feelings again, but they didn't stay. It's like a reminder of the blackness."

"You are doing great. You've had a lot of loss in a short time. Funerals get easier as time passes, but they still take me on a brief spin through the pain. The good thing is they remind me to keep my heart open to all the richness life offers."

"And that's why you wanted to come out here tonight?"

He thought for a moment. "Partly. Maybe mostly. I feel grounded again when I connect with nature."

She sighed. "Me too."

Several days later she stopped at the Brutus Restaurant and Seafood Market to pick up some fish for dinner. Standing in the line up, she watched a man walk in wearing yellow tights, a white and black striped shirt and a metal colander on his head.

Whoop, whoop. Crazy encounter alert! Everyone, check your 9 o'clock!

She counted the number of people ahead of her.

He stood behind JJ in the line up. She heard strange shuffling noises then he cleared his throat. "Me, me, me. Doh, ray, me, fah, so, lah, lah, lah – laaaaah."

JJ closed her eyes.

Where's my anti-fruitcake repellent when I need it?

She leaned out to look past the person in front of her.

Any chance of getting outta here before this goes slam-bang crazy?

She glanced down at her leather anklet.

Fat lot of good you did – the talking ABM and now the singing spaghetti strainer. For sure the cops will lock me up if they find me at another nut up.

She heard him pump a spray bottle. She ducked and turned to check if he sprayed something on her.

He smiled. "Pretty lady!" He held up what looked like water and sprayed some in his mouth.

She turned back to check on the lack of progress of the line.

Please, please, please. Try to contain yourself until I'm gone.

He tapped her shoulder. "Pretty lady?"

She ignored him

He tapped again. "Pretty lady?"

She turned.

"I'm Luciano Pavarotti." He held out his hand.

Of course you are. She gave a quick smile. "Hi," and turned away.

He tapped. "I'll sing Madame Buttertart for you."

Excellent. I can't remember the last time I heard Madame Butter-
tart."

He cleared his throat. "Baa, baa, baa, ba-na-na-na –" At top
volume he sang his version of Barbara Ann.

The woman in front of JJ turned around to look at the colander-clad Pavarotti then glanced at JJ.

"Ba-na-na, please take my ja-aa-am!"

JJ gave the woman a what-can-you-do look.

The woman pointed at her. "Hey, I know you."

Pavarotti wouldn't be ignored. "You got me rippin' and a-
ridin', slippin' and a-slidin' ba-ba-ba ba-na-na!"

Leaning forward JJ said, "I don't think so."

"Yeah, you're that reporter who wrote those lies about
me."

At increasing volume Pavarotti continued his serenade.
"Went to the store, looking for some more!"

This is getting out of hand. Wonder what the book says about
when you're surrounded by nutters. "I'm not a reporter. I work at a
resort here in town."

"Of course, you would lie about who you are. You ruined
my life."

"Saw Ba-na-na and I slid across the floor!"

"I– "

"JJ!"

Both women turned.

"Movin' and a-groovin' Baa-naa-naa!"

JJ said, "Hi, Sydney."

The other woman said, "Sydney, do you know this
woman?" pointing at JJ.

"Tried gorilla glue! Cement on my shoe! Then some home-
made goo, but I knew they wouldn't do!"

Sydney glanced at Pavarotti then leaned in. "Hi Cindy. Yes,
this is JJ McCurdy. She works at the Plantation."

Pavarotti belted out the finale. "Ba-na-naaaaah!"

Finally! Robin Hood's merry man is done. I think his tights cut of the oxygen supply.

The woman nodded toward Pavarotti. "Thank heavens. Listen, I'm sorry. You look like the reporter that came by the house."

"No worries." She nodded toward the fish counter. "Looks like it's your turn."

Sydney said, "Sorry JJ, I'm late for a dinner engagement. I'll catch up with you later."

I really want to know why I'm a magnet for cosmic weirdness. I'm like a walking banana in a jungle of starving monkeys.

The notice of a registered letter sent her back to the post office. She looked at the return address – the familiar post box in Big Pine Key. It sent a shock wave through her peaceful world, stirring that uneasy feeling again. It had been more than two months since the last package. The contents of the box in her closet had slipped from her mind. She opened the envelope to find a bunch of photos.

The first few were taken of her graduation, receiving her diploma, with her classmates, and the celebration afterward. The next ones were taken the following day when she married Cam. There were several outside the church. The ones taken inside during the ceremony disturbed her. *Is this from someone we invited to the wedding?*

Then there were photos of the day they brought little Lucas home. But the most alarming photos were of Cam's car on the road after the crash that killed him. His blood covered the windshield.

She felt sick.

From the closet, she got the box out, dropped the latest photos and envelope in and stuffed it back in the closet. "You hold no power."

Lying in bed that evening, the image of Cam's blood haunted her thoughts.

Oh Cam. I'm so sorry. I hope you didn't suffer.

She thought about the last months of their life together.

We lost our love, didn't we? We barely talked. You tried to reach me, but I was numb. I'm sorry I abandoned you. I couldn't see my way out of the darkness. And you died alone. You died amid our brokenness. I shouldn't have chilled you out. Your last days shouldn't have been so alone. What an epic failure. Cam, I'm so sorry. God, tell him I'm sorry.

A deep down guilt settled in. Her heart ached for her inability to apologize and make it right. She felt sick over her failure. She lay awake ruminating.

A few days later one of the new guests booked an appointment for a massage. As she walked with him to one of the outdoor rooms she noted his Cheers Boston ball cap.

"So, Mark, are you from Boston?"

"I'm in Boston now, but I'm originally from San Simeon, California."

"What? That's where I'm from! At least until I was 14. Small world."

"How old are you? Sorry, I guess that's not a question guys should ask."

"No, it's okay. I'm 27."

"Me too. We must have been in the same grade."

"Cambria Grammar?"

"Yes!"

"What's your full name? Maybe I remember you."

"Mark Russell."

She thought for a moment. "Yeah, you were really good at sports."

"That's me. And what was your name back then?"

"Jennifer Jaye McCurdy. Mostly people called me JJ."

"Yeah, I remember you. You were a little cutie. It disappointed me when you moved away because I never got the chance to ask you out. Wow. JJ. That was a long time ago."

They chatted about things they remembered and where life has taken them both. She recounted her story without tears, and knew the icy grip of grief eased. When he left she said, "Good to see you again, Mark."

He looked at her a long time. "Yes, I can see in your face that young JJ I knew. You look great despite all you've been through. It's good to see you again. It's great to run into someone I know. Thanks JJ."

She looked out her bedroom window Friday morning. The grey skies disappointed her. She hoped for sunshine. Jason invited her to dive a local wreck to celebrate her certification. She checked her phone for the detailed weather report. They forecasted scattered showers for most of the day, then clearing by late afternoon.

Mid morning she drove to Jason's. He didn't answer the door, so she wandered around to the waterfront and found him stocking the fridge on the boat. "Hey Jason."

"JJ. How are you?"

"Good. Anything I can help with?"

He came up from the galley. "Yeah, I'll get you to bring down my cameras and I'll get the tanks."

As Jason pulled the boat from the dock he said, "Want to steer us out?" He showed her where to head then brought in the bumpers. Popping below, he grabbed two bottles of water and returned to the wheelhouse. He cracked them and handed one to her then took over the wheel.

"Where are we going?"

"The Cayman Salvor. It's about 90 feet down. It's a salvage ship they intended to sink, but it went down prematurely. It lay on its side until hurricane Katrina righted it. I brought two cameras, one for you if you want to take some pics." He pointed to the smaller camera on the bench seat.

Turning it over in her hands she said, "You will teach me to use it?"

He pointed, "There's the on-off switch."

She flicked it on and pointed at him. "Does it work out of the water?"

He grinned for the camera. She clicked.

"Okay how do I view the photos?"

He showed her. "Do you know about f-stops and shutters

speeds?"

"I took a photography course in college, but it's been awhile since then. You might need to give me a refresher."

He showed her how to meter and manually set the shutter and aperture. She snapped off a few shots of him piloting and looked at the results. "Oh this is a superb camera." She showed him her first photos.

"I must be careful. You'll be stealing my job."

She laughed. "Not quite."

She experimented with the settings. She stood in the back with bent knees trying to stabilize the camera to get a good shot of the islands.

He called back to her. "If you're getting hungry, there are bagels, cream cheese and smoked salmon in the fridge below."

She went below, assembled the food and brought it to the wheelhouse.

It rained. The sun broke through briefly. It sprinkled. It poured. Nearing Key West, he steered between the islands flipping on the wipers again. "It's a monkey's wedding."

She looked around at the islands. "Is one of them called monkey's wedding?"

He looked puzzled, then smiled. "No, monkey's wedding refers to the crazy changes in the weather. Another Nana phrase, I'm afraid."

"She sounds awesome. Where does she live?"

"Unfortunately she passed away last year."

"Oh I'm sorry."

"I saw her a few days before she died. So that's good. And I know I'll see her in heaven."

She thought about the Indian urchin that died in his arms with the Hindu burial. *Jason probably wonders if he'll see that kid in heaven or if he was of the age of accountability.*

South of the islands he steered west. Finally he powered down, shut off the engines and tied up to one of the mooring buoys. He gave her a few more instructions on the camera then they geared up and plunged into the world below. He led them to the wreck. She stayed close to him, not wanting to give him cause to worry about her. He checked the settings on her camera to ensure the exposure would be right. They swam along the length of the ship, Jason snapping a number of shots. He signalled for her to stay where she was then took a few of her with the wreck.

They spent an hour exploring. When they surfaced, he asked what she thought.

"Love it! I'm so glad I got my certification. What a gift to make a living from spending time in this world. I can't wait to see your photos."

Onboard, Jason downloaded the images off of both cameras onto his laptop and they sat going through them, hers first. He commented, "You have a good eye."

"Thanks, but I took pictures of what I saw you shoot."

"Still, you've composed them well."

"Thanks. Now let's look at yours."

They both liked the ones of JJ in silhouette near the wreck.

The sun set as the sky cleared. "How about Greek salad and munchies?" He turned on some music. They stretched out on the benches, propped up against the bulkhead and watched the sun sink. Jason foot tapped to the changing beat as he sang – that quiet sporadic way people do who unconsciously sing.

As the sun kissed the horizon she sat up. "Can I have this dance?"

He took her into his arms and slowly they moved to the rhythm. As he sang, the vibrations resonated in her chest. She wasn't sure what she liked more, the dancing or his voice touching her inside. A faster song allowed him to spin and dip her. They laughed together as the last of the sun disappeared.

She turned her head up to the sky drinking in the unpolluted view of the stars. Standing behind her he whispered, "In the darkness she sees the beauty in the stars, and their twinkling hope touches her soul."

She drew in a deep breath. "I love the Keys. It's the first place I've bothered to really look at the stars. They are beautiful out here."

She leaned on the rails looking out to the horizon. After awhile she said, "I love the rock of the boat. Do you ever sleep out here, under the stars?"

"I've slept under the stars in many places, but not on this boat yet."

"I can see why people chose to live on a boat instead of land."

"I spent a month on a research vessel on the Mediterranean. And yeah, I loved sleeping in the intoxicating effect of rocking waves."

"Who is this singing?"

"It's all Kenny Chesney."

"You like him."

"A lot of his songs are about island living. He's been a favourite of mine for years. I think he's only done one song I didn't like."

"Your voice is a lot like his, maybe deeper, but just as pure and smooth. I like the way you sing along without thinking. And if your not singing, you're humming. When you're focused on something, you hum."

"I wasn't aware. There was always music in my home growing up. My parents always sang. I guess it rubbed off."

"I like it. It's a happy soul that lets the music out. I think I'm becoming a fan of Chesney."

"Haha. My kind of girl."

As the *Cool Change* pulled into Jason's dock, a person slipped away into the darkness. The old Land Rover pulled away. "I'll give you one thing, Jason. You have persistence. That may be your undoing. Things are going to get hot. Don't say I didn't warn ya."

CHAPTER 16

Sunday, Dan drove Ang to the airport in Miami. She flew out to Europe for a two-week tour with Jerry of his hotels then attend a week-long conference in Rome.

Monday, JJ noticed Mark had booked another massage. Afterward, he invited her to Key West for the day.

Before they left mid-morning on Wednesday, JJ picked up another registered letter. She had a bad feeling about this one. This time it contained a business card – Peaches N. Sunshine, drag queen artist. She furrowed her brow and checked her dresser. *No, the one she gave me is still here.* She set it aside. Underneath were another series of photos. Several were of when she stopped on the roadside to sketch the bird after leaving the mainland. Her hands shook as she looked at the next images – of her and Jason leaving and returning from the wreck dive just a few days ago.

This is getting pretty close to home. Who is this sending this stuff? What does it mean?

Whoever it is, they know about Jason. That's not good. Oh God, please protect us. Don't let anything happen to Jason. You can't put him into my life then take him away. Please, I'm begging you. Look after him. And give me some clarity on what I should do about all this.

She waited, but no thoughts popped in her head.

She packed it all away and drove to the Plantation House to meet Mark. He drove a silver Ferrari rental. They drove around the town then wandered the downtown area. They ate a late lunch at Jimmy Buffet's. He excused himself to go to the washroom before they left. She waited on the street. After 10 minutes she began to worry. She scanned the restaurant then asked the waiter to check the washroom, but no one was there.

She stood on the street waiting another 15 minutes. A blond woman approached her and said, "You're not so special."

JJ said, "Sorry, can I help you with something?"

"No, you've done more than enough. Now it's all about me."

"I think you've got the wrong person."

"You'll never forget this encounter, now will ya?" She walked down the street laughing.

JJ muttered, "No, I don't suppose I will. Weirdo magnet alert. Zeee-ooooow boom. Incoming crazy. I think you warrant a gardylunatic."

She looked up and down the street, but saw no sign of Mark. She went back to where they parked the car. It was gone.

"Now what? Did he ditch me?" She waited another half hour, but he didn't show.

She dialled Jason and got his voice mail. "Hi Jason. It's JJ. I need a favour. I'm stranded down in Key West. Could you come get me? Call me when you get this. Thanks."

She sat on a bench on the street, trying to sort out what happened.

Mark doesn't seem like the kind to just ditch me here. But here I am. And he's gone with the car. If I see him back at the Plantation, I will give him a piece of my mind.

She felt a twinge in her heart. *I hope nothing happened to him.* Then she remembered the empty parking space.

But how could something have happened to him? He got in the car and drove off. No, he's looking like a real jerk.

She watched the passersby for awhile.

And what's with all these weird packages? There's been more weirdness since I left Sioux City than the whole rest of my life put together. Peaches singing at the gas station, the lady setting her hair on fire, the champagne cork hickie, Pavarotti in the fish market, the man trapped in the bank machine, this unforgettable *woman who thinks I'm not special, the gift ball of nothing, the box of coal, and the constant stream of packages from someone anonymous. Why is my life so different from everyone else? All the deaths around me? Weird*

*people and weird packages? I'm pretty sure none of this happens to
other people. What is all this about? Why is weirdness a part of my
life? If I had my choice, I'd rather not the weird, thanks.*

Her phone rang. "Hi Jason, thanks for calling back."

"You're in Key West?"

"Yeah. Can you come get me? I'm in front of Jimmy Buffets."

"I'm on my way. It'll be about an hour."

"Okay. Thanks."

"No problem. See you soon."

She stood up when she spotted his Land Rover. He pulled
over and she hopped in. "Thanks Jason."

"No worries. What happened?"

"Oh, this guy staying at the Plantation is an old grade
school classmate. He's vacationing alone and invited me to
keep him company for the day. We had lunch. Everything
seemed fine. He went to the washroom and just never came
back. The waiter checked but he wasn't in the bathroom. I went
back to the car, but it was gone. That's when I called you.

She buckled up. "He doesn't seem like the type to just ditch
me here, but here I am. It's like I'm a magnet for weird people."

He laughed. "What do you mean?"

"Well, while I was waiting, weirdo woman comes up and
tells me I'm not special, and I'll never forget her. And then
there's the creepy packages."

"What creepy packages?" He glanced at her, concerned.

She sighed. "I've told no one about them. They're just too
weird."

"Like what? Dead pigs or something?"

She laughed. "No, mostly a lot of photos of me – throughout my life. Like today's package had pictures of when I came
here. And photos of you and I on the boat the other day when we
went diving."

His brows knit. "I don't like the sounds of this."

"I don't much like it either."

"What have you done about it?"

"Nothing. I'm hoping it'll just go away if I ignore it."

"When did they start?"

"Shortly after I got here."

"What's the return address?"

"A post office box in Big Pine Key."

"Do you know anyone there?"

"No.

"So photos of you here. Anything else?"

She told him about the stuffed rabbit, the newspaper clippings about a couple killed in a fire and her father's funeral, the photos of kids she didn't know, of all the childhood photos taken while she was unaware, of the picture of Cam's blood on the windshield, the ball of nothing and the coal. "When I say it out loud, it sounds bad."

"Uh yeah! I think you need to talk about this to Mike. This is beyond weird, and well past creepy."

"I keep thinking this will be the last one. They're bound to stop if they're not getting a rise out of me, don't you think?"

"No. I don't think this is about getting a rise out of you."

"What do you think it's about?"

"I don't know, but I have a bad feeling about it."

"I'll think about it. I don't want to provoke whoever it is by involving the police."

Jason pulled over onto the shoulder. "I'm really worried about this. Promise me if you get another one you'll go to Mike."

She looked out the window thinking.

"I promise I'll think about it."

He looked at her a long time.

She finally looked at him.

"I'm worried JJ."

"Okay, I promise to talk to Mike if I get another one."

"Okay."

He pulled out. "Thanks for promising me."

After a long silence she said, "You're right. It is pretty creepy."

He cleared his throat. "What I said was that it's *beyond* creepy."

"Yeah, I was trying to make it not quite so bad as that."

When he dropped her off he walked her to the door. She said, "Dinner Friday night? I'd like to thank you for rescuing me."

"You don't need to thank me. That's what friends are for, but yes, I'll come."

She unlocked the door. "Come early. I'll be serving appetizers on the lanai – meaning the back deck."

He laughed. "Sounds great."

"See ya, Jason."

"Lock up, hey?"

"I will. Bye"

"Bye." He waited until he heard the deadbolt before he left.

CHAPTER 17

She had her weekly meeting with Eulah. She mentioned her feelings of regret around Cam.

"Tell me more about that."

"After Lucas died, I shut down. Basically I emotionally abandoned our marriage. Cam didn't deserve my punishment for our losses. He was hurting as much as me, and when he reached out I didn't love him enough to give him a little piece of me. I cut him off. I'm not a good person. I don't think I deserve another shot at happiness. What if he needs me and I cut him off too?"

"Do these last days truly define your relationship?"

"No, I guess not. We had a decent enough marriage before Lucas died. Then it fell apart."

"What were you dealing with in those last days?"

"I felt like I had no heart left, like love was violently ripped from me, leaving me a bloody pile of discarded garbage. The days were black. I don't remember much of what happened. I just know I was lost."

"Imagine yourself, not as you, but as a neutral bystander. How do you think this bystander sees your actions? Would they see it as a failure on your part?"

She thought for a long time. "I'd see two terribly hurt people who didn't know how to deal with all the pain. They both needed something that neither could give."

"Mm-mm. So from that perspective, what do you say about not comforting Cam?"

"I guess in my depth of hurt and pain, it would be impossible to support another hurting person. I had nothing to give."

"Death seems to bring with it a mindset that travels directly down the regret road. Soon a ticker tape plays a steady feed of self-reproach. But you need to see that warped view is but one perspective of the situation. There are far more realistic views than those that grief feeds you. "What do you think about this bystander's viewpoint?"

"Yeah, I see I couldn't do anything more than I did, any more than Cam couldn't do anything more than he did. I don't fault him for not helping me. I guess I shouldn't fault me for my inability to help him."

"So you based your regret on an irrational expectation you have of yourself. Do you think in light of this new insight you can release yourself from this regret?"

She nodded. "I think this regret holds me back from trusting myself as a reliable friend."

"How so?"

"Regret says I'm incapable of being there for someone else."

"And what do you think of that statement now?"

"Those events that brought me to the lowest point in my life are not likely to happen again – I hope. And I've learned a lot since then. I am a different person now."

"Do you expect yourself to be perfect?"

"No."

"I want you to really consider this question. Do you expect you will never make any mistakes?"

"I don't want to hurt anyone."

"None of us do. But does that mean you must never make a mistake?"

She laughed. She thought for a moment. "No, I don't have to be perfect. I guess that caring and loving doesn't mean no hurt, it just means my heart is intending good."

"Okay more homework. I want you to write a letter to yourself. Think about things since Cam died. Think about your life now and how you're handling both his and Lucas' deaths. Imagine you are Cam writing to you from heaven. What would he say to you? When your regret rears its ugly head, read this letter.

"And there's a few affirmations from today you can include on your mirror, like 'I'm not perfect, but I have a good heart.'"

In the afternoon Mike stopped by her office. He knocked on the open door.

"Mike! Come on in. What are you doing here?"

"I'm afraid it's police business." He pulled out his notebook. "Do you know a Mark Russell?"

She had a sick feeling. "Yes, he's a guest of the resort. I gave him a couple of massages. It turns out we were classmates in grade school. We went to Key West yesterday."

"When did you get back?"

"Well, that's the weird thing. We had lunch, he went to the washroom then he ditched me. He took off with the car and left me there."

"Did you see him leave in the car?"

"No. When he didn't come back from the washroom I looked for him. I went to where we parked in case he was there, and the car was gone. I haven't seen him since."

He nodded and jotted down more notes.

"Did he mention anything about someone wanting to do him harm?"

"No, we talked about his work as a sports writer in Boston. It sounded like a pretty ordinary life. Did something happen to him?"

"They found him this morning crammed into the trunk of the Ferrari. He was murdered. You were one of the last people to see him alive."

She paled. Her eyes brimmed with tears. He came around the desk and squatted beside her chair. "I'm sorry JJ."

She nodded.

He leaned in and hugged her for a long moment. "You going to be okay?"

She nodded. "He was a good man. Find who did this."

"We will."

She watched Mike leave then turned to look out her window.

And another death to add to my list. Really reaching to the depths this time by wiping out a childhood friend. God, when will this stop? How much do You think I can take?

She headed down the beach to her favourite isolated spot. Hugging her knees, thoughts of Mark rolled around her mind.

I'm sorry Mark. I thought some unfair things about you. You were a good man. And your life ended far too soon. Goodbye, my friend. I won't forget you.

She played with a fallen palm leaf. Tears flowed. She stared out to sea, to where the sky and sea disappear into each other. "I am not the grim reaper. Death doesn't follow me." She paused. "It's getting hard to say that and believe it. Mark comes to me for a massage and now he's dead. God, I need supernatural thinking here. The reality around me is a lot of death. So what do you say?"

She closed her eyes to focus on her inner voice.

This is not your fault, little lotus. Death does not flow from you. Keep your eyes on the life and light I've placed around you.

Half an hour later, she returned to work, her heart and mind clear of destructive thoughts of death.

When she got home she found another notice for a registered letter. She looked at it a long time then tossed it on her dresser. After dinner, she sat at the table with paper and pen. She wrote, "Dear JJ. It's Cam –"

She straightened up, and mentally put herself in Cam's shoes. Through tears and laughing, she completed her homework.

She read the finished letter.

I love you, JJ and always will. I'm sorry I couldn't be there for you when you needed me. It was something neither of us understood and we couldn't see beyond our own pain. It's okay though. Both of us are in a better place. Heaven is good. I'm good.

And I see you are in the Keys. You always loved the ocean. I'm glad you're there. It's where you should be. Your life is blooming in ways it never did with me. I loved you so much. But I always knew you were so much more than I deserved. You held back from what you were meant to be because of me. So I'm happy that you're now finding yourself and flourishing.

I want you to jump into life. Take a big bite. Shoot for the best. You are now free to reach for the stars, my girl. Life is short so live it to its fullest. Be sure in old age you don't say, "I wish I had –" Go do it all.

Don't think all these negative life events are tearing you down. I see the woman you are becoming, and though those things have scarred you, you are exquisitely beautiful. There's a new depth to you – a depth of strength, a depth of love, a depth of wonder. The man who gets you is a lucky man.

Walk close with Jesus. You will find life there. And I want you to surround yourself with things and people that bring happiness. Go on with your life. You have my blessing. Love you and I'll see you someday. Until then, go big, then when you've reached your destiny and done all God created you to do, I'll see you on the other side.

Cam

Fresh tears ran. She loved the grace found in that note – the grace she found within herself. She folded the paper and tucked it in an envelope, and put it in her underwear drawer. The sketchbook caught her eye.

Oh little bird, what do you have to show me? Ah the green chest. A heart full of regret. Like lungs full of congestion, you leave a heaviness on my chest and you make it hard to breathe. I see a lot of homework ahead. I think like congestion regret will be a difficult one to clear out.

The next afternoon, the doorbell rang. She called out, "Hey, Jason. Come on in."

He came into the kitchen with a smile and a bottle wine. "Hey, JJ."

"I hope you're not allergic to strawberries. I didn't think to ask."

"No allergies. And there aren't too many foods I don't like.

Where's your corkscrew and I'll open the wine."

She pointed to a drawer. "Oh, hang on. I want to show something before we settle in." She grabbed his hand and took him to her bedroom. "See?" pointing to where the stars hung. "I look at them every night."

"Like Van Gogh's starry night." He pointed to a line up of paintings leaning against the wall. "This is your work?"

"Yes."

"This is Indigo and her sculpture? Oh JJ. It is beautifully sad and touching, an impossible mix of tranquility and sorrow. It's really good."

"Thank you."

He moved further along the collection. "You could sell this one. What's it called? Oh yes, *Wonder and Delight*. You have a way of engaging imagination. I can see the wonder and delight of these two cherubs."

He moved down the line and squatted down for a closer look. "Is it dry? May I pick it up?"

"Sure."

He picked up *Argonaut*. "I like this one – a lot."

"You should. It's you."

He looked confused.

"It's the image that popped in my mind when you told me about growing up on the coast."

He studied it, finally setting it down. "If you ever want to sell it, let me know." He stood up. "Hey, what's that on your dresser?"

She spotted the registered letter notification.

"Is that what I think it is? Did you talk to Mike yet?"

"No."

He opened his mouth, but she stopped him. "I didn't talk to him yet because I don't know for sure what it is."

"So you've avoided picking it up so you wouldn't break your promise?"

"I haven't had time."

He grabbed the notice and her hand, and hustled her out

to his car. "We've got just enough time to get there before they close."

When the clerk handed her the large envelope he glanced at the return address, and gave her an I-knew-it look.

Back at her place, she dumped the contents on the island counter. Two halves of a ripped photograph lay on top of the pile. He picked up the half with a young girl. Someone wrote "Hated" across the top and a broken heart in black marker. He looked at the other half with an infant in a stroller. "Loved" topped the image, with scattered pink hearts.

"Did the previous photos have writing on them?"

"No." She left to get the box out of her closet.

He glanced through the pile of items on the counter – a box of matches, a newspaper clipping, and some official looking documents at the bottom.

She set the box on the counter, showing him the things in the order they arrived.

He returned to the latest items, picking up the generic matchbox, looking it over then setting it down. The newspaper clipping announced JJ's wedding to Cam. Someone used a red marker to draw blood drops on it. He handed it to her and picked up the first document. It was a birth registration issued by the State of New Mexico. He read down. "Do you know a Kenna Bodine?"

"No." She took the document. "I don't understand. That's my –" She reread from the top. "That's my date of birth."

"Were you born in New Mexico."

"No. My family was from California."

He picked up the next document. "Okay, this looks like your birth registration. Jennifer Jaye McCurdy."

She looked at it. "Yeah, but this says I was born in New Mexico – same hospital and doctor as Kenna. This is really strange. It doesn't make any sense."

"Do you have a twin sister?"

With furrowed brows, she shook her head. "No."

The last document was issued by the State of California.

Jason said, "These are adoption papers." He read through then set it on the counter. "It's your name on here." He pointed to the date and location of birth on the adoption papers and the identical ones on the birth registrations.

"I don't understand. Is this saying I'm adopted?"

"Yes. If these are legit."

"I'm really Kenna Bodine?"

"It looks to be your birth name. But you are JJ. That's who you were raised as and who you are."

"Wait. Bodine. Isn't that the last name of the couple who died in the house fire?" She rummaged through the pile and pulled out the newspaper clipping. "Yes, Brande and Robbie Bodine. My parents died in a fire started by an arsonist. This stuff – " She picked up several photographs and let them fall. "All of this is about me."

He rested his hand on her back, between her shoulders. "Now, can I call Mike?"

CHAPTER 18

Mike stood at the counter with Jason looking over all the items. He studied the photos for a long time then looked away, finger tapping the counter.

Jason said, "What do you think?"

"Did JJ tell you about the murder of Mark Russell, a guest she went to Key West with?"

He glanced at JJ sitting with her legs tucked up on the couch in the living room, her moist eyes staring out the window.

"No."

Mike filled him in on the details.

"So there are these crazy packages *and a murder*?"

Mike nodded. "I have a few questions for JJ." They headed for the living room. Jason sat beside her, his arm on the back of the couch.

Mike sat on the edge of the chair beside them. "I have a few more questions about Key West, if you're up for answering them. I think it could be related to all these packages."

She sniffed and nodded.

"Okay. When you were there with Mark did you see anyone hanging around?"

She thought. "No."

"No one bothered you or Mark?"

"No."

Jason said, "There was that weird woman."

"Oh yeah."

Mike perked up. "A woman?"

"Yeah. I was standing on the street. I'd found out Mark wasn't in the washroom. This woman comes up and says some crazy stuff, then leaves laughing."

"What did she look like?"

"I don't know. Blond. Maybe 34 or 35 years old. About my height I guess."

"This is important. What *exactly* did she say?"

She thought for a moment. "She said something like I'm not anything special. I asked if I could help her. Then she said something about I'd done enough and now it's all about her. Then she said I'll never forget meeting her."

Mike looked directly at Jason.

Jason rubbed his face.

The doorbell rang. Jason said, "I'll get it."

Mike drew in a breath. "We have a witness who saw Mark being strong-armed down the back alley by a blond woman in her 30s. They thought they saw a gun. We found one fingerprint on Mark's watch. It traces back to a sealed juvenile case. We are working on getting the courts to release the information on this person. I think she could be the same person who spoke with you.

"I think she knocked Mark out, stashed him in the trunk, then came and talked to you."

A shutter ran down JJ's back.

Jason returned with a package. JJ considered it for a moment then turned to look out the window. A torrent of dread filled her heart. "You open it, Jason. I don't think I can."

He pried open the box and peered in. "It's a glass."

Her brows furrowed. "What?"

He pulled out the glass and the colour drained from her face.

Mike said, "Let me see," and took the glass and all the packaging. "There's no indication of who it's from. I've seen these before. Generally it's a gag gift."

Jason said, "This doesn't feel like a gag."

JJ said, "What kind of idiot sends someone a glass with a bullet embedded into the side?"

Jason said, "This isn't from an idiot. And it's no gag. I don't like the sounds of this. I'm concerned JJ is in danger."

Mike said, "Wait. Here's a note." He unfolded the paper. "You are not made of glass."

Jason said, "That's a threat."

"Prior to the bullet glass I would have said it could all be coincidental – having been approached by a blond in the vicinity of Mark's murder, and while these photographs and things have a degree of underlying threat, I wouldn't have been really concerned. But the bullet glass and note elevate my concern. You're here alone?"

She nodded. She tried sniffing, but crying left her congested.

Jason said, "You can't stay here." He looked at Mike to add his support.

"I wouldn't advise it."

She said, "I can stay at the resort."

Jason said, "No, you'd have no protection there."

Mike said, "The problem with the resort is the unobserved access to you especially at night when there's no people around. I can arrange for some police protection during the day, but overnight would be a problem. We're just a small division." He looked at Jason. "If Jason is okay with a guest, I think that would be a better option."

"Absolutely. You can have your choice of guest rooms."

She stared out the window.

Mike said, "We'll stay on this. We'll get whoever killed Mark and whoever is sending these things."

She whispered, "Thanks, Mike."

"I'd like to take all the items from the packages with me. I'll give them back as soon as we've had a chance to investigate."

She nodded, still staring out the window.

The guys packed up the items and Mike walked to the door with Jason. "I'll keep in touch. Other than when she's at work, don't leave her alone. Drive her to and from work. I'll post an officer at your house in the evening and at the resort when she's working. I didn't want to scare JJ, but this is serious. How did her husband die?"

"A car crash."

"I don't like the drawing of blood drops on the newspaper clipping of their wedding announcement and the photo of the car crash."

Jason said, "This is nuts."

"Call me if anything concerns you."

Jason nodded. "All of it worries me. But thanks. I'll call at the first sign of anything new."

Jason returned to the living room. "Come on JJ. Let's get you packed."

She got up. "Thanks Jason. This is just far bigger than I thought. It's overwhelming."

"It'll take time to get your head wrapped around it all."

"How could I get this far in life and not know I was adopted? I'd have thought that would be something someone would mention somewhere along the way. Just when I feel like I'm getting my feet under me, life seems to delight in knocking me down again – and again, and again."

He pulled her into his arms and hugged her while she cried.

He said, "This doesn't change anything. You are not a different person now than you were an hour ago."

"My whole childhood was based on a lie."

"Did your parents love you?"

She nodded.

"Then the rest is history – it's just the facts, that's the encyclopedia version of your life. But the part that matters, family, love, the joys of childhood, well you lived a rich life, right?"

She thought for a moment. "Yeah, I had a good childhood with my parents."

"That's the part that matters. That's the story of your life. That's what made you who you are today, not these legal papers."

"I think I have more Eulah homework coming on this one."

He smiled. "Yeah, this is the kind of thing that requires homework."

She squeezed him then stepped away. "Thanks for being here."

While she packed, he locked all the windows and back door. He popped into her bedroom. "Don't forget your bathing suits."

She looked at him.

He shrugged. "You never know. A huge humpbacked whale could swim into the bay and you're gonna want to go swimming with him." He grinned. "Bring that blue number. It's my favourite."

She laughed. "Okay, I'll bring bathing suits – *in case of humpbacked whales.*"

When they got her settled at his place, he asked if she was hungry. She thought she could handle toast and tea.

While Jason worked on his laptop, JJ sipped her tea. "I don't like the name Kenna. I don't feel like a Kenna."

He thought for a moment then typed something. "Kenna means born of fire."

"Well, isn't that appropriate, considering the arson that killed my birth parents. What does Jennifer Jaye mean?"

He tapped then looked up. "A beautiful fast lady."

She threw a cushion at him.

He laughed. "I'm not kidding. That's what it says."

"It does not."

He moved beside her. "See? Jennifer means fair one and Jaye means swift. I just put it in today's language."

She leaned her head on his shoulder. "What does Jason mean?"

"Healer." He closed the laptop and put his arm around her.

"You and Mike think this is serious, that I'm in danger? What did he tell you at the door?"

"He said I shouldn't leave you alone, to drive you to and from work. And there'll be an officer nearby when you're at work."

"See, that scares me. It means you guys think I'm in danger."

"We are not to live in fear. And God said He will give us

His abundant and supernatural peace. But that doesn't mean we should act foolishly. Yes, I think there is a certain amount of danger, and it isn't wise for you to be alone, but you need not be afraid. God's still in control."

He looked at her head resting in the crook of his shoulder. "Would you like me to pray for peace?"

She nodded.

He held her hand. "Thank you, Jesus, for standing with us. You know all the details of what's going on here, and we ask for your wisdom in making decisions. Keep JJ safe, tucked under your wings of protection. Fill her with your peace that is beyond understanding. Let it flow, as she needs it. Let her sleep in your peace. Thank you for your Holy Spirit that infuses us with your love and joy. We thank you precious Saviour."

She said, "Amen."

The next morning he came into the kitchen to find JJ buttering some toast. "Good morning."

"Good morning, Jason."

He started the Keurig for a coffee. "How'd you sleep?"

She smiled. "I slept great. Thanks for praying last night. I feel at peace with everything." She poured boiling water from the kettle into a mug.

He squeezed past her to get the milk from the fridge. "Milk?"

"Please." She held up her mug.

He took a deep drink of his coffee. "When do we need to leave for work?"

"Soon. About 15 minutes?"

When he dropped her off, he asked when to pick her up. "Let me check the schedule. I'll text you."

"Okay. Have a good day."

"You too."

Mid morning she got a text. "No sign of humpbacks yet."

She tapped back, "Are you sure you know what to look for?"

"Something big and grey?"

"I was thinking more along the lines of bubble nets."

"You read the Geographic!"

"I do now."

"Good answer."

"Can you pick me up at 5?"

"See you then."

"ttyl"

She pulled together a report for Ang and Jerry on the growth of the spa with phase one implemented. The numbers looked good – an increase of 10% over the previous year. She knew Ang would be happy to forward it to Jerry.

As she walked out toward Jason's car, a man followed her out. Jason said, "Who's that guy?"

She glanced over and waved. The man waved back. "Mike's assigned bodyguard. He dressed to blend in. He's just making sure I get in the right vehicle."

Jason nodded at him. "Do you mind if we stop at the fish market? We can pick up something for dinner."

"Sounds good. You can meet Pavarotti if he's there."

He chuckled. "What?"

"Yeah, colander-clad Pavarotti. He gives spontaneous concerts there. The last one was Madame Buttertart."

"I'm afraid I'm not familiar with that variation."

"Yup, just one of the crazies who seem attracted to me."

"Ahh." As he pulled out of the parking lot he said, "You have tomorrow off?"

"Yup. You can sleep in."

"Have you ever been in a helicopter?"

"No."

"Interested in a ride along the Keys?"

"Sure!"

"Then we need to be up and out the door by 9:45."

"You do the best things ever."

"I'm just trying to impress you."

"It's working."

They sat on the back deck and enjoyed their grilled fish.

They put their feet up on the rail and watched the boats in the bay, until the moon rose over the water. He said, "This is very hygge."

"Is that another grandma word?"

"It's a Nordic word. It's a kind of a state of mind, a state of being, cozy with friends, Danish zen thing."

"Well, hue-gah right back at ya."

From the darkness evil watched and raged.

In a dank motel room, the light of one room spilled out onto a mustard yellow Land Rover.

"Hygge, is it? Danish zen? I give you some Danish zen, right between the eyes with my handy dandy hygge shooter."

The lone guest picked up Beretta handgun off the musty bedspread. "I show you a real state of being. Just a cozy time with friends – you, me and 9mm of zen."

CHAPTER 19

The next morning while making her tea JJ spotted Jason sitting in the weathered red chair down by the water. She wandered down. "Good morning, Jason."

"Oh good morning, JJ." He closed a notebook. "How was your night?"

"Another good one, thanks. Looks like a clear day."

"You'll get a good look at the islands today." He stood up and walked her back to the house. She noticed him scanning the area.

At Old City Helicopters, he introduced her to his friend and pilot, Jake. While Jake took care of the paperwork in the office, Jason helped her into the front seat, handing her the head set. She threw on the shades she'd permanently borrowed.

Before she put on the headset he leaned on the doorway of the chopper. "Jennifer, the fair one."

Laughing, she said, "Not swift today?"

"You will be soon." As he put on his sunglasses, he glanced around.

Once he settled in the back seat she turned around and said, "Where is Jake taking us?"

He pulled the head set off one ear. "Sorry?"

She copied him, exposing one ear and repeated herself.

"We'll go up to Key Largo on the south side of the islands, then down to Key West along the north."

She nodded and covered her ear again.

Jake settled into the pilot seat, flipped a bunch of switches, looked at JJ and said, "Ready?"

She put her hands to her ears, surprised to hear his voice through the headset. She gave a thumbs up.

He fired up the engines. Moments later they were airborne. He dipped the nose and banked left.

"Woohoo!"

Jason laughed. "That's a mic you're yelling into."

She looked back at Jason. Then rested her hand on Jake's arm. "I'm sorry."

"It's fine. I turn my volume down before I do anything exciting."

He rocked the chopper left and right to much laughter. Jake turned his head toward Jason. "Hey, buddy?"

Jason leaned forward. "Yes?"

"I think you've got an adrenaline junkie on your hands."

She looked back at Jason and nodded her agreement. "I love a good roller coaster."

Patting Jake on the shoulder he said, "Then go ahead and give us a ride."

And he did.

After lunch Jason brought his laptop out to the great room that looked out over the bay. He settled in to answer his emails and do some work on his latest photos.

JJ put in her earbuds, turned on some music and played a game on her phone. Absorbed in the game, she started singing along with the music.

Jason looked up from his work, and listened until he identified *Drift Away*, the song Dan gave her. He bent to his work smiling.

After a couple hours, he closed his laptop and stretched out on the couch. His breathing soon fell into a rhythmical pattern.

She tiptoed past him to the kitchen and made a tea. Sitting at the windows she watched the activity on the bay and thought about her life – where it's taken her. She thought about the letter she wrote as Cam.

That letter's a great answer when regret tries to take hold. I didn't let Cam down any more than he let me down. Oh green chest of my bird, your grip on me is gone. The ticker tape of regret will no longer play in my heart. And I've got ammunition if you come back.

That letter is a cleaver exercise. I connected with my deep inner voice. Some hidden desires surfaced. Stepping away from my defences and myself I finally said things I've always longed for, but held back. Yeah, it was about self-forgiveness for the past, but the amazing result of that exercise is clarity. Desires I put away long ago are flaming to life again. I see hope for my future. Yeah, good one Eulah.

She got a paper and pen. Returning to the view of the bay, she wrote a letter back to Cam.

I loved you, Cam. You'll always hold a special place in my heart. I'm glad you're in a better place. I will replace that picture of your blood on the windshield with you happy in heaven. Thank you for giving me that.

You're right. I think I've found the place I'm meant to be. I'm discovering happy here. I'm sorry I couldn't find a way to bring all of me to our marriage. But in those few years of marriage, I grew up. Losing you and Lucas was almost too much for me. But I think I gave up a lot of the important bits of me for our marriage, and that wasn't good for either of us.

I've found solid ground here in the Keys – ground I'm sinking my roots into and I'm starting to live again.

I hate the saying what doesn't kill you makes you stronger. It breezes over the part of being shattered by the darkness and abyss – the crushing weight of emptiness. It doesn't acknowledge the number of souls that don't survive the winepress of deep loss. It doesn't speak of the work and determination to get through. Or how you emerge bruised, battered and scarred. The one good thing isn't becoming strong, it's the paradox that deep wounds and their exquisite scars open your heart to feel a deeper, broader love.

I promise you, I will grab life with both of my hands. I have a friend that's helping me through the grief. And I have a friend who is showing me how to live a full rich life. He's invited me to taste, fly, swim, dance and sing. These happy stars shine the bright light of hope. He's a good friend. So yeah, I'm going to be okay. I'm coming out the other side of that valley of shadow of death that took me past death's portal.

There's some crazy stuff going on but I will hang on to all the good that God is placing in my life. It will not break me. I've come too far to be destroyed by things that don't matter. Jason's right. The real stuff is love, laughter and putting your heart out there again with people.

I'm sure you and Lucas are hanging out together. I always thought you'd be a good dad, so teach him to be a man equal to you. And someday you'll introduce me to our grown up boy. I choose now to let him go and leave him in your good care.

I'll visit with you in my thoughts and remember the good days, but you two now walk a different journey than me. So I will say "Bye for now," to both of you. And it's time for me to live out my life on the path before me.

Until we see each other again

JJ

In her bedroom she put the letter in an envelope and tucked it in her luggage case with the letter she wrote from Cam. She returned to the great room with her sketchbook. She turned to the bird.

So what comes after the nasty green congested chest of regret? An orange neck and shoulders. Hmm. The part that holds up the head. Orange is a positive colour, not like the sickly green of regret, right? The front of the bird got the most light. So what is orange?

Jason drew in a deep breath then stretched. "What time is it?"

She checked her phone. "It's almost 5:30."

He rolled on his side. "I'm afraid I haven't been a good host."

"Don't apologize. You don't need to entertain me. I had a good afternoon. I got in a bit of thinking time."

He sat up. "Are you hungry?"

"I'm getting there."

"You up for stir-fried steak teriyaki?"

"Ooo that sounds good."

He stood up, interlocked his fingers and stretched out his hands, and headed for the kitchen. She followed.

"How about some tunes?" He pointed to his iPad.

She tapped his music app. "Which playlist?"

"Aw, my favourite – Chesney."

Scanning through the lists she said, "There's about 50 Chesney playlists. Which one?"

"Not quite 50."

"Okay 15."

He laughed.

She lifted up the tablet to show him. "How about the fav songs one?"

Starting the rice, he set the timer. From the freezer he pulled out a large steak "Mom would be disappointed in me for making this without marinating the meat for the afternoon, but it still turns out good. I add extra sauce to the veg mix."

She laughed. "Sounds good."

He got out the cutting board and a lethal looking knife and sliced the meat. He nodded toward the fridge. "Get out whatever vegetables you like."

With a stack of food on the counter waiting to be chopped, she asked for another board and knife.

He watched her chop a stick of celery. "You're pretty good with that weapon."

"You're pretty good yourself."

He tossed her a carrot and took one himself. "Race ya."

She positioned the carrot and knife. He said, "Three, two –" and he started chopping.

She hip bumped him to slow him down. "You cheated."

"It's like the ladies' tee at the golf course. I'm a guy. You gotta give me a head start."

She gave him another hard push.

He scrambled for his footing. "Now who's cheating?" He pushed her away, pulled her cutting board closer to his, and stood in her way.

She pulled the towel off his shoulder and snapped him on the bare leg.

He said, "Hey, hey. No fair."

"Oh we're long past fair."

Amidst laughing he said, "Done! Let's see how far you got.

Oh, not even half."

She snapped him again.

He grabbed for the towel and missed. She ran.

He gave up and looked down at his leg.

She came back. "Is it fatal."

"If I pass out from the pain, do you know first aid?"

"I think I can throw a bit of ice your way."

"Good to know I'm in competent hands." He picked up his knife and started chopping again. Cautiously she approached and pulled her board back. He gently hip bumped her. Bumping back, they hip danced for a few seconds. They chopped in happy silence.

When the opening strains of *Sing 'Em Good My Friend* played, Jason let out a low mmm. She listened to the words about an old man selling a guitar to a young man. With love of his life near death, he'd come to the end of his world. He told of holding the beautiful old hand of his love, heart, and soul. The young man vows to sing of the pain, then sing of the truth, then sing the music still held in that old guitar.

She made it through one verse before tearing up. She held her hand to her mouth, chin quivering with emotion. He opened his arms and she stepped in resting her head on his shoulder. He whispered, "This one gets me every time too. I see me holding my nana's hand for the last time."

She wiped at her rivers soaking his T-shirt. They slowly moved to the sad song, each letting the forge of sorrow give another hammer blow to their hearts and temper their steel.

She thought, *This song is right. Grief is first a song of pain. Then with the diminishing pain, it's a song of gritty, cold, hard truth. When the balm of truth quietens your heart and you can see things honestly, then you can sing a song, a good song of life for those you've lost. The pain is almost done with me. I'm coming into my truth. And I know one day I'll sing my song of life.*

With the last strains of the song, he stepped back. "I keep it in my playlist because it reminds me of Nana."

The rice timer rang.

They did a quick stirfry of the meat and vegetables and served their plates. The stars beckoned them to the back deck.

"Tell me about your grandma. You've mentioned her a few times."

He nodded. "She was a fantastic woman. She passed all that goodness to my mom. I spent many of my summers with Nana. She kept me on the straight and narrow in my teens. And she introduced me to her Saviour.

"When I was older and moved away from home, I still spent a couple of weeks a year with her. She said it was to fatten me up. She was the queen of peach cobbler. I'd come in from an afternoon of surfing and she'd have a warm cobbler waiting for me. She was the first woman to steal my heart from Mom.

"And then cancer laid claim to her. They gave her a few short weeks. I was on assignment in Philippines at the time. I flew back as soon as I got the news, then spent three 20-hour days in the hospital with her. Every time I tried to say goodbye to her, I couldn't choke out the words – I couldn't bring myself to the finality of goodbye."

He looked out to sea, then rubbed his temple and looked down shaking his head. He shifted in his chair.

"When I finally said goodbye, she held my hand. She said – "

He coughed. "She said, 'It's not goodbye. It's see ya later.'" His voice broke.

He let out a long breath. "She patted my hand and made me promise I would never walk away from my faith, that she would see me in heaven.

"I took a photograph of our hands that day. It hangs in my bedroom. I'll never forget that amazing woman.

"That's why I listen to a song that brings tender memories."

"She sounds lovely. She helped turn out a good man."

The moon travelled much of the sky while they talked, laughed and imagined new constellations in the stars before retiring.

She awoke just as the sky hinted at morning, then rolled

over and fell back asleep. She didn't get out of bed until 10. The house was so quiet she looked out at the weathered chair to see if Jason was there. It was empty. She found a note on top of a mug with a teabag. "I'm in the workshop with a pottery class. I've locked the doors and I've got my phone. Call me when you're up. J."

"Hey, good morning JJ. How're you feeling?"

"Good morning, Jason. Good. I guess I was tired."

"I'm not surprised. It was late when we went to bed. Help yourself to whatever you can find in the kitchen. I'll be down here in the workshop with a class until noon."

"Okay. I'll make lunch for us."

"Sounds good. See ya in a couple hours."

"Okay, bye."

After class, Jason came through from the garage. He heard the playlist from the previous evening rocking through the house before he got through the door. Coming down the hall, he heard her singing. He called to her, but she didn't hear him. He rounded the corner to see her dancing in the kitchen. She was preparing lunch. He leaned against the wall.

What was it she said? It's a happy soul that lets the music out.

While she grooved at the fridge, he slipped past and got his camera. He crouched at the edge of the room to take several photos – swing dancing with the fridge door, belting out a chorus into the spoon, singing and pointing across an imaginary crowd, and his favourite, an impassioned air guitar.

When the Sun Goes Down, a song with a steel drum, Caribbean sound came on. He set the camera down and settled against the wall. As she spread the mixed tuna on the bread, she swayed with the rhythm. She adopted Chesney's accent then slipped into Uncle Kracker's voice. With a final smear of tuna, she gestured a rapper thumbs up singing one of the final lines replacing Kenny with Jason."

He murmured, "There's *my* girl."

He picked up his camera and slipped down the hall.

When she went to bed that evening, she found a close up

photo of herself – mid sway with eyes closed and a heartfelt look as she sang into the spoon. Jason wrote, "It's a happy soul that lets the music out." A sticky note said, "I saw a woman happy in the moment and couldn't resist the shot." She set it standing up on the dresser.

Past the pain, singing a song of truth. Ah, I know what orange means now. In the light of the receding storm it is honest acceptance – of the journey, of truth. Oh God, I'm glad to reach the sunlight. Thank you for bringing me here. I'll be happy to stay in this place a long while. Don't go thinking we need to hurry along.

Wednesday morning she stayed to join Jason, the young woman teaching the class and the kids from the resort while they made their clay lantern masterpieces. The kids enjoyed the instructor's easygoing manner. JJ sat alongside the kids with her own block of clay. When finished she joined Jason at the wheel and watched while a beautiful vase formed under his gentle hands. She found the changing shapes mesmerizing.

Soon a crowd of kids gathered around him. He patiently answered all their questions then invited one kid to try it. Bent with heads close together he instructed the young girl until a pleasing bowl formed. Several more kids wanted to try it. And he took the time to work with each one. When they got back to the resort, the kids excitedly told their parents they wanted to be potters when they grow up.

This explains all the positive comments on the program.

On their trips back from work, they stopped by her house regularly to pick up the mail, but no new packages arrived. The days passed in this happy bubble of peace and laughter, but in the shadows hate boiled over and plans escalated.

CHAPTER 20

On Saturday morning she spotted Jason in the old weathered chair. He seemed to be sleeping and she wondered if he spent the night there. Awhile later she noticed him writing in his notebook. Fifteen minutes later he headed to the house. "Good morning, JJ."

"Good morning, Jason."

He dropped the notebook on the table. "I need a coffee."

She looked at the notebook binder. One of his photos of sailing filled the see-through cover. In bold letters it said, "Life Abundant," and his name.

Maybe I need to start a journal.

"Feel like a toasted bagel?"

"Sure." She joined him in the kitchen.

"Tell me about that weathered red chair."

"What do you mean?"

"It sits on the lawn like a hairless aardvark at a beauty pageant."

He chuckled. "I never noticed the hairless aardvark aspect, but I guess so. It was here when I bought the place. Before I could get rid of it I found myself doing much of Eulah's homework there. I guess it's the place where life makes the most sense."

"And you keep a journal?"

"It's something I picked up from Eulah. It's a journal of my relationship with God. I write the things He shows and tells me, and of the conversations we share. At first I didn't write it all down, but I'd forget things. And I think what God says to me directly is important, so now I write it all down. Often I read a month or two back and I see patterns emerge, and a bigger message that I'd miss without journaling."

"Eulah mentioned it to me as well. I didn't think I had much to write down. And I'm not much of a writer."

"I tune in to God's voice more when I have a pen in my hand – and I'm sitting on the hairless aardvark."

She chuckled.

"And it's not about the quality of writing. It's about keeping track of all that God shares with you."

His cell phone rang. "Hey, Gunner."

As he listened he looked at JJ. "Hang on a sec."

"Up for a dive this aft?"

She eagerly agreed.

"Sounds good. You'll bring the tanks?"

"Okay. See you guys after lunch."

"Dan, Mike and Gunner are coming over. Gunner's bringing a new friend."

She perked up. "A *girl* friend?"

"He didn't say." He smeared jam on his bagel. "The boat will need a tank up. We can go when we're done eating."

He piloted the boat around the east end of the island to the marina. They waited in the line up for two boats ahead. JJ hopped onto the dock with Jason as the attendant hooked up the fuel pump. He chatted with the young attendant like old buddies. She wandered down toward the dive shop. He kept an eye on her, ready to follow if she decided to go inside.

Two good ole boys staggered out of the shop and stopped to talk to JJ. He didn't like the way they positioned themselves on either side of her and headed down.

One grabbed her arm. She struggled to get free. Jason broke into a run.

"C'mon honey. We'll show you a good time."

"Let go of me."

"Ah Sweet Cheeks, don't be like that."

Jason pulled the creep's hand off JJ. He swung at Jason and grazed his face. Jason shot off a quick hit, knocking the creep off his feet. He turned to the creep's friend to back him down as well, but the guy held his hands in the air.

Jason dropped his fists. "Pick your buddy up and don't come around here again."

"Hey man, we didn't know she was with you. No offence meant."

He growled, "Offence taken. Whether or not she's with me, grabbing a woman is not acceptable." He looked at the creep struggling to his feet. "Get out of here."

He said to JJ, "Let's go." They walked back to his boat. He paid the attendant.

The teen said, "Those two have been bothering several people. We called the cops, but they said it'd be half an hour before they could come."

"I think they're done bothering people."

He tucked his credit card in his wallet and helped JJ aboard.

Once away from the marina she said, "I'm sorry to have caused trouble for you."

He looked puzzled then shook his head. "This wasn't your fault. Those boys just needed to learn a little respect."

She touched the cut on his cheek.

He said, "How bad is it?"

"Just a shallow cut."

"Yeah, he didn't really connect."

"If you have rubbing alcohol aboard, I'll clean it up."

He pointed to a cupboard.

When she'd cleaned the cut, he pressed his face in several places. "Just checking if wearing a mask will hurt."

"It's above where the mask would sit, I think."

"Yeah, I think it'll be okay."

"My hero."

"Not really. I lost my temper. In my heart I was ready to take them both out. I didn't need to knock the guy off his feet." He nodded toward JJ's hair. "He saw Jennifer, the fair lady and liked what he saw. That, I can understand. Grabbing you wasn't cool, but then me letting loose on him wasn't cool either."

"Well, I'm glad you appeared when you did. He was a big boy. I think you did the only thing that would stop him."

"Well, thank you for not thinking bad of me." He waved at a passing vessel and powered up the boat. "Lord, forgive me for hitting him. Forgive me for my anger. Thank you."

He steered into his bay. "Just so you understand, defending you is not wrong. And I don't feel using force is wrong. I will always defend you with whatever is needed. Using force beyond what was necessary with a drunken fool was wrong."

When the guys arrived, Dan took one look at the developing bruise and said, "Hope you laid him out."

Mike asked, "What happened to you?"

"A couple drunks thought they'd drag JJ off for a bit of fun. I changed their minds."

"Good man." He turned to JJ. "You okay?"

"I'm good."

Gunner came around the vehicle with a couple tanks and a dark-haired beauty. "That'll shine up nice in a day or two." He handed Jason the tanks. "This is Becky. Becky, this is Jason – and JJ."

JJ noted Gunner wore her favourite blue canvas shoes.

And they match his shorts and shirt. I wonder, does the presence of Becky have anything to do with his newfound fashion coordination?

Dan said, "Now that we're all together, there's a local band playing tonight at the Hurricane. Anyone interested?"

Becky said, "Is it the Wayfarers? I hear they're great. I'm in."

JJ smiled when Gunner followed with a quick, "Me too."

Jason looked at JJ, then said, "We're in too."

Mike said, "I'm in too. I need to keep my eye on this big fella." He pointed his thumb at Jason's cut cheek.

They got the gear onboard and headed off to one of the nearby reefs. JJ sat beside Becky. They chatted about the usual things – where she moved from, what she does, how she likes her new job. JJ thought Gunner found a keeper.

As Jason helped JJ with her tank he said, "That Neanderthal bruised you."

"Yours is worse. I'm glad that's all he did."

"Me too."

They did their safety check and plunged into the depths. *This will never get old*, she thought. They moved along the outer edge of the reef. Gunner gave the signal to stop. He pointed and gave the shark signal. A huge hammerhead swam into view. JJ touched Jason's arm. He looked at her huge eyes. He gave her the okay signal. She nodded, but moved in a little closer.

Although her breathing sped up, she held steady. It placidly swam by within 10 ft.

Onboard he asked what she thought.

She said, "So amazing!"

"I noticed you slid in behind me."

"You said you'd do anything to defend me."

"And you figured he'd be full after chowing me down?"

"You are a bit more meaty than me. I saw him giving you the eye. I think I saw him lick his chops."

"You'll be glad to know hammerhead attacks are extremely rare."

At the bar, Becky and JJ headed off to the bathroom. When they came out, Jason was standing nearby and walked them back to the table. JJ went to the bar to ask for a refill on pretzels and Jason joined her. She looked at him. "What's the deal?"

"If you attract a couple drunk bums at the dive shop, I can't imagine what you'll attract at a bar." He signalled a couple of beers to the bartender.

She looked him up and down. "I seem to have attracted one barfly already."

He turned toward her and leaned on the bar. "That happened long ago at the grocery store when you said the colours are better here."

The beers arrived. He handed her one, raised his toward her and took a drink.

"Is that true?"

He stood up, set his beer down, and backed her into the bar, placing one hand on either side. "Jennifer Jaye, you've stolen my heart. But I'll wait for you until your ready." His eyes locked with hers, then he stepped back "In the meantime, I'm happy to be your homework." He picked his beer off the bar. "Let's get back to the table."

What just happened?

JJ sat down. Absently she looked back at the bar. Conversations swirled around her without registering.

When the band started playing, Becky grabbed JJ and headed for the dance floor.

The first slow song sent them back to the table. Jason spun JJ around. "My turn."

Once swaying to the beat he said, "JJ, I don't want to lose you as a friend. That stuff I said at the bar – I shouldn't have said anything. Just forget about it, okay?"

"What you said – is that how you feel?"

"How about we talk about that when you feel the same."

After a couple of turns she leaned in to his ear. "Let's talk soon."

Her words, her breath sent goose bumps down his neck. He let out a deep breath.

She smiled.

Man of sea and wind, you've stolen my heart too. I need to be sure you will not get hurt – by me or by the craziness around me.

The following week carried on the same as the first. Every morning she found Jason sitting in the old weathered chair, writing. He drove her to and from work. Their laughter-filled evenings and long talks late into the night made JJ almost believe nothing bad could ever happen again.

Mike came by late in the week. He brought all the mailed items back. Sitting at the table he said, "I've confirmed the validity of these documents." He handed her the birth registrations and adoption papers. He pointed to one of the newspaper clippings. "This was your birth family."

"So Kenna Bodine is my birth name?"

"Yes."

Jason said, "How about catching the lunatic doing this?"

"That P.O. box number doesn't exist, so it's impossible to trace it.

"As to Mark's murder, we haven't had any luck getting the courts to release the information we want. We've been combing through the Keys looking for the suspect and have come up empty handed. We're always a step or two behind. But there's been no sign of her for over a week. I'm starting think she's left the islands.

"I believe there's a link between Mark's murder and these packages. I have my suspicions about who the blond woman is, but with no evidence, I'd rather not say what I think. What I will say is that she's gone for now, but it wouldn't surprise me if she shows up again sometime. I know that's not what you want to hear."

"Ang is back this weekend. Is it safe to go back home?"

"I don't know what to tell you. It *looks* like she's left. And you can't live in hiding forever."

"Okay, well I think I'll go back home." She looked at the concern on Jason's face. "Like Mike says, I can't stay here forever."

"No, what he said was you can't stay in hiding forever. Listen, I understand what you're feeling, but I don't like this. There's a lunatic out there with their scopes on you. And I don't like some crazy person coming after you one night leaving you and Ang to defend yourselves."

"I'll put you on speed dial."

"You mean I'm not there already?"

She laughed. "Mike, how much longer can I have police protection?"

"We must pull the guys."

Jason said, "Oh man, I don't like any of this."

JJ said, "How about we take it one day at a time? If anything happens that is concerning then we can talk about where I should live then?"

"Then expect to see me around a lot. And you need to

promise to tell me about anything *I* might consider concerning."

Mike said, "If another notice for a package comes in, let me know and I'll have forensics pick it up. We'll check it for fingerprints."

Under a red western sky, a powerboat navigated out of Banana Bay marina loaded with groceries, bottled water, charts of the waters, a shovel, a package of zip ties, a roll of duct tape, and a longstanding hatred.

"Your time will come, Princess. Soon you will pay."

CHAPTER 21

"I didn't expect you up so early."

Ang stretched. "I didn't either, but I can't sleep thinking about all the work waiting for me. Do you mind getting Jason to pick you up after work this week? I think I'll stay late to catch up."

Inwardly, JJ smiled. "No problem."

She settled into their new routine, stopping for groceries and dining on her back deck. He stayed until Ang got home.

On her first day off she and Jason piloted the *Cool Change* to a reef north of Sugarloaf. When they got back on board, JJ spotted a disturbance of the water about 20 feet off the starboard. "Jason, what's that?"

A turtle head popped up. It struggled to catch its breath before disappearing.

Jason said, "It's a turtle and I think it's caught on some netting that's pulling it under."

"We have to do something. Can we cut it free?"

"It's illegal to get any closer than we are right now." He went into the wheelhouse and made a phone call to the Turtle Hospital. "They'll be here shortly. They said to see if we can snag the lines and pull them up. Maybe we can keep him up if we hold the weight of the lines dragging on him."

When they stabilized the lines, and the turtle no longer struggled to surface JJ said, "Look at the tumours on its head."

"That's the virus that causes the tumours to develop."

"Oh the poor thing. It can't even see. It's amazing it's still alive."

When the rescuers arrived, they cut the turtle free and brought it aboard their boat. It would to go to the hospital to treat the virus and remove the tumours. The lead rescuer said, "You found him, so you get to name him."

Jason looked at JJ. "You spotted him."

"It's a male?"

"Yes. He's an older juvenile male, probably around 20 years old."

"Oh my goodness. Well he looks kind of like an English butler. How about Humphrey?"

"Humphrey it is. Thank you for calling us. If you stay in touch, we can let you know when we plan to release him. It won't be for at least a year, but you're welcome to join us for the release."

JJ waved as they drove Humphrey to the Turtle Hospital. "Now that was awesome. We saved a turtle's life."

That evening, JJ opened her new journal and poised her pen to write.

Okay God. I'm ready. What do you want to say?

She wrote as thoughts entered her mind and the dialogue that followed.

You are like Humphrey.

Really? How?

Caught in the netting of mistaken assumptions, drowning in turbulent thoughts, and blinded by false perceptions. It's time to treat the virus and remove the tumours.

You need to explain all that to me. What are the mistaken assumptions and false perceptions? How do I treat the virus and remove the tumours?

Assumptions are things you think are true, but have no basis in fact. Tell me your thoughts on the grim reaper.

She laughed.

Yeah, Eulah pointed that one out to me. I get that it's wrong, but it sure seems that there's far more people dying around me than anyone else. So what do you say is the truth about all this death?

I did not bring death to this world, but now that it's here, I command full control over it. People dying around you is not your fault. You can trust Me to provide the full extent of days to those you love.

It sure feels like it has something to do with me.

Circumstances will soon reveal the truth. Know that I'm telling you this ahead of time so when all is revealed you will know I am God and you can believe what I tell you.

Then what about false perceptions?

You are forming an opinion that perhaps your marriage to Cam was a mistake. My children do not always make the best decisions in life, but I always turn the negative into good. The truth is that you loved Cam and you have a son here in heaven. You will spend eternity with him. Your sweetness that Indigo sees in you matured through your time with Cam.

So you see pink sweetness too? Am I really cerise?

You are, and I adore it.

Okay, well how do I treat the virus and remove the tumours?

The virus of lies will continue to infect you unless you fill your mind with my truth. Eulah has you on a good path. Bring your concerns to me and I will tell you the truth. Not everything is what it appears to be. Remember that. Circumstances can lead you to believe false things. I know the beginning, your beginning, from the end. I can tell you the truth. Think about the Red Sea. The people thought they were trapped against the ocean, but the truth was that I would part the waters for escape. When facing several feet thick walls at Jericho, it seemed impenetrable, but the truth was I would tear down the man-made fortress. There are times when your situation will look impossible, but remember those circumstances are not my reality. Place your trust in me.

And the tumours of disbelief will continue to blind you to my truth. Stand in faith that I am God and I do not lie to you. I will expose the lies and together we will remove the disbelief that is blinding you. Clear of blindness, you could avoid the false perceptions and the netting of mistaken assumptions. Immerse yourself in truth. It pushes out all turbulent thoughts. Continue to walk with me.

She stopped writing and looked over her notes.

This is definitely not me talking. Thank you God. Help me in my unbelief. Keep showing me where I'm mistaken.

As Jason held open the door to the funeral home JJ muttered, "I'm not the grim reaper."

A middle-aged woman excused herself from several guests and approached them. "Would you happen to be JJ?"

"Yes, I am."

"I'm so glad you came. I'm Jedediah's daughter, Kiera. Dad spoke of you often. He treasured the painting you did for him. I want to thank you for making his final days a bit brighter. He sat in his chair with the painting for hours. The first time he showed it to me he spent the entire afternoon telling me stories of him and Mom – many were stories I never heard before. So you've given me a good memory too. That painting will be a family treasure. Thank you so much for your kindness. And thank you for coming today."

As the woman moved on to speak with others JJ thought,

Thank you God for the idea. It never occurred to me that it would have such an impact. Kind of cool that through me You blessed this family. The Conch Republic is a good place to put down roots.

At the end of the service JJ signed the guest book. As she waited for Jason she thought, *In the orange light of the receding storm, the truth of loss trumps the pain of grief. It is good to sojourn in the land of honest acceptance. Honest acceptance of great loss is not an easy place to get to, but it's a relief to be done with the anger, anguish and regret. Hello sunshine. Goodbye storm. The bird is escaping the abyss.*

One evening over dinner Jason said, "So you moved to Iowa after college?"

"Yeah."

"What was that like?"

"I packed light."

"That's an interesting answer. What do you mean?"

"I didn't take much of me. I didn't let much of who I am out – like going on a six-month vacation with just an overnight bag. "

"And here in the Keys?"

She thought for a moment. "I brought all my luggage. And I've unpacked most of it – the artist trunk, the connection to nature suitcase, the friendship valise, even the God-relationship duffle bag." She paused briefly. "There's a few pieces I'm nervous to open, but I've got it all here."

He cocked his head. "I'm intrigued. What still –" Jason's phone rang. "We haven't finished this conversation."

JJ muttered, "Luggage open. Underwear everywhere." *Now that my friend is a fantastic example of not keeping the barn door closed. That conversation took a quick and unexpected turn to places even I've dared not go in my heart. Who knows what would have come tumbling out of my mouth without that interruption.*

"Hello."

"Hello, Jason."

"Oh hey, Sam."

"Sorry to bother you in the evening, but we have an emergency. Jamie was going to Galapagos. We're doing a story on some research on the endangered penguins. Unfortunately, he got an infection from a bad scrape with coral and is in hospital in Hawaii. You'll meet the research vessel at Guayaquil, Ecuador in four days and be aboard for eight days. Tell me you can do this."

"Ahh." He looked at JJ and scratched his forehead. "This is not good timing."

"I'm slammed. I really need you to go."

"Can I call you back?"

"I need to know tonight."

He got off the phone and ran his fingers through his hair. "JJ, that was my contact at NatGeo. They desperately need someone to go to Galapagos. I'd be gone for, well it would be 10 days with all the travel. Thing is, I'm not comfortable leaving you right now."

"You should definitely go."

"If anything happens to you when I'm gone – I don't know."

"I'll be fine. Nothing's happened for a long time. Mike said that whack-job has left the Keys."

"You have a terrible habit of understating the bad points. He said he *thinks* they've left. They may be lurking, waiting for an unguarded opportunity."

"Okay, I promise to never be alone."

"Why am I having trouble thinking this is a good idea, even an acceptable idea?"

"Honest. I promise there will not be one minute I'm alone, except, like, when I'm in the bathroom."

"If they weren't desperate, I wouldn't even consider this."

"I really think it'll be okay. Nothing's happened for almost a month now. Go. I'll be fine."

"We'll talk every night. I want to see that the fair Jennifer is okay."

"Deal."

He called back and confirmed he would go.

The first night he Skyped from the hotel in Ecuador and the second anchored off Whale Bay of Isla Santa Cruz. The third night he sent her a movie of the scenery from the remote west side of the islands. They talked about her workday and his time with the penguins. "JJ, hang on." He spun around looking behind him.

She heard a lot of background noise.

"I'm sorry JJ. I've got to go. I'll call you tomorrow."

She didn't hear from him the following evening. She sent several texts, but received nothing back.

Oh God, this better not mean something bad has happened. Please, please, don't do that to me.

She lay awake imagining all the things that could have happened. They all ended with Jason dead.

After signing off with JJ, Jason charged upstairs to utter chaos.

"Get the RIB down! Go! Go! Go!"

"Get on the light!"

"Are you sure you saw someone?"

"Where? Where? Which way?"

"Are there still people onboard?

"Hurry with the flare!"

He stopped one of the crew. "What's going on?"

"Someone was onboard the boat!

The flare gun fired, lighting up the fleeing boat briefly. The overhead spotlight quickly located the boat and traced its departure. Three crewmembers hopped into the small RIB in the water and tried starting the engine to no avail. Helplessly, they watched the boat disappear into the dark distance. The captain teamed people up for a deck-by-deck search of the vessel.

Jason and his search mate, Ryan, headed down to the berths and engine room. They checked each room looking for anything disturbed, missing or out of place. The upper deck chaos died down by the time they got to the engine room. Ryan opened the door. Immediately, the fresh air caused a fire in a bucket in the middle of the room to explode. The ship violently rocked to the side, bringing the deck almost to the waterline. It remained severely listing to the starboard.

The explosion blew both Ryan and Jason up the stairs and 25 ft. along the passageway. The fire roared out from the engine room. Jason pulled an unconscious Ryan to the deck just ahead of the flames. Within a minute the waterline reached the deck. Everyone got off with just the clothes they had on – no cell or satellite phones. They couldn't access the lifeboat on the side in the air, leaving the one that wouldn't start. They placed the most injured in the RIB and the remaining crew took to the water. Within 15 minutes the ship slipped beneath the waves.

They remained in the water for over 28 hours before being rescued by a small yacht. The Ecuadorian coast guard airlifted everyone to the hospital on the mainland.

At 2:24 am JJ's phone rang.

"Jason?" Her heartbeat pounded in her ears.

"Is this Jennifer Jaye McCurdy?"

She moaned, "No, no, no."

"Ma'am?"

"Is this about Jason? Is he okay?"

"Yes, ma'am. This call is regarding Jason Williams. You are Jennifer Jaye McCurdy?"

"Yes, yes. Is he okay?

"Yes, ma'am. I'm with National Geographic Human Resources and Jason has you listed as one of the contact people in an emergency. There's been a shipboard fire leaving the crew in the waters for over 24 hours. A small tourist boat discovered them and the coast guard airlifted them to the mainland. They have checked Jason out in the hospital and we expect they will release him tomorrow morning. We've arranged a flight for him. He should be back tomorrow evening."

"He's in the hospital? For sure, he's okay?"

"Yes ma'am. He's okay."

"Can you tell me why he's in the hospital?"

"I'm not sure. That's not information I have."

"He said you'll hear from him as soon as he can get to a phone. Unfortunately, he lost his cell phone in the incident."

"And he'll be back here in the Keys tomorrow?"

"His flight lands in Miami tomorrow afternoon."

"Okay, thank you. What's your name?"

"I'm Brianne Richards, ma'am."

"Thank you, Brianne, for calling and letting me know."

"You're welcome."

The next day her phone rang in the late afternoon. "Hello, Jason?"

"It's me."

"Oh what a relief! It's so good to hear your voice. How are you? Are you okay? Where are you?"

"I'm badly bruised, but the doctor gave me a clear bill of health. I'm in Miami now talking on my new phone. You're my first call."

"I can come get you."

"My parents will be here in a few minutes. When NatGeo called, Mom and Dad made arrangements to meet me here.

Human Resources called you too, right?"

"Yes. It was two or three in the morning, but I'm grateful they called. I worried when I didn't hear from you."

"I'm sorry you were worried, but I'm glad they called. I added you to my emergency contact list before I left. Listen, Mom, Dad and I are staying in the city for the night then they're dropping me off at home tomorrow morning. I've told them about you and they wanted to stay and meet you but they have a prior commitment. They send their apologies and asked that I tell you they'll be back soon to meet you."

"Meet the parents, hey?"

"Mom said, and I quote, 'Is she an imaginary friend, dear?'"

She snickered. "She sounds awesome. Seriously, I would have enjoyed meeting your parents, to see who you came from."

"Well, maybe it's a good thing it is delayed. It takes a bit of prep for people to my family. "

She chuckled. "What does *that* mean? You make them sound like the Bluths from *Arrested Development*."

"No, nothing like that. They are – we are close knit. It's just that everyone is fast and funny with their words."

"So more like *Everybody Loves Raymond*? They sound great."

"Yeah, on steroids. We know one another well – too well. There's a lot of laughter and teasing. If you can dish it out and take it they'll adore you. We can be normal, but I know anytime any of us kids brought someone home, it would be a crazy night. Our guests found it intimidating and many never came back. As a result, all my in-laws are just as bad as my family. They're the ones that survived the test. Thanksgiving and Christmas are quite the experience."

"So kind of like a three-car pile up between Giggles, BooBoo and Chick Jagger?"

He grinned. "Yeah. I don't know why I'm worried. You'll do fine. Anyway I gotta go. Plan on dinner tomorrow night, my place."

CHAPTER 22

She arrived at 6 p.m. with a foil-covered dish.

Jason opened the door. "Hey now, what's in the dish?"

"Hi. Yes, I'm good. Thanks for asking."

"It *is* good to see you." He rubbed her shoulder.

"It's really good to see you too."

They walked to the kitchen. "This is a surprise for dessert. I need to put it in the oven to warm it up. And you can't peek."

They swapped the chicken Parmesan in the oven for the dessert. "After floating on the ocean for a day, and eating hospital and airport food, I decided to tank up on a little pasta. Could you grab the salad in the fridge? And we can serve ourselves."

"I notice you're moving slowly. How badly injured are you?"

"Just bruised, and some sore muscles, but nothing serious."

"So, no dancing tonight?"

He chuckled. "It might be a week or two before I'm up for the dance floor."

After eating their meal Jason said, "So, a little tea or coffee with whatever is in the oven?"

They took their dishes to the kitchen. JJ got the dish out of the oven. "So I know you spent over 24 hours floating on the water and I remembered you speaking of coming home after a day of surfing and your nana had warm – "

"Peach cobbler!" He peeled off the foil. "Oh you are spectacular! Thank you." He grabbed her face and kissed her.

After dessert they headed back for the deck. She said, "Those bruises are quite a fashion statement."

"You like this look?"

"Not really. I don't think splotchy black on a sickly yellowy-green works for you. It clashes with the whole windswept beach blue thing ya got going."

"I'll make a note of that." They settled into their usual chairs, Jason more carefully.

"What happened down there in Galapagos?"

"While you and I were chatting I heard a commotion on deck – a bunch of banging and shouting. That's why I signed off so suddenly. I went up to utter chaos on deck, everybody shouting and rushing about. Someone boarded the boat without us knowing. One crewmember set off a flare. We could see someone in a small boat powering away, but we couldn't get our runabout boat started. The captain initiated a deck-by-deck search, to check for anything amiss. I followed one of the guys down to the engine room. We found a bucket blazing with fire in the middle of the floor. When the door opened, it flashed over and blew us down the passageway.

"The explosion destroyed the ship. Thankfully no one was badly hurt."

JJ sat forward in her chair. "Why was there a fire in a bucket?"

"A fire in the engine room is extremely dangerous. No one in their right mind would intentionally set a bucket on fire in there. And since there were no buckets like it onboard, the conclusion is that whoever boarded the ship started the fire."

"Are you saying someone set the ship on fire *on purpose*?"

"That's how it looks."

With a confused look she said, "Did they catch who did it?"

"No. They got away."

She rubbed her forehead. "Do they at least know who it was?"

"No."

"So a ship you were on was boarded by some unidentified person. They set it on fire and the whole thing ends up burning down? And you're left swimming among hungry sharks for 24 hours?"

"Well more specifically the explosion blew a hole in the hull sinking the ship. I think it would have sunk whether I had been onboard or not. And there weren't any sharks."

She stood up at the deck rail, shaking her head.

He gingerly sat forward. "What's wrong?"

She kept shaking her head. She banged the rail several times.

"JJ – "

"I can't do this. I just can't do this. Not again." She pushed past him, ran through the house to the driveway with Jason limping close behind.

"JJ, can we talk about this?"

On the driveway she whirled around almost bumping into him, eyes full of tears.

"Oh honey. What's wrong?" He held her shoulders, but she shrugged him off.

"This is already breaking me. Don't make this any harder."

"Tell me what we're talking about."

"This! You! And exploding boats. I can't face *another* round of everyone-who-JJ-loves-dies."

"But I didn't die. I'm okay." He reached for her hand. "Wait – did you say you love me?"

"Don't joke. I'm serious."

"I am too. You love me? This isn't quite how I envisioned us talking about our feelings for each other."

"Jason, please."

"Okay, let's talk about what's upsetting you, but I'd like to come back to this bit about you loving me afterward."

She squeaked out, "I'm sorry," and got in her car sobbing.

"JJ, don't leave like this."

She mouthed the words, "I'm sorry," and drove away.

When she got home she turned off her phone, noting the calls from Jason. She fell into bed, clutching the pillow.

God, how could you do this again! I thought You bring life. Where's the life in this? Jason was almost killed. Okay universe, you win. I'm cutting anyone out of my life that means anything to me.

God, You can stop this whole death thing here and now. I've learned the lesson – no one more needs to die because of having a relationship with me. I'm done. My heart can take no more.

For a week she ignored Jason's calls and avoided Ang in any context outside of work.

Jason glanced at his phone. "Hi, Mom."

"Hi, sweetheart. How are you feeling?"

"The bruises are pretty much gone, so doing better."

She paused. "I hear hesitation. What aren't you saying?"

"Just something between JJ and me. I'm just trying to figure out women, or one in particular."

"Well, since I am one, maybe I can translate. What happened?"

He let out a long breath. "I don't know. We had dinner on the deck like we often do. She asked about what happened in Galapagos. I gave her an abridged version. Then she asked a few questions. Then she stood up and announced she couldn't handle another person dying and left in tears. But I didn't die. Now, she won't talk to me. I don't know if I should just go over to her house and make her talk or keep calling or what."

She thought for a long moment. "You know, from all you say about her and her past, then it doesn't sound like she's running from you."

"It sure looks that way."

"I think she's running to protect you."

"What does that mean?"

"Well, she loved her dog. It died. She loved her parents. They died. She loved her grandmother. She died. She loved her baby. He died. She loved her husband. He died. I'm thinking she's fallen in love again, and now you've had a brush with death. I think she's running because she wants to cut you free before you die."

"That's crazy."

"Yes, but from her perspective, it makes sense."

"So what do I do?"

"A spooked young filly requires a calm and steady approach and they always settle down."

"Mom. I'm a guy. And JJ's not a horse. Stop speaking in metaphors and just give me your advice. I can't afford to get this wrong."

"Sometimes you sound just like your father. Okay. Communicate your heart in a clear, steady way. No pressure, just in a way that says you are not going anywhere. Don't let her fear push you away until you've had a chance to talk it through. Then if she wants to end it, you must let her go. But I don't think deep down she wants to end it. She's overwhelmed by her fear of you dying and she suffering another broken heart. It's clouding her thinking."

"Thanks, Mom."

"When you work it out, Dad and I would like to visit and meet this one."

"Okay. Well that will only happen if I get this sorted."

"I'll be praying for you and JJ. And let me know if there's anything I can do."

"Thanks Mom – for everything."

"Love you, Jason."

"Love you, Mom. And say hi to Dad for me."

He hung up the phone. "Alright JJ. I won't let you push me away."

CHAPTER 23

JJ checked the time and closed down her computer. Ryan would be there any moment. She glanced at her phone and read the text from Jason. "Chesney's just not the same without your air guitar. Miss ya. Can we talk?" JJ looked out her window at the bay. *Miss you too, man whose soul sings.* She put her phone in her purse.

"Ryan. Good to see you again."

"JJ." He set down the magazine. "Ready to go?"

He took her to a restaurant in Key West. The waiter led them to a patio table under trees strung with lights. Champagne chilled on ice at the table. She took one look and said, "Ryan, this is too much. You remember me saying about being friends only, right?"

"I remember." He held the chair for her.

He tried to pour her some champagne, but she held her hand over her glass.

"Okay." He set the bottle back in the chiller. "JJ. I know what you said. And I understand." He put his hand on his chest. "Honest."

Her head tilted. She opened her mouth to speak.

"Here's the thing. I can't stop thinking about you. I want to have one night where I can show you why you should reconsider. One night."

She shook her head. "Ryan, I'm sorry. It's not you. And all of this is attractive. You're attractive and anyone would love this life you offer. But there's just no way. I'm dealing with a lot of stuff, and it wouldn't be fair to get involved."

He nodded. "Yeah. Well okay. Plan B for the night. How about we talk about the new program we are rolling out for preferred customers."

Business is your plan B? "Okay. Business I can do. Is the Plantation House really a preferred customer? We're a new account."

"You're one of *my* preferred customers."

"Uh-huh. So you don't have a plan B."

He dropped his head. "I tried."

"So how about we skip the date, and forget business, and spend the evening as friends."

"Yeah, okay. Sure. How about some champagne, as friends?"

He poured them each a glass. She said, "To no-cost friendships."

He held his glass for her toast then set it down when he heard it. He looked her in the eye. "You're not a no-cost friend. Any decent friendship involves an exchange of giving. You should never settle for a friendship without investment and return, without cost."

Her eyes brimmed.

"What's going on, JJ?"

"Nothing." She stared through the trees to the ocean. "I'm grieving for a number of people, and just last week I almost lost another dear friend. I'm in a place where I need to cut the ties. I can't handle any more loss. So, I can't get involved with anyone right now. I can't afford to give anything of my heart and lose it."

"We're not talking about you and me anymore, are we?"

She shook her head.

"Listen, I don't know or understand what you're going through, but I know you are exceptional. And if there's a special guy out there that already has a piece of your heart, then he's probably waiting with open arms to help you through whatever this is. I know I would be."

She let out a shaky breath and wiped her eyes. "How about we enjoy a good meal and talk about what kind of girl lives in your dreams."

"Okay. To dreams – yours and mine."

She hesitated.

"C'mon. You don't need to tell me your dreams, but you can toast them."

That night the image of Jason waiting with open arms haunted her sleep. She woke up tired from a night of ruminations.

The next morning before she headed to an outside massage room a text message pinged.

"Grilled fish on the deck tonight? Let me know what's on your heart." She rubbed her eyes with the palms of her hands.

This is so hard. Jason, you're making it very difficult to protect you. I can see you stretched out on the deck chair. Oh man of island chill, I miss eating with you, talking with you, laughing with you – really just about anything with you. But I can't face life if anything happens to you. This is killing me, but going to your funeral would be the end of me. I'm so sorry. She put her phone on the desk upside down without responding and walked out the door.

A handsome couple in their 60s approached holding hands. *Why does it have to be a couple in love?*

JJ held out her hand. "I'm JJ. I'll be your therapist today."

"Oh hi dear. I'm Carlie and this is my husband Lance."

Once on the tables, JJ asked, "How long are you two here for?"

"We both retired this year and decided to celebrate. Not sure how long we'll stay, maybe ten days or two weeks. We haven't decided yet."

They talked about their recent retirement, their four kids and one grandchild and things to do in the area.

JJ watched them leave and thought, *If only I could –* She remembered her letter to Cam and her promises to grab life to max. *I can't keep that promise. I can't put another person's life at risk just for a short burst of happiness. No. Door closed.*

The next morning, she took her laptop out to the lounge to work for awhile. Carlie and Lance strolled down the beach and stopped at the bar to get coffee.

With mug in hand, Carlie said, "Good morning, JJ."

"Good morning, Carlie. What are you two up to today?"

"We wanted to book more massages with you. That's the first time we've had one and I think Lance is hooked. Could we have you again?"

"Sure. Just book it at the front desk. They can put it on my schedule."

"Do you mind if I sit a minute?"

"No, have a seat." She closed her laptop.

"I was wondering if you'd mind doing me a favour."

"Sure."

"Lance wants to book some deep sea fishing, but I'm not interested in hours of trolling for some fish you can get in a can. I have three daughter-in-laws that I'd like to do a little shopping for and I'm wondering if you'd go with me to the shops. I could use a young woman's perspective."

JJ thought it a bit strange, but Carlie seemed sweet. *And it would keep me away from Ang.* They arranged to go to Key West the next afternoon.

She met Carlie in the lobby. As she got in the rental car, a text message arrived. "Fair Jennifer, mine eyes dost long for thee. Missing you like crazy. Call me." She turned off her phone and directed Carlie out to the highway. Looking out her window she almost laughed remembering when Jason called her a beautiful fast woman.

I know you love me. Oh Jason, I'm crazy about you too. You are a paradox of chill and excitement, of deep thoughts and easy laughter – you are Cognac, the man of smooth and spicy. Please understand. I have to let you go.

The two women chatted about work life and retirement. JJ settled in, letting herself enjoy the moment. They visited several stores for the perfect gifts for her adult kids and one grandkid. While Carlie talked to one cashier, JJ felt a pang of regret.

So many years without my mom woven through the chapters of my life.

They stopped for a late dinner. Carlie said, "So how do you like island living?"

She thought about Iowa and said, "It's taken me by surprise

how much I love it here, but the warmth, sunshine and the chill lifestyle grips my soul. It isn't hard to put roots down. It's like an irresistible pull."

And then there's Jason. He's rather irresistible too.

"Chill lifestyle? In teen lingo, chill can mean casual hook ups."

"Carlie! Aren't you a bit of straight fire."

"That's me, dropping low with my homies."

JJ laughed. "I guess troubled teen social work let's you in on all the slang."

"It does indeed. It's a whole different language."

"Well, I think you're Gucci."

Carlie laughed. "Thanks dear."

The waiter stopped to check on them. Carlie asked for a top up on her coffee. "So, anyone special in your life?"

Yes! Yes, the most amazing man fills my life, but I have to leave him. "Yes. Sort of. I guess it's complicated."

"Oh I'm sorry to hear that."

"Me too. He's quite amazing. He's full of life."

"It sounds like you don't want it to be complicated."

"No I don't. But circumstances can push you in a lousy direction."

"Like I tell my teens, complications involving others don't get resolved without communication. It might be hard to start, but if both of you want this to work, then it's worth at least trying." She dabbed her mouth with her napkin. "Life is too short to let a good one go."

Before she could think JJ blurted, "And it would be an even shorter life for him if I stayed."

"I don't understand."

"It's just that I have a long, long trend line of family and friends dying. Young. Old. Doesn't matter. They all die. And I don't want this guy to die. He almost did and I don't think I can handle another death right now."

"That sounds like quite a dilemma, but he sounds worth it."

How is it that I'm telling you all this? Is it because you're here for a few weeks then gone out of my life? Yeah, I guess everyone needs a safe place to dump their load. Sorry Carlie, I actually like you. I don't mean to dump on you, but – gardyloo!

"He's definitely worth the risk, but I'm absolutely terrified. It's been a long road, but I'm finally stepping back into life after losing my family. So I have to be strong to protect both of us. Anyway, enough about me. Tell me more about your work with teens. It sounds challenging."

In bed Carlie's words rolled around her head. "Life is too short to let a good one go."

Sometimes I wish my life was short and just put me out of this misery. God, where are you in all this? How could you let death get so close to Jason? I thought I was getting better. Now I'm terrified. I can't regress back into the abyss. I just can't do that again. Please, don't let Jason die.

A week later JJ headed to the outdoor lounge for a cup of tea. She was checking her email when a text came in. "Been awhile since we've spent time on the water. I think I'm going through withdrawal. How about a tour around the Key? Please, let's talk." She could almost smell his cologne and see the ocean breezes blow through his tousled hair. Her heart ached.

I miss you so much, man of wind and sea. More than I can contain, and yet, I cannot bear to see anything happen to you. This is tearing me apart.

She looked down toward the bench hoping to spot Eulah then remembered she was on vacation.

God, I need an answer to this today. I can't go on like this.

Carlie popped by just before lunch. "Lance has gone for a helicopter ride. I wasn't up for an intimate afternoon with an airbag, so I'm on my own today. I've got a table in the restaurant. Care to join me?"

They ordered and settled into chatter about the weather. JJ asked about their plans for the rest of the week.

"We signed up for the sunset cruise out of Key West and

booked the night in a hotel there. And Lance talked me into some dive lessons. I have visions of being the appetizer at a shark frenzy."

JJ laughed. "I've taken up diving since coming here and I can tell you, it's spectacular. It's so peaceful and stunningly beautiful. I've encountered sleeping nurse sharks and a very uninterested hammerhead. I'll tell you, my strategy was to always keep another person between me and the shark."

"Oh that's good. Then I can be the entrée."

"Oh my goodness. You are too funny."

"Oh that reminds me. Lance asked me to invite you to dinner with us tomorrow night. It's our last night here before we head to Key West we wanted to take you out."

"That would be lovely, thank you."

"Now before you say yes, I have to tell you – us includes my son."

"Is this your unmarried son, by chance?"

"Yes, but I'm not trying to set you two up. Like you, he's not looking for a date either."

"Carlie, I know you care about me. And you're so sweet and kind. But you *know* I'm not looking to meet anyone right now."

"Oh I know, dear. You don't need to worry. He's not some misfit living in my basement. And he's not some kind of throwback with pink hair."

"Wha -" She laughed then straightened up. "It rather sounds like a family night."

"Oh don't leave me with two men who want to talk about fishing, the latest in car dashboard technology and who is going to win the world series."

"Oh you poor thing."

"Join us, please. You are such a lovely girl. I hate to see you struggling with whatever this is. A evening of distraction isn't going to hurt. It might help shine a light on what's going on in your head and heart. Or maybe not. Either way, it's just dinner. And Lance would enjoy a dinner together before we leave."

"Okay. When and where?"

"How about we meet in the lobby at 7 tomorrow?"

Grateful that Ang and Dan were out on a date, she sat on the back deck. "God, we need to talk. I really need to hear from you. I've tried to let go of Jason and my heart just clings to the life and hope he brings into my world. I can't seem to walk away. But after dealing with my parents deaths, then my grandmother, and another round of let's-wipe-out-everyone-I-love when both Lucas and Cam died, I cannot handle yet another round of losses. And its really coming up on round four if we count my real parents who an arsonist wiped out.

"Arsonist. Hmm. Is that who is sending me all this stuff? Some crazy lunatic that had a hate on for my parents? No, no, no. I can't think about that now.

"This came close to another round of loss and I just can't handle that. And that whole boat explosion? That terrifies me. I'm so scared it's all going to happen again. I need to hear from you that I can trust You to protect Jason – that You will not take him from me. I can't keep trying to run from something that's got a tight grip on my soul. My heart aches for a life of joy and happiness. But I'm terrified of losing Jason, then losing myself permanently to the abyss. So I'm coming to you with my heart and my hopes and Jason."

In her head she heard,

My hand of protection sheltered him. You can trust me, my lotus. You need to stop running and rest in me. Take a look at your bird. I want to show you something.

"Will you promise Jason will be okay?"

I promise you I take care of all of my own and that includes Jason. You can trust his life in my hands.

"How can I trust this is You speaking and not just my desperate hope?

Read what I've written to you.

She opened the Bible app on her phone and read Psalm 140, where she left off days before. There was a link to a verse in 2 Samuel. She read chapter 22 three times. Then committed several verses to memory "The waves of death overwhelmed me; floods of destruction swept over me. The grave wrapped its ropes around me; death laid a trap in my path. But in my distress I cried out to the Lord; yes, I cried to my God for help. He heard me from his sanctuary...my cry reached his ears. He reached down from heaven and rescued me; he drew me out of deep waters."

"God, I'm crying out to you. Hear me. Please rescue me from these deep waters. Protect Jason from death's trap. Thank you for giving me these verses. I'm holding You to them."

I have heard the cries of your heart. And I will always pull you out of the deep waters. I will always rescue you. No matter how impossible things appear, I will provide a way through. Now, take a look at the eyes of your bird sketch.

"They are surrounded by a black band."

Yes. Your vision is tainted by fear. Even in the bright sunlight, the fear masks the truth. I am the truth. I speak truth to you. I am the God of life, of impossible rescues, of protection. I am everywhere, even the deep waters. I am with Jason too, providing rescue and protection for him. Your fear is blinding you to the truth of my promises.

"Forgive me, Lord. Help remove the mask of fear that blinds me."

For the first night since the boat explosion, she slept well.

CHAPTER 24

A few minutes to 7 she waited in the lobby for Lance and Carlie. Another text message arrived. "Are you looking at the stars tonight? Yeah, me too. Missing our nights under those twinkling lights. We'll talk soon, right?"

Oh man of stars, hope and life, thank you for sticking with me.

She typed an answer. "I miss our nights under those twinkling lights too. I miss you Jason. Sorry for my silence. Been working through some things. I can't meet you tonight. Going out with a guest and her family for dinner. But I'm off tomorrow. Could we meet and talk sometime tomorrow?"

"Tomorrow for sure. How early are you up?" She smiled.

Lance interrupted her thoughts. "JJ, how are you this evening?"

"Hi Lance, Carlie. I'm good, thanks. You're both looking pretty island chill tonight."

"Carlie bought me these crazy flower shorts. It's probably the last chance to wear them and not look like a hippie hula princess."

Carlie hugged Lance. "How about a quick demonstration of a hippie hula? Not sure what that is."

He mixed Saturday Night Fever disco with hula's swinging hips to the delight of both ladies.

As they walked out to the car, JJ quickly tapped on her phone, "How does 9 a.m. sound?"

"It sounds perfect." She put her phone away.

The waiter seated the three of them and took their drink orders. They chatted about their vacation when JJ heard a familiar voice.

"JJ."

She spun around.

"Jason!" She jumped from her seat. "I'm so sorry."

He whispered, "Hey, you're the girl I met at the grocery store, right?"

"I am."

He bent to kiss her. It started a gentle brush of lips, then enflamed to a deep connection of two hearts.

He pulled back to look at her. Then she remembered her tablemates.

"I'm sorry. Lance, Carlie, this is my – my boyfriend Jason. Jason, this is Lance and Carlie."

Jason turned to the couple and said. "Mom, Dad. I see you've met my girl."

Stunned, JJ said, "Jason is your son? Carlie, did you know all along?" She turned to Jason. "Did you know about all this 'Come out to dinner and meet my son who doesn't have pink hair,' thing?"

"Pink hair? No – " He rubbed his forehead. "Mom, what have you been saying? No. I thought I was just meeting Mom and Dad for dinner. I'm as shocked as you. I told you my family is kind of nuts." He turned to his mom. "That's my best feature? I don't have pink hair? That's the best you could come up with?"

"I had to think on my feet."

"You might as well have said I don't wear a stuffed parrot on my shoulder. That's equally valuable information, don't you think?"

"Jason, really."

Lance chimed in. "But you did have Goggles, the one-eyed goldfish. That thing lived for years."

JJ snickered. "Goggles?"

Jason said, "Dad, you're not helping here."

Carlie turned to JJ. "I'm sorry JJ. Jason talked non-stop about you in Miami – "

"It wasn't non-stop."

"– then he asked my opinion on what sent you running. Mostly I wanted to meet the one woman who captured his heart. Then I saw your pain. Maybe it's time to talk through whatever is worrying you. Call this an intervention."

"Mom, you make it sound like we're a pair of strung out addicts. We're not glue-sniffing teens needing an intervention. There's a reason I live three states away. You won't remember this with your *dementia of convenience*, but when I asked you to give me a woman's perspective, I didn't say, 'Hey could you come on down here and royally screw things up for me.'"

JJ's eyebrows stretched up her forehead as she bit her upper lip, trying not to laugh.

Carlie said, "Dementia of convenience? I have no idea what you're talking about. Who are you again?"

Jason shook his head and laughed. "I'm the one without pink hair, remember? You're nuttier than a jar of roasted peanuts. You bring out the nutty in everyone around you – look at Dad off talking about Goggles the one-eyed fish. And Dad, what's with those shorts?"

Lance said, "It's my last night as a hippie hula princess. I can show you the dance." He scraped back his chair.

"No, Dad. I don't even want to imagine what that looks like."

JJ said, "I saw it. He's pretty good."

Jason shook his head. "Unbelievable. I didn't think it was possible to out-crazy past parent encounters, but you two have outdone yourselves." He kissed his mom on the cheek. "You need to dial back your campaign for more grandchildren. Coming down here is way over the top."

JJ said, "Jason, it's okay. Really. From the perspective of having no family, I think it's kind of sweet they're here."

He sighed. "Okay. I love you Mom and Dad, but you two are not helping at all." He turned to JJ. "What do you say we leave Pinky and the Brain to their meal, and we grab a pizza and sit under the stars?"

"Okay." She rested her hands on Carlie and Lance's shoulders. "Thanks for the dinner invite. Meeting your son is not what I expected at all, but I've rather enjoyed the evening so far, you know, the hula dance thing and talking about Goggles the one-eyed goldfish. I'm sorry to bail on you two, but I'm sure you understand. We'll be seeing more of each other – soon I hope."

"Love you, dear."

Without hesitation, she kissed Carlie on the cheek. "You too, Carlie."

As they left JJ heard Lance say, "Pinky, are you pondering what I'm pondering"

Carlie laughed. "I think so, but this time you put the nylons on the orangutan."

Jason said, "Can't say I didn't warn you."

JJ said, "They are lovely. They're not as crazy as some of the people I've run into lately."

"Yeah, Peaches and Pavarotti make Mom and Dad look normal."

"And don't forget about the guy in the bank machine."

And the bridesmaid at the restaurant with Ryan, and the interpretive dance of Dancing Queen. Maybe God used all those other wacky occurrences to ensure I was primed to meet his parents. Maybe it's all about not running away in fear, but I'm meant to settle in and enjoy life's ride. Maybe God is just bringing a little unpredictable fun into my days. What was it? Oh yeah. Whimsical. The window that lets in sunlight and colour. I guess these strange events could be called whimsical. Lance and Carlie are fairly colourful. I enjoy their fun. Maybe I need to stop fighting and enjoy God's whimsical journey.

Walking into the house with their pizza Jason said, "Want to take the boat out into the bay and dine to the gentle rock of the waves?"

"Are you trying to ensure I can't escape?"

He laughed. "No, I hadn't considered that."

"Then dinner on the bay sounds good."

The last light of day faded as they stretched out on the bench seats with a slice and a soda. JJ looked up. "Star light, star bright, first star I see tonight. I wish I may, I wish I might, get the wish I wish tonight."

"What is it you wish for?"

"Oh you don't get your wish if you tell what it is." She sighed. "What I want is for no one to die unexpectedly." She turned to face Jason. "You've brought light and life to the darkness of my world. I didn't realize how much of life I'd been missing. Even before Cam and Lucas died, my life wasn't full and happy. It's been a very long time since this kind of joy has been a part of my days, like since I was 13. The joy, laughter, dancing, diving, all of it is like a lifeline in the lonely emptiness of grief, and I was hanging on to it for dear life. But the other end of that line is attached to you. When you told me the details of the explosion, the line was no longer anchored to something secure. I can't face falling back into the abyss. I'd be forever lost in the black, empty void if something happened to you.

"So, I thought I better cut my ties to you before something terrible happens. I couldn't live with myself if you died like everyone else around me. I wanted to protect you."

Jason sat up. "But you can't protect me. The power of life and death lies with God."

JJ sat up to look at him. "I know. I struggle with that. I wonder why God is allowing everyone around me to die, like Mark, Nic and Jedediah, although he was old. So maybe he doesn't count. It feels like God hates me, and everyone around me is paying the price."

Jason started to say something.

She stood up. "I know that's not true, yet the fear rises and there is no rational logic that will quell it. I'm still dealing with this fear, but God and I have had long discussions about you and this fear. So, I'm choosing to trust God that He has a shield of protection around you, and that hanging out with me will not kill you."

"So – you want to hang out?"

She leaned against the back of the boat. "I want to talk about our feelings for each other."

He joined her at the back of the boat. "Oh, *that* conversation. I recall you declaring your love for me right before running out. I'm happy to finish that conversation, but before we do, give me your hand."

She offered her hand. "I promise I won't run this time. You made sure that is impossible."

He grinned. "Oh, I'm not worried you'll run. I just wanted to hold your hand."

She bumped him with a quick shoulder check. "You're sneaky. I must keep my eye on you."

He wagged his eyebrows. "I think you should keep both eyes on me."

"You're not taking this conversation seriously."

"Ah you want serious. Okay I'll start." He scratched his chin. "Well, as I mentioned at the bar, you got me way back at the grocery store when you said there's better colours here. You intrigued me."

"And you got me with your photographs, the manatees, the turtles – and the diving – well, the helicopter ride too – and the dancing. And honestly, I'm intrigued by the man who doesn't walk around with pink hair and a stuffed parrot on his shoulder."

"What can I say? One can't choose family."

"I envy you with so much family who love you. It's a lonely journey without the love, the laughter, the joy – without people that will be there at the airport when you've been blown up in the Galapagos. Even the crazy family get togethers sound fantastic."

"Aw, JJ. I'm sorry. You're right. Family brings a richness to life – even if they are a bunch of nutters." He cocked his head. "I know a cure for that jealousy. We could make you a permanent member of the family."

"Dial it back, there Zippy. You do know dashing means charming. It doesn't mean accelerating the relationship to breakneck speed. I just caught up with talking about how we feel. Your miles ahead of me again."

"Best way to keep you moving in the right direction."

"Well, I'm still at the let's admit we have feelings for each other and figure out what this is stage."

He turned on some music and offered her his hand. "Okay. I admit, I have feelings for a beautiful fast woman."

"You're such a goof. The apple doesn't fall far from the tree, even though you don't want to admit you're an apple."

CHAPTER 25

A couple evenings later, Jason picked JJ up from work and drove them to a local beach where a crowd gathered. "I have a surprise for you." He grabbed two cameras from the back, handing her one. "C'mon, let's go get some photos."

"Okay. What are we taking pictures of?"

He grabbed her hand and pulled her along. "You remember Betty from the turtle hospital? And Tango, that huge turtle we saw at the hospital? Well, today is Tango's release."

Six men brought Tango out from the back of the turtle hospital ambulance in a tub. The crowd gave a big aww and several woots.

JJ said, "Oh, he looks really good. That's amazing considering all the tumours. Look at him. It's the first time he's seen the ocean in a long time."

They floated the tub on the surface of the ocean as they walked to hip deep water. Tango smelled the salt water and popped his head up.

He remembers the good life he led out there – the freedom, swimming just for the sheer joy of it, exploring the depths, and chowing on fresh seafood. What that virus stole from you now is restored.

She looked into those ancient mariner's eyes.

I'm like you. I lost much of what made life worth living, remaining blind to my affliction. But now I see more clearly. Now I too smell life ahead.

She snapped off several close ups of Tango's eyes. With the ocean splashing his face, Tango clamoured to get out of the tub.

Yeah, I get that. I don't much like the abyss and I'm pretty eager to get out too.

So without too much fanfare, Betty pushed the front of the

tub down into the water and Tango swam out to sea.

Thank you Tango for sharing your life with us, even briefly. Now go, live a long happy life. I will too.

Driving home on one of the residential streets, someone left an old, weathered, blue Adirondack chair on the curb for garbage pickup. JJ tapped her window. "Hey look! Another hairless aardvark."

"Aw, poor thing."

"They are so rare, it's a shame to throw it out."

"Not everyone appreciates the beauty of aardvarks."

"Bye little one. I hope your life isn't over."

Later, when examining their photos, one of JJ's close ups caught a drop of water rolling down Tango's cheek, like a tear of joy at seeing his beloved ocean. Jason said, "This is a fantastic shot. It's the kind of happy coincidence all photographers hope for on every shoot. You could sell this one."

"It's my favourite one I've taken. I don't think I could sell it though. It'd be like selling a part of me. Tango's release is like my coming back to life after a long journey through the darkness of loss. A splash of his natural world touched his face and called him back. A lot like island life is splashing my heart and calling me to a rich full life."

Friday, another gift awaited JJ on her desk. She tore off the birthday wrapping paper, opened the box and pulled out a ball cap.

Cheers Boston. Now where have I seen this before?

A card fell out of the cap. "A gift from an old friend. Happy Birthday, Princess."

Unable to remember where she'd seen one before, she set it on top of the filing cabinet and carried on with work.

Jason waited in the parking lot to pick up JJ for a Netflix night. At his house, he told JJ to go on in while he got his camera bag out of the back. He followed her through the garage door and down the hall to the kitchen. She turned on the lights to the sound of "Surprise!"

Ang stepped forward. "Happy Birthday, JJ."

Shocked, she stared wide-eyed at the crowd while they sang. "Thank you, everyone. Y'all got me. I thought Jason and I were going to binge on Netflix. I guess that's tomorrow night."

Jason leaned into her ear. "Consider your weekend booked. Doubt there's time for video binging."

She looked at him.

"That's all I can say for now." He turned his attention to his guests. "Let's get this party going."

People quickly loaded up with pizza and gathered in the great room. When they finished, colourful gift bags appeared. "Aw, you guys are too much." She thought of her promise to make a great life and live it to the fullest with good friends. A lump formed in her throat. She quickly turned her attention to the first gift bag. There were lovely cards, and wonderful gifts, many handcrafted.

Ang gave her a spectacular tie-dyed shirt in shades of cerise, blue and fuchsia. "I love it! It's just how Indigo describes me." She hugged her friend whispering in her ear, "Thank you so much for this gift, organizing the party, and sharing your friends with me. Getting me here has brought me back to the land of the living. Thank you more than my heart can say."

"You're welcome, dear friend."

She opened a card from Jason, then looked in the bag and lifted out a heavy box. She removed a bunch of tissue paper to see a piece of pottery. She carefully pulled it out of the box to much oooing and ahhing. It was a bowl-shaped piece, painted in a deep ocean blue. On the outside were many cherry coloured shards giving the illusion of shattered pottery put back together again. "Oh Jason, it's a stunning piece of artwork. I love it! It's like me – my broken heart made lovely again. I will treasure this forever. You made this, didn't you?"

He nodded. "All but the cerise paint. Indigo mixed that for me."

The crowd erupted with compliments.

"Thank you so much, Jason." Ang placed it safely on a

nearby table. JJ looked over all the gifts and cards. "Thank you so much, everyone. This was a wonderful surprise. What means the most is that you all have opened your hearts and lives to welcome me in. Because of you I feel like I've found the place where I belong. You all mean so much to me – more than I can adequately express. Thank you for being my friends."

Ang and JJ were the last to leave. Ang said, "Thanks Jason for the idea and your help in pulling this together. I think for once I pulled off a true surprise party."

JJ said, "You did. I had no idea. Now what's this about my weekend plans?"

He said, "Ah, your birthday surprise continues all weekend. I'll pick you up around 11 tomorrow morning. Pack for over-night."

"And where are we going?"

"It's the kind of weekend that's really best as a surprise. Trust me on this."

She turned to Ang. "Do you know what's planned?"

She smiled and shrugged. "Let me carry some of these out to the car for you," and disappeared with a load of gift bags.

"Okay I can wait, international man of mystery. Thank you again for this absolutely lovely gift, doubly special because you made it." She leaned in to give him a kiss. He pulled her in close. They held each other for a long moment.

She leaned back and let her eyes drink him in. He kissed her again. "Goodnight, JJ. I'll see you tomorrow. I promise it will be –" He searched for the right word. "An unforgettable weekend."

"Unforgettable?"

"I don't think there's a word adequate to describe what's coming this weekend. I think special, in the paradoxical sense."

Her brows knit. "I don't understand."

"In this case, I think a cliffhanger is a good thing."

She picked up the remaining gift bags. "Okay Austin Powers, see ya tomorrow."

"Groovy, baby."

The next morning he picked her up and drove her back to his place.

"What are you up to?" She noticed a rental car in the driveway. "Now who does that belong to?"

"Brace yourself. Please know I warned you."

She squinted her eyes. "You warned me?" Her eyes opened wide and she grinned. "It's a Pinky and the Brain weekend! Carlie and Lance are here?"

He nodded. "Until dinner Sunday."

"Oh my goodness. This is the best birthday ever."

"I hope you still say that tomorrow. I did tell you it could be crazy."

"But they're your family. And they've come here for a weekend with me." She gathered her bags and hurried in the house. She gave Carlie a big hug. "Oh Carlie, so good to see you."

"Happy Birthday, JJ."

"Thanks. This is awesome."

Carlie squeezed her hand. "I heard it was your birthday and we immediately made arrangements to spend the weekend here. I'm afraid the guys have cooked up plans."

JJ laughed. "Whatever they are, I'm very glad to spend my birthday weekend with you. Thanks for coming down. It's a great surprise."

Lance came out from the bedroom hallway wearing his colourful, flowery shorts.

JJ said, "I'm beginning to think you actually like those shorts, Lance. Good to see you." She hugged him.

He stepped back to do his hippie hula dance again to the delight of both Carlie and JJ.

"Thanks for sharing that, Dad. It's now burned into my memory."

Lance started again.

"Please stop. Listen, do you have any other shorts with you? Perhaps if you can't get those hips under control, you should change into something less inspirational – something in say, black."

Lance grabbed Jason and hugged him. "So good to be here, my boy. Life! Isn't it grand?"

"Try to contain the crazy gene for the weekend, hey? I don't want you two to run JJ off before we have a chance."

"I thought you'd prefer the hula to me telling her all your childhood secrets, like when you thought your stiff dead hamster was sleeping like Uncle Frank after a night of party Kool-Aid."

JJ snickered. "Party Kool-Aid?"

Carlie said, "That's Uncle Frank code for rum and coke."

JJ said, "You thought your hamster was sleeping off a drunk?"

Lance said, "What was that thing's name? Oh yeah. Superham."

JJ couldn't help laughing. *Goggles, the one-eyed goldfish and Superham, the dead hamster. That's hilarious.*

Carlie said, "He even made him a little superhero cape out of a Solo cup. It stuck up in the air like a giant sail."

Jason said, "I was five. How long have you been sitting on that little gem, Dad?"

"All your life. I have a truckload of stories. Just waiting for someone to tell them to."

"Excellent. This is what happens when you're the last one to bring home a girlfriend. Well, Monty, I guess I'll pass on door number two, mortifying childhood stories. I'll take what's behind door number one – humiliating behaviour in public."

Holding up an imaginary microphone Lance said, "Humiliating behaviour in public it is. And because you've been such a good sport, we're including everything in the big deal! I'm going to throw in the childhood stories for free." He hugged JJ. "It's going to be a great weekend."

They spent the day wandering around Key West, laughing and enjoying each other's company. After dinner, Carlie pulled out a boxed gift and card. In the envelope, she found a gift card for an online art supply store.

Carlie said, "I heard you like painting, but I didn't know what you have and what you need. Splurge on things you wouldn't normally get."

"Thanks, you two."

She opened the box. Inside was a beautiful blue stained-glass rectangular table lamp. "Oh my goodness. This is lovely. Thank you both so much. To share my birthday with both of you makes it most special. Thank you for the thoughtful gifts. They're perfect."

Jason pulled out a small box. "I have another gift for you."

Lance whispered loudly to Carlie, "Ooo, this looks interesting. Steady yourself, old girl. This could be what you've been waiting for." He patted her leg. "Or maybe you already know something about this?"

She elbowed him in the side. "No, and neither do you, so put a sock in it."

JJ looked at the small box, worried about what awaited inside. She stalled by telling his parents about the handmade gift Jason gave her the night before. Tapping the box she glanced at Jason. *He's leaning back, looking island chill. That means it's probably not the big one, right?*

She opened it to find a small velvet jewellery case. Her concern escalated. "This isn't the kind of gift that comes with a really big question, is it?"

Jason looked momentarily puzzled, then grinned. "You have nothing to worry about. That kind of gift will never share the same space and time as Dad's hippie hula shorts. I promise to make it abundantly clear before I spring that kind of jewellery on you. This is the kind of gift you give to your girlfriend who loves nature."

With that, she opened the box. It was a leather bracelet with a silver loggerhead turtle on the band. He said, "His name is engraved on his belly."

"It's Tango. Aw, I love it. Thank you. Help me put it on."

Lance drummed the table. "Ah the tango. Baa-daa-dum-dum-dum-dum-dum. Baaaa-daa da–"

Carlie said, "I love the tango. Maybe we can find a Latin dance club after dinner. You can strut your stuff, Lanciago."

Jason rubbed his forehead. "Okay *Lanciago* and *Carlita*, there'll be no stuff strutting. You two are like a pair of minions at the monkey house. For your information, Tango is a turtle we watched released back into the ocean."

JJ touched the textured silver shell. "Definitely a good birthday with some pretty special people." She lifted her wine glass. "You all have been so wonderful. I love the gifts, but even more I love that we are spending this weekend together. As you know, I don't have family so it warms my heart that you came all the way down here just to spend the weekend with me. Thank you for that gift too. To a wonderful couple and their amazing son."

Carlie said, "And to the wonderful woman who doesn't mind hanging out with a couple of old hippies."

Lance clinked everyone's glass. "To the gal who appreciates the finer points of interpretive hula dancing."

Jason said, "To the rare woman who actually enjoys my family's squirrelly side."

Sunday evening after his parents left he said, "I have one more gift."

"Oh Jason, no. You've been so generous. I don't need anything more. The hand-crafted bowl means so much to me." Touching the leather on her wrist she said, "And you gave me a piece of a shared memory, one that represents my coming back to life."

He held her hand and touched the turtle with his thumb.

She said, "And then the special gift of a weekend with your family."

He groaned. "They are *special.*"

"I really loved my birthday weekend. Your dad cracks me up and your mom goes along with all his fun. Your childhood must have been a blast. I really like them."

"And they quite like you. The nuttier they are, the more

they are enjoying themselves. Anyway, back to my last gift. I think you'll want it when you see it."

"Okay. Where is this irresistible present?"

He walked her out to the side of the house.

"It's Mrs. Hairless Aardvark!"

"I went back to rescue her."

"You're right. I love it."

"We can take it back to your place tonight."

She sat in the weathered old blue Adirondack chair, fondling the rough arms. "I think she needs to stay here with her mister. They can sit together watching the world pass by. And I'll have my own chair here when I visit – if you're okay with having two."

"If you ever want it at home, let me know."

He moved it waterside beside his old red one. They sat together holding hands and chatting about the weekend with Lance and Carlie.

The following week they played mini golf with Ang and Dan. Ang brought Ultimate Mini Golf challenge cards. For every round they drew one card from the deck and everyone had to do what the card instructed. One round they each had to take a selfie. On another they had to compliment every other player. The two guys really enjoyed this one.

Jason said, "Dan, that's a spectacularly skilled miss. It takes real talent to miss a two-inch putt."

Dan said, "And it takes exceptional skill to make it bounce off the windmill blade and land right back where you started."

On another round they had to take the even number shots with eyes closed. Jason sunk his ball on the second putt.

JJ said, "You peeked! You are such a cheater. Does your mama know what a cheater you are? I could call her up and tell her. She and I are like that." She held up two crossed fingers.

He picked his ball out of the hole. "Yeah, now that is all kinds of disturbing." He spun his finger over his head. "The lab-is-about-to-blow warning bells are going off in my head. Kiss me before the end of the world." He leaned over. "Love ya, babe."

Bent over her swing, Ang's eyebrows shot up at hearing his last comment. *Oh JJ, we do have some talking to do tonight.*

Unobserved, a yellow Land Rover sat in the parking lot, the driver watching the group closely. "Laugh, my princess, laugh. Your happiness tells me it's time. I will have you."

CHAPTER 26

On Saturday, JJ and Jason borrowed a couple paddleboards and launched from the north end of Sugarloaf to go to the Great White Heron Wildlife refuge. It was a nice afternoon paddle across calm waters sheltered by the string of barrier atolls and keys on the north side of the bay. Halfway out a pod of dolphins circled their boards. They both sat down to watch the antics of the boisterous mammals. One popped its head out to get a close up look at JJ. It clicked while she stroked its chin.

She glanced at Jason. "What is it about being with you? Great animal encounters happen when you're around."

"I don't know. Even as a kid, wild animals knew I was a safe person. Maybe that's what led me to work for the National Geographic."

"Manatees, turtles, dolphins, manta rays, sharks, people at the auction want to talk with you and want to work with you, even the resort kids in the pottery workshop want to hang with you. Indigo calls you Cognac. I call you the man of sea, wind and sun. I can't figure out what it is, but it's a naturalness, a connectedness to life, peace – you are so at ease with everything. How do you live that way?"

He pulled her board in close. In a low voice he said, "I've found a paradox of strength and quiet peace in God. When I spend time with Him, His personality flows through me and the world finds Him irresistible."

She knit her brows for a moment. "That's the time you spend in the hairless aardvark in the mornings. What exactly do you do?"

He loved her name for his weathered chair. "A variety of things. Sometimes I listen to instrumental music, close my eyes and just spend time with Him."

She cocked her head.

He smiled. "Spend time with Him for me means I let him put visuals in my head. It's sort of like when you get a spontaneous thought that you know isn't yours. You open your mind to whatever visuals He wants to share. They just pop in."

She thought of her visions, like Whimsical, Wonder and Delight and the colourful bird. *All those visions are from God? Wow.* She thought about the vision of the tiger Eulah shared with her.

"Other times I'll ponder a bit of scripture that really stood out while I was reading. I listen to what God has to say about it for me. And sometimes I'll journal a conversation with the Lord.

"The more time I spend, the more likely I will be filled up and it all overflows to others. Over time, I have become more like Him. This is the man you see today. I'm far from perfect, but I am a better person than I was."

"I'd like to be a better person."

He looked directly in her eyes. "I think you pretty spectacular already."

She reached over and rested her hand on his thigh. "Thanks, Jason. But I'd like a big dose of that peace and quiet you have, no matter what's going on around you."

"He's always at hand, waiting for that kind of relationship with everyone."

She glanced over the ocean and the nearby keys thinking about the ways of connecting with God. "Hey look." She pointed to the nearest island. "What is that?"

He looked in the direction she pointed. "I don't see anything."

"Something on the beach. It went into the trees."

"Shall we go see?"

Leaving their boards and paddles on the beach, they headed inland, looking for footprints in the sand.

"Did it look like an animal or bird?"

"More like a four-legged animal."

"Maybe a Key Deer?"

"I don't know if it was as big as a deer."

"They are rather small. Look here. Raccoon footprints."

"Yeah, maybe it was a raccoon."

They looked up in the trees. He pointed to their right. "Look over there. That's a heron's nest."

"Hey, I see movement. Could that be baby herons?"

"Probably. We can sit here awhile and see if one of the parents come." He pulled his camera out of his backpack. Their quiet pause paid off. A white heron landed with a gullet of fish for the squawking youngsters.

They gradually made their way back to the beach and slowly wandered down to their boards. After several minutes of walking JJ said, "Isn't this where we left our boards?"

They stood looking at the board marks left in the sand. They looked up and down the shore, then out over the ocean. There was no sign of anyone.

She said, "Do you think someone came by, saw the boards unattended and took them?"

"I don't know. I guess so." He put his pack down and unzipped a side pocket, pulling out his cell phone. He held it up high. "No service." They walked down to the bottom point of land. It eventually registered one bar. He dialled, but the call wouldn't go through. "I'll try a text. Maybe that will go through." He tapped out a message, asking for a pickup and detailing where they were. He hit send and waited several seconds, only to be notified that it couldn't be delivered. "I think we'll have to flag down a boat." He put the phone back in the pack. "Let's go back and look around. Maybe someone just moved the boards."

They got back to where the boards had been. Jason set down the pack to take a look in the nearby trees.

She picked the pack up to follow him. "I don't want it to disappear in the Bermuda triangle like the boards."

He laughed. "Fair enough."

"Jason look. There's a boat."

They both ran to the waterline, yelling and waving, but the

boat continued on its way. JJ dug through his pack pulling out her bright pink T-shirt and flowery shorts. "Maybe waving these will attract more attention."

She handed him the shorts. He reached for the T-shirt instead. She held the shirt just out of reach and threw the shorts at him. "You could try a hippie hula dance if you like. I won't tell anyone."

He threw them back. "I'm more of a Miami Vice coloured T-shirt man than a hippie hula dancer guy."

"Uh huh. Oh here comes another boat." They shouted and waved the colourful clothing, but this one passed by as well.

"They don't see us when they're heading the other way. We might need to wait for one coming more toward us."

They heard a noise behind them and turned. A blond woman stood with a gun and shovel. "Looking for your boards?"

CHAPTER 27

JJ stood frozen by the sight of a gun pointing at them.

Jason studied the gun. *Looks like a Beretta 9 mm.*

JJ moved beside Jason. "That's her! That's the crazy woman from Key West."

In a falsetto voice the woman said, "Oh Jason, protect me from the crazy lady."

Jason stepped in front of JJ.

"And I expected nothing less from her Prince Charming." She cocked her head. "You know that everyone who loves her ends up dead? It doesn't look good for you."

Jason said, "What do you want?"

"What do I want?" She scratched her forehead with the barrel of the gun. "What do I want? Well, let's start with introductions. I mean, if you're thinking of marrying the princess there, best you meet the in-laws. Hi. I'm Kenna's sister, Kellie. Good to meet ya, Prince Charming."

She waited for a reaction. "You do know the princess cowering behind isn't JJ. She's Kenna, my little sister. But she was never much of sister. I wouldn't expect much from her, if I were you. Look at her track record. Just sayin'.

"Let me tell you about when we were kids. You know, everything was fine until that darling princess came along. She stole all the attention for herself. After about 8 months it became quite clear our parents didn't love me. It was all about Kenna."

She sniffed. "So I dealt with them. I taught them a thing or two. It just took one match, and poof. Problem solved." She laughed. "Poof! I like that one.

"Next thing I know I'm stuck in foster care, and Princess is adopted. Again, people love her and not me. What's wrong with me?" She assumed a model pose. "I'm gorgeous, right?"

She looked at Jason and snapped her fingers several times. "Hello? Anyone home? I asked you a question."

"I'm listening, but you're just not saying anything interesting."

She nodded. "You want interesting? Let's see. I poisoned her dog, and then her adoptive dad. Is that more interesting?"

She waited for an answer. "No? Tough audience. How about I did in Grandma too." She stepped around to get a better view of JJ. "You listening, Princess? Yeah, all those people died because of you.

"And then there was Cam. You got the picture I sent you? I took it right after he crashed. I was there. I made it happen. Not bragging or anything, but the crash was even more spectacular than I'd hoped. Just couldn't resist a snap or two for the family album."

She looked back at Jason. "What'd you think? Pretty good photography, hey? Maybe you could get me a job at the National Geographic." She smiled. "We could go on photo shoots together. Yeah, I'd like that. I'd like that a lot. Say, I've got an idea. Let me take care of the princess once and for all. Then you and I can do all that stuff, you know, diving, dancing under the stars, sipping wine on the deck, travelling to exotic places. Yeah, you and me. I think I'm onto something here.

"Oh, and the boat fire down at the Galapagos. That was me as well.

"Tell you what. Take this shovel." She threw it at him. "Start digging."

He threw the shovel down. "No."

JJ said, "Jason –"

Kellie imitated JJ. "Oh Jason." She pointed at the shovel. "Pick it up."

Jason didn't move.

She shot just in front of his feet. "Consider that my final warning. Pick it up and get digging."

He complied.

"See? I'm very easy to please. I'm telling you, I look ahead and see nothing but good times for you and me. Oh, I'm gonna need you to make the hole a lot bigger." She indicated a hole about 10 ft. long and 3 ft. wide. "That's big enough for the Princess, don't you think?"

He dug as instructed, surreptitiously watching for an opportunity to take her out.

"You know, Prince Charming, you're kind of blowing my plans. I had a special tombstone island in mind for her. But hey, for you I'm willing to be a little flexible."

After 20 minutes of digging Kellie said, "Yeah, that looks good. Man, you're a great partner in crime. You're sure you haven't done this kind of thing before?"

Jason stood looking at her.

"Throw the shovel over there."

"Good. Now, JJ?"

Jason said, "Get behind me JJ."

Kellie said, "Oh relax, my love. Don't get your panties in a twist or in your case your whities in a tightie. I just want her to get your boards. They are just behind those trees. Bring the paddles too."

While distracted with directing JJ, Jason charged at Kellie. She caught the movement in the corner of her eye and pointed the gun at his chest. "You're a frisky one aren't ya? Settle down tiger. Lots of time for frolicking later."

She told JJ to put the boards and paddles in the hole. She looked at Jason and laughed. "What did you think? It was a grave? I guess it is of sorts. Rest in peace, that happy life Kenna thought she had with Prince Charming. Now pick up the shovel and fill it in."

When the job was done she threw Jason's backpack at him. "Put a couple shovelfuls in there."

With the pack weighted with sand Kellie said, "Now, throw it into the water."

He tossed it out, watching his camera and new cell phone

sink to the bottom of the ocean like his last one.

My insurance won't believe I've lost a second one in the drink along with thousands of dollars of equipment.

Kellie said to Jason, "Now, my love. I'm sorry, but I have to tie your hands." She waved the gun at JJ. "Princess?" She handed her a zip tie. "Tie him up."

"No."

She shot at her feet.

That's two shots, he thought. *Long way to an empty magazine without her killing us.*

JJ took the zip tie. Jason held out his wrists.

Kellie said, "Not in front, darling. Hands behind your back, my tiger."

He put his hands behind his back, turning for JJ to tie him up. He whispered, "It's okay. Remember, it doesn't matter how it looks. God is still in control."

She said, "I'm so sorry you're involved in this."

Kellie pushed her back. "Yeah, yeah. Prince Charming and I don't want to hear your bleeding heart crap." She checked the tightness of the tie. "Really Princess, you need to workout," and pulled it hand-numbingly tight. She circled Jason. "You're a looker, aren't ya."

She drew her finger down his sweaty face. "Yeah, you're mighty fine." She caressed the damp curls of hair at the back of his neck. "I bet you think fairy tales come true. Boy and girl meet. They fall in love, and happy ever after. Yeah, I just can't shake the feeling that it will not be a happy-ever-after for you two."

He held still, keeping his eyes focused on JJ.

"I'm serious, I really don't see things working out with her. I'd be good with a hook up, you and me – you know, if she were to die."

His jaw clenched.

"Ah, that one got ya. Hmm. Now, what was it that excited you? The hook up or Princess over there kicking the bucket." She watched him closely. Jason concentrated on giving no reaction.

She laughed. "Yeah, I think you're interested in a bit of Kellie time." She ran her hands over his chest.

"You're one of those silent types – not much of a talker. Well, that's okay. I'm not much interested in all that get-to-know-ya stuff anyway. See, you and I are made for each other, cut from the same cloth."

She touched his lips. "I wonder –" Grabbing the back of his neck she pulled him toward her and roughly kissed him. He strained against her pull then stepped back.

She wiped her mouth. "Don't be like that. You're making me think you might not like me. You haven't been listening. I don't like it when people don't like me." She circled behind him and picked up the shovel. "No, that just won't do." She lifted the shovel like a baseball bat and leaned into her swing.

JJ yelled, "Jason, look out."

He started to move, but Kellie landed the blow and he dropped to the ground with a force that snapped the zip tie. Blood oozed from his head.

Kellie stumbled back a step. "Whew! That felt good. I really connected." She looked up at JJ. "It's always *so* satisfying when it's someone *you* love." She checked his pulse. "Aw sorry Princess, no pulse." She leaned in and gave him a long kiss. "Go quietly into that unending night, sweet prince. There'll be no happy ever after." She placed his hands over his chest, like a person in a coffin.

JJ stared for the briefest of moments, then turned and ran. Not sure where to go, she focused on getting away from this lunatic. She headed north.

"There's nowhere to go Princess." Kellie followed JJ. "Don't make me shoot you."

Spotting Kellie's boat, JJ ran as fast as she could. She jumped in and pressed the start button. Nothing happened. She frantically pressed every button, flipped every switch and moved every lever.

"Looking for these?" Kellie held up the keys. "I like sports as much as the next person, but we'll not be doing this catch-me-if-you-can thing again." Waving the gun she said, "Come on out and lie face down on the beach."

JJ got out the far side of the boat and for a moment she thought about swimming out to sea. A shot zinged past her ear. She turned around and complied.

Kellie put her foot on JJ's back while she blindfolded her and zip tied her hands. She dragged her over to the boat and pushed her in. With JJ lying down in the bottom of the boat, Kellie drove for half an hour. When beached, she pulled down the blindfold and hauled JJ through a treed area to a shack, threw her on the ground and tied her feet.

"So now, Princess. We finally get time alone to talk. I'll start. As you know, you have flung pain into my life over and over again. Everyone loves little Kenna and forgets all about me. And I've spent my life teaching all these people a lesson. Like dead Jason. He learned it is fatal to like you better than me."

Jason is dead. God, I thought I could trust you. Life finally allowed some joy my way. But here I am deep in the abyss again. What I love is ripped from me – dead, like all the others. Well, I'm done. I just want to die. I can't do anymore of this life.

"At first I was angry with you. I hated you. I wanted you to suffer, to feel the pain when people you love go away. And I thought if I'm not going to have a happy life then neither will you."

Lord, please take me home.

"Yes, I took those photos of you and your adopted parents. I have more if you want to see them. Maybe we can have a photo album night where we go through all those memories."

So many of my loved ones are in heaven with You. Please bring me home.

"And that stuffed rabbit? That was yours before the fire. All my toys were utterly destroyed, but of course the Princess' toys come through undamaged.

"And then, what I consider the pinnacle of my efforts at making you suffer was the car crash where Cam died. Yeah, that was spectacular. Loved the blood splatter pattern on the windshield. I have to tell you, he was still alive when I got to the car. Want to know what he said?"

I want to be done with this life. Please God, if you don't step in and do something then show me what it will take to speed this whole thing up and bring it to its inevitable end.

"Of course you do. I went to confirm he was on his way out. I couldn't have the ambulance come and rescue him. But there was no need to worry. He lived just a few brief moments then died. Right there. With me holding his hand."

Kellie looked up to the roof of the shack, lost in her memories. "It was absolutely – satisfying, a deeply pleasurable thing to be right there when your husband died. He was with me, not you. He was calling for you when I took his hand. Then gripping my hand he professed his love. So deliciously sweet. I killed him and he tells me he loved me."

Really, Lord. This nutcase has interfered in my whole life. Haven't I paid my dues? I have no interest in continuing on this earth. Even if there is nothing beyond this life, I'm still done.

Kellie laughed, wiping spittle from her mouth. "That just made me want to kill another of your lovers. It is the only thing that quells my hatred for you. So, now I've killed Jason." A shutter brought a deep moan. "Oh, that felt so primal. I felt the vibration of the deathblow through my hands and right up my arms. Yes, that was very satisfying."

I've had enough insight into the world of a lunatic brain. Please bring this to an end.

"But now I'm getting to know you. I've waited so long to reconnect with you. I sent you so many mementos to remind you of our relationship. You are the only family I have left. And now I'm the only family you have left. You see? All we have is each other. So let's treasure this time we have together."

JJ muttered, "You're sick."

Kellie checked her forehead. "Nope, no fever. I'm as healthy as a horse. Thank you for caring. Oh you mean *mentally ill.* I've heard that before. Don't put much stock in that psychobabble crap."

An alarm went off. Kellie looked at her phone. "Oh dear. I have to cut short this wonderful reunion. I have an appointment, but I'll bring back some dinner and maybe we can reminisce over drinks tonight." She touched JJ's cheek, but JJ pulled away.

Thank God she's on another topic. Really. Thank you, God. Sweet relief. How sad is it that I'm reduced to finding this something to be grateful for?

"Don't you dare pull away from me. How much more clearly do I have to spell it out for you? People that don't like me don't live long. You saw what happened to Jason when he pulled away. You're not too swift, are ya?"

Swift. JJ's eyes welled up as she remembered the conversation she had with Jason about the meaning of her name.

Oh Jason, I am so sorry that knowing me brought your death. Perhaps Kellie will kill me as well and you and I will have all of eternity to rest in joy and peace, far from this rotten world. I believe I'll see you soon.

Kellie put the blindfold back in place on JJ and left.

When JJ heard the boat pull away, she prayed out loud. "I see that it's not You God that caused all those deaths, nor was it me. But You told me to trust You about Jason. Now he's dead. Please, just take me home. I'm done with this life."

But I'm not done with you. Trust me. Right now, you cannot imagine what I have in store for you. My plans always work ugly things together for the good. I know from your perspective that is hard to believe, but put the little bit of faith you have in me. I am bigger than all of this. Remember the Red Sea and Jericho?

"Put my trust in You? I thought You told me You would look after Jason, that he was safe in Your care. You even had me memorize Your verses of promise. You ask too much – trusting You again, after failing on Your promise.

Remove the black mask of fear. Tell me those verses.

"The waves of death overwhelmed me; floods of destruction swept over me. The grave wrapped its ropes around me;

death laid a trap in my path. But in my distress I cried out to the Lord; yes, I cried to my God for help. He heard me from his sanctuary...my cry reached his ears. He reached down from heaven and rescued me; he drew me out of deep waters."

Hold on a little longer. I have heard the cries of your heart. I heard them before you even uttered them. And I'm reaching deep into your life and bringing things together for good. Even now I am drawing you out of these impossibly deep waters. Do you remember Humphrey? Do you remember the tumours, the virus and the entangling nets? Do you remember Tango's release? What did you say about your photo of him?

She thought about her Tango bracelet and how he sniffed the ocean and clamoured to return to his happy life. "We talked about assumptions, turbulent thoughts and false perceptions. You talked about how I was mistaken to think the grim reaper walks beside me killing those I love."

And?

"And now I know it was Kellie and the evil in her heart that wreaked all that destruction. It was not my fault."

So, now you have proof that I was right. It was a mistaken perception. And what did I promise you?

"I can trust You to provide the full extent of days to those I love."

And when you insisted all this death is your fault, what did I tell you?

"Circumstances will soon reveal the truth. Know that I'm telling you this ahead of time so you will know I am God and you can believe what I tell you." She pondered that for a moment. "So this is the circumstance through which I come to know what's really going on."

And I told you that would happen before it happened so you would know, today, right now, that I am God and you can trust all that I tell you. Will you fill your mind with truth, even in this place? JJ, remove the black mask of fear. I tell you again, there are times like now when your situation looks impossible, but remember, this impossibility is not my reality. Place your trust in me.

"Do you always win every argument? Not sure I like that."

She thought she heard God laugh. *You're a tough little nut to crack.*

"Really? You're comparing me to a cracked nut? I'm not the cracked nut in this situation."

See? It can't be all bad. You still have your humour. You are my sweet cerise lotus flower. I'm lifting you to the surface of the water. You are about to bloom – gloriously, spectacularly, peacefully in My warm sunshine of joy. Your head will be filled with the pure yellow of celebration and joy. You can get there kicking and screaming, or you can rest in My gentle hands. I love you so much, My dear one. Wait until you see how all of this will work out to a long life of blessings in My care.

"Your solution better be really great because right now with Jason dead, and me lying here in the mud, tied and blindfolded in a shack on some deserted atoll in the hands of a serial killer – I think I'm justified in saying my life has hit rock bottom. This is worse than the bottom of the barrel. I don't want to go through the grief thing again. I just don't have the strength for that. So I'm expecting something beyond amazing. You know, that thing about no eye has seen, nor ear heard, nor entered into my heart. That thing."

I'm dealing with the stalking tiger. Her time is done. Watch her disappear. She will no longer touch your life. Rest in Me.

CHAPTER 28

Groggy, Jason rolled over and pushed up from the sand. He felt his head. Sticky, but no longer bleeding. He slowly rose to his feet and scanned the area.

"JJ?"

He looked at the sand and followed the footprints north. "Oh JJ. What happened to you?"

He stood looking out over the ocean. "God, I've never needed an answer more than now. Please, is JJ okay?"

He felt an assurance fill his heart. "Okay, then I need You to get me off this island and bring help."

He walked to the northern most point of the island and waited. He spotted a boat coming from the west. He pulled off his shirt, waving it and yelling to attract attention. The boat slowed and turned toward the island. "Thank you, God. Thank you."

"You okay, buddy?"

"Thanks for stopping. I need to call the police. I've been assaulted and my girlfriend has been kidnapped."

"Hop in. Shelley, get the phone from the glove box."

He dialled 9-1-1 and told his story, and gave his location. He asked if they would transfer him to Mike. After several long minutes, Mike came on the line.

"Jason, they told me what happened. Where are you?"

"I'm on Galdin Key, north of Sugarloaf and southwest of the Heron refuge. Listen, it was Kellie, JJ's sister. She's taken JJ and I think she's on one of the islands. You gotta get out here and start looking."

"I'm was at the marina on other business, so I'm boarding the police boat now. I'll be heading out to you in five minutes.

And I've activated the Coast Guard search and rescue. Hang on, Jas. We'll find her."

He could hear Mike talking with someone in the background. "Okay, the captain says we can pick you up in 15 minutes."

"Thanks Mike."

The couple stayed with him until Mike arrived. He thanked the couple and hopped aboard the police power boat. Insisting JJ was still alive he pressed Mike to quickly find her. One of the officers took a look at the cut on his head and checked Jason's pupils.

"It's not deep, but the scalp will bleed a lot. You really should get checked for underlying damage or issues."

"I will once we find JJ."

The man nodded, thinking to keep his eye on Jason for any sign of a brain bleed.

Mike worked with the captain to plan a search of the atolls and islands in an ever-expanding radius.

After circling a couple of nearby islands, looking for a boat or evidence of recent traffic, Mike began to wonder if they would find JJ alive.

CHAPTER 29

Jason leaned on the bulkhead of the boat. "Oh God, where is she? We desperately need your wisdom."

He paced the back of the boat. "C'mon JJ. Where are you?"

Inside the wheelhouse, Mike got a call from another search team. "Sir? We've got an abandoned boat. There's some blood and a blue leather bracelet. Over"

Mike called Jason back in the wheelhouse. "They've found an abandoned boat. Was JJ wearing leather bracelet? Blue?"

"She wore a blue leather anklet. Yes! That's her!"

Mike answered on the mic. "That's hers. Where exactly are you? Okay. Keep looking. We're on our way. Over"

The helmsman pointed the location on the map.

Jason traced the line from where they found him to the abandoned boat. His finger absently tapped the map. "I know where they were going." He pointed to a small island a couple miles further. "Head here."

The pilot looked at Mike.

Thinking about the blood in the boat, Mike focused on Jason. "You sure? We get this wrong and it could cost JJ her life."

"I'm sure – Mike, I'm sure."

Mike nodded to the helmsman. "Go. As fast as you can."

Jason sat down, running his hands through his hair. "Oh God, please keep her safe. Please protect her, shelter her. Help us find her. Give her your peace."

A several minutes later the team radioed Mike. "We fished a blond out of the water. How long until you can get here? Over."

Jason jumped up. "They've got her?"

Mike spoke into the mic. "Is it JJ? Over."

"She says so. I'm sending you a photo. We'd like you guys to identify her. Over."

Mike pulled out his phone and opened the image. Jason turned the phone to see. "It's not her. It's Kellie – the lunatic who took her."

Mike keyed the mic. "It's not her. Repeat. It's not JJ. It's Kellie Bodine. Hold her. We should be there in 10. Over."

"Jason, when we get there I need you to stay out of it. I'll let you be there while I question Kellie, but you must control your emotions. She plays head games, and I don't need you engaging with her. I'm only letting you in on this because you might hear something that would help us find JJ."

Jason nodded. "I know."

"Buddy, this will be the hardest thing you've ever done. She will push on all your buttons. You gotta stay cool."

"I got it. I won't let her get to me. I just want to find JJ."

"Okay. Then let's go find her."

"Thanks, Mike."

They boarded the boat where Kellie sat in cuffs with a bandage on her forehead.

Mike thought, *It may not be JJ's blood. She might still okay.*

Kellie moaned when she saw Jason. "Great, it's Prince Charming." She nodded at Mike. "And his trusty stead."

Ignoring her connotation Mike said, "Kellie Bodine?"

"You don't know?"

"Did you get that cut from JJ?"

She shrugged. "Don't know how that could happen. She's dead. Her perfect little life is over." She grinned at Jason. "Guess you'll have to settle for me."

Jason felt rage rise, but kept it from registering on his face.

Mike moved closer, using his size as intimidation. "You could do yourself a favour and tell us where she is. It'll go easier for you in court."

She looked up directly at Mike and leaned her head toward Jason. "So he can mourn her death? That's no way for Prince Charming and I to start our new life together."

Jason clenched his jaw.

Mike said, "You want to start this new life with a clean slate. Where is she?"

"I told you. She's dead."

"I don't think so. I think you're like a cat with a mouse. I think you're having too much fun toying with her to let her die."

"Well, aren't you the cleaver one."

"So where is she?"

A slow smile crossed her face. Her eyes turned cold. "I hear dehydration is really the way to go." She leaned out to look past Mike. "They say it's a euphoric experience."

Jason muttered, "We don't have time for this." He headed for the wheelhouse.

"Oh c'mon honey. Don't leave mad. Let's kiss and make up." She watched him leave. "Love you, babe." She made kissing noises.

Jason closed the door behind him, shutting her out. "Can I see the area charts, please?"

Mike said, "Okay. Now it's just you and me. With the long list of murders, capital punishment is a very real possibility. Help us and I'll talk to the D.A. on your behalf."

"Ah the sweet kiss of death." Her voice hardened with resolve. "Suicide by order of the courts. Sounds pretty good. You think I want to live this crap life? Go ahead. Kill me. You'll be doing me a favour."

Mike nodded to the attending officers. "Take her back to the precinct and book her – kidnapping and attempted murder. There will be more charges as we investigate."

As they helped her board the other boat she sneered, "You'll never find her. At least not in time."

He joined Jason in the wheelhouse.

Jason tried to read Mike's face. "Did you get anything from her?"

"No. But I'm sure JJ is still alive. And we're close. Kellie's worried we'll find her." He looked at the numerous islands and atolls in the area and said to the helmsman, "Call in all the police boats in the Keys, and get as many Coast Guard boats as you can. We need to search this entire area."

Jason pointed to the same island as before. "Here. Mike, she's here."

"What makes you so sure?"

"Kellie said the island would be her tombstone. Look at it." He tapped the island several times. "It's the shape of a tombstone. It's the only one like that. I checked. Mike, please."

Mike signalled the helmsman and they were underway at top speed.

Jason whispered, "Baby, hold on. We're on our way." He rubbed his hands down his thighs. Feeling he couldn't breathe he headed outside and paced the back of the boat.

The boat screamed toward the beach. At the last second, the helmsman threw it in reverse, stopping the boat in the shallows. Jason charged over the side with Mike and the team behind him. They spread out down the beach then started into the trees. Running as fast as the terrain would allow, Jason yelled, "JJ! It's Jason. Where are you?"

Hearing one of the guys down the way yell, he hurried in that direction. Several officers stood outside a ramshackle shelter with the door open. He pushed his way inside. JJ sat on the ground, a blindfold pulled down around her neck and cut ties around her ankles. An officer bent behind her to cut her hands free.

Jason squatted in front of her. "Hi."

"Jason." Her eyes filled with tears.

He wiped her cheeks. "You're okay now."

One of the officers handed Jason a water bottle. He cracked it open and handed it to JJ, noting her wrist wounds as she drank.

She struggled to her feet. "Get me out of here."

He helped her up. The officers cleared a path.

The water curdled in her stomach leaving her retching outside the shack. Leaning on Jason, he guided her to the beach.

Mike and the team bagged the evidence. It took several trips to get it all aboard.

Over her shoulder, he watched the evidence procession for a moment then looked back at her face. He pulled her into a tight embrace.

Pressed against his chest she said, "I thought you were dead. Kellie checked your pulse and said you were dead." She sobbed.

"I'm right here. And I'm definitely alive."

She put her hands on his face. "You're real."

"Yeah honey, I'm real."

She dropped her hands to his chest. "You found me."

"It's been a lifetime, but I've found you." He held her face, searching her eyes.

Her eyes filled with fresh tears. "I can't believe you're alive."

"It's all over now. They've got Kellie in custody. You're safe now." He pulled her in and gently pressed his lips to hers.

She could feel his heartbeat. Her head swirled then everything went black.

Jason caught her before she fell to the ground unconscious.

One of the passing cops said, "Nice one. No girl ever fainted over any kiss of mine."

Mike gave the young man a stern look then joined Jason at JJ's side. "Is she okay?"

"I think it's just a faint. She could be low on electrolytes."

"Let's get her onboard. We've got some Gatorade."

Mike arranged for a rescue helicopter to take both of them to the trauma hospital in Miami.

CHAPTER 30

Jason pulled into the dive shop parking lot. "These guys have everything, tons of wetsuits and scuba gear."

JJ nodded and hopped out of the Land Rover.

Jason's phone rang. "Hello?"

"Hi Jason, it's Mike."

"Oh hey Mike. How are you?"

"Good. I've got some news for you."

"Sure."

"Oh hang on. I have to put you on hold."

Jason called to JJ walking ahead. "Mike says he has news, but he's put me on hold."

They sat down on a bench.

He said, "I can't believe it. The cop shop plays muzak."

Spotting something in the empty parking space in front of them, JJ indulged her curiosity and investigated. She brushed the white sand away and picked up multiple pieces of obsidian glass. Sitting on the bench she assembled them on her lap.

"Yeah Mike, I'm still here. What's up?"

The two larger pieces fit together, but the smaller pieces took several attempts to find the right fit.

"Uh-huh."

It's a heart, I think. Who would want a black heart?

"Oh my goodness. Well –"

She fit together all the pieces.

A badly broken black heart in the white sand.

"Yeah, okay. Yeah, she's right here. I'll tell her. Thanks, Mike."

When he hung up she said, "What's the news?"

"Kellie was scheduled for sentencing tomorrow. They

found her dead in her cell this morning. It was suicide."

She bent her head. "Look what I found while you were getting the news."

"A broken heart."

"A discarded black heart that ended up shattered. It's many pieces discovered in the white sand of the Florida Keys. Kind of like Kellie, don't you think? Discarded. Shattered. And finally exposed in the white sand of the Keys. "

"She's got some pretty sharp bits."

"Deadly bits." She tried pressing all the pieces tighter together. "There weren't any deadly points until she was crushed."

"As a child."

"Yeah." She played with the pieces. "I think I'm going to keep it. This is how I want to remember her. I have more sympathy when I see her this way." She continued looking at the shattered lava glass. "Do you remember that ripped in half photo of Kellie and how she drew a black heart in marker?"

His eyebrows briefly flashed up and he nodded.

"Perhaps God showed this to me so I can find my way to forgiveness. Not that I'm there yet, but maybe seeing her this way will make it easier. She was badly broken before she did any harm. Just getting close to others, her sharp points inevitably injured."

"And killed." Jason went back to the vehicle and ripped a piece of paper out of his notebook. He folded it into an envelope. "Put them in here."

She carefully swept them off her leg into the open pocket. "Thanks."

Sitting with her journal in her aardvark chair, she pondered Kellie's suicide and the events leading up to it. She remembered Eulah's tiger vision.

One meaning of the tiger was my fear of losing Jason, but Eulah felt there was another meaning. Like Kellie, that she-tiger stalked me my whole life, constantly knocking me down. But in the shack, God, You said her time is done – that she'd never touch my life again. And now she's dead. She disappeared like the tiger.

But there was something about the colours. God, this vision was from You. So what do the colours mean?

She poised her pen, ready to write.

The dark yellowy-green was envy. She envied the love and attention you received and let it take a deep root into her heart. It caused the first break. The pink was a passionate hatred. It brewed and boiled within her cracked heart, shattering it into shards. Envy and hatred set her on her evil course.

She paused her pen. "And I'm a cerise blooming lotus flower. That's quite a stark difference." She looked out over the bay. "It's amazing how love transforms. But for Your grace, this black heart could be me."

Yes, everyone starts out with a heart bent away from Me, but you chose life. You chose truth. You chose Me. And that's made all the difference.

JJ thought,

Thank you for pursuing me. Thank you for putting Eulah and Jason on my path.

She watched a sailboat motor out of the bay.

God, forgive me for my hatred of Kellie. I don't want this hatred to fester and damage like it did in Kellie. Please sweep away any sharp, black bits in my heart and help me grow the sweet bits.

Jason quietly approached. "I brought you a tea. Mind if I join you?"

"Thanks." She smiled and nodded.

They watched several boats pass. She reached for his hand. "I really like my aardvark chair. It's one of my top three birthday presents ever."

With his thumb he adjusted the Tango turtle bracelet and smiled.

CHAPTER 31

Six Months Later

The radio station organized a Community Karaoke in the Park evening. Dan and Jason arrived at 6:30 to pick up Ang and JJ. On the way Dan told them he had an early shift in the morning, so he'd be the designated driver.

Tables were filling up fast, but they found one near the front. The guys headed to the bar to get drinks for everyone. When they handed the girls the beers, Ang said, "Here's to JJ's one-year anniversary in the Keys."

JJ's eyebrows shot up. "I guess it has been a year. Cheers everyone." Three beers and one bottle of coke clinked.

They danced, talked and laughed.

An hour later, the boys visited the bar again and came back with four beers. It surprised Ang to see Dan with a drink.

He said, "I'm only having one. Don't worry."

Jason left the table and headed for the stage. JJ looked at Ang and Dan. "Do you know what he's up to?" Ang shook her head.

Jason took the mic, and adjusted the height. "Hi everyone. I'm Jason."

The rowdy crowd answered, "Hi Jason!" He laughed.

Behind JJ, two guys set up a video camera. They gave Jason the thumbs up.

He nodded. "How many people here are with someone they love?"

The crowd erupted. "Yeah. Me too." His bass voice vibrated the speakers.

"There's a lady here tonight who has totally stolen my heart."

A female voice to the left shouted, "Say it ain't so, Jason."

Looking toward the voice in the dark he leaned into the mic. "Sorry."

He turned toward his friends. "JJ –" He pointed to her. "This year has been – amazing." The crowd hooted.

He held his hand to his chest. "You fill a hole and make me complete. So I dedicate this song to you." He nodded to the DJ.

JJ sat stunned, her hands covering her gaping mouth. Ang looked at Dan and mouthed, "Did you know anything about this?"

Dan smiled and nodded behind her. She glanced back and saw the camera. She whirled back to Dan. He held his index finger to his lips. "Shh."

The DJ spun up the song *Ends of the Earth*.

Jason sang the opening line about life being an endless river taking him to unimaginable places. He winked at JJ, then pointed over the crowd while rocking out the rest of the verse.

JJ said, "He's imitating me." She caught his eye and pointed back at him and mouthed the word brat.

When he came to the chorus he sang to her, inviting her to follow him to the ends of the earth, that there's a world of things for them to see. He followed the sweet chorus with an amazing imitation of her air guitar. She shook her head.

The next verse he described the fantastic life they can have together and asked her not to leave him to explore alone.

In the third round, he proclaimed his willingness to die for her, and told how real life isn't about standing still, but getting out there. The final line he changed to, "Come with me into the unknown."

He invited her to the stage. The crowd went crazy. While she walked to the stage, he pulled a velvet box from his pocket and said, "This is the kind of box that comes with a really big question."

The crowd exploded.

She froze in front of the stage. She mouthed, "Is this what I think it is?"

He squatted down. "I promised to give you a heads up. So, yeah, this is what you think it is. Now, just head to the stairs over there." He helped her onto the stage and returned to the mic. He looked out to the crowd. "This is JJ."

From the back someone yelled, "Nice choice, man."

"Thank you." He positioned both of them in front of the mic.

He looked deep into her eyes. "JJ–"

Her eyes flooded with tears.

"You going to be okay?"

She nodded, wiping her eyes.

"Baby. My bohemian rebel with the tears, I love you and I can't imagine my life without you. You bring quite a bit of – excitement."

She laughed, wiping a fresh flood of tears.

Wiping her cheek he said, "Hang in there, I'm almost done." The audience laughed.

"You love me even though I don't have pink hair or a stuffed parrot. And though I cannot fathom it, you really like my nutty family."

He opened the box. "Will you spend the rest of your life with me wandering this earth, diving the oceans and dancing under the stars? JJ, will you marry me?"

She nodded.

He pulled the mic in close. "Sorry honey, I didn't hear you."

"Yes, yes."

He held her shaking hand and placed the ring on her finger. "Love ya, babe."

He gave her a long, passionate kiss. It slid into a hug. He whispered, "Love you with all my heart," while giving the thumbs up sign to the crowd. They exploded in howls and cheers.

He stepped back, looked out over the audience, held his hand on his heart, and leaned into the mic. "Thanks y'all."

To whistles, hoots and clapping he helped her down off the stage. They sat down to two piña coladas. The celebrations lasted into the wee hours of the morning.

On the way home Dan looked in the rearview mirror to see Jason mutter something then kiss JJ. He watched for a couple of seconds, then flicked the mirror up and reached for Ang's hand.

She said, "You don't have work in the morning, do you?"

He smiled. "No."

Jason pulled JJ tight beside him, closed his eyes and rested his head on hers.

She touched the ring on her finger.

I've finally reached the yellow head of celebration and joy. Thank you God for staying with me as I journeyed through grief. Thank you for bringing me out of the darkness of grief and restoring hope. And for delivering into my life things I couldn't imagine one year ago. Thank you for a family I can call my own. Today, I entrust them to Your care. So, what lies ahead?

A vision appeared. She and Jason were on a sailboat with a billowing yellow sail. Jesus was at the helm as they navigated down a misty river with no end. The distant shoreline on either side could barely be seen. The sun hung low in the early morning with all the promise of a bright summer day.

They tied up at a platform in the middle of the river. As the boat rocked against the mooring, crates were loaded onboard. Destiny labelled one crate, Revelation another, and several colourful crates were labelled Promises. Many she couldn't read the label.

With all the crates aboard, the platform workers tossed off the lines and Jesus set the boat to autopilot. He sat down at the back with the crates, Jason and her. "Let's open the destiny crate and see what's inside."

Jason pried off the side panel letting it fall to the deck and stood back. He reached for JJ's hand.

The brightness almost blinded her. Then she noticed there were pictures in the light, like a projector flashing images – a rainfall of vividly coloured pearls roared down. They became real pearls that poured out of the image, bounced all over the deck then floated away in the river. Next there was a huge sea turtle that swam out of the image, over the boat and into the mists ahead leaving a trail of turtle eggs that became hatchlings. JJ and Jason gave them away to passing boats. And finally a 20-foot oceanic manta ray at a feeding station glided out of the image, circled around eight times then positioned itself to swim permanently under their boat. Its enormous wingspan could be seen on either side.

What does it mean - the pearls, the turtle and hatchlings, the manta ray?

She waited then smiled. *Ah.* She closed her eyes with a sigh.

The End.

THANK YOU

If you've enjoyed *White Sands, Black Heart* won't you please take a moment to leave me a review at your favorite retailer? Thanks! Your review will help other readers decide on this book! Tell your reader friends about this book and share a story.

You can also visit SerenityMcLean.com for her full list of great fiction.

In times of grief and loss can be crushing. But God doesn't want our lives to be filled with sorrow. Thankfully He provides hope in the face of hopelessness, light in the land of desolation, and peace amidst our sorrow, anger and regret. The Bible tells us to think on things of goodness.

> *And now, dear brothers and sisters, one final thing. Fix your thoughts on what is true, and honorable, and right, and pure, and lovely, and admirable. Think about things that are excellent and worthy of praise (Philippians 4:8).*

I hope you found yourself thinking about God, your relationship to Him and your walk with Him while reading this book. What we do in this life sets us up for our eternal life. Invest your spare time thinking on the things of heaven. Keep your eyes fixed on that eternal light at the end of the valley of darkness.

In the meantime, imagine big and keep reading!

OTHER BOOKS

From the Heartwarming and Inspiring Collection

The Flawless Life

Weeping Dune

Never Midnight

Leaving Lost

Final Moments Series

Rainswept

Veiled Agenda

ABOUT THE AUTHOR

Serenity McLean grew up in Ontario and moved to western Canada in 2004. She returned to Ontario in 2017. With a Masters degree in Adult Education, Serenity worked in various roles at several colleges. She also worked in the Information Technology sector predominantly in project management. She wrote her first fictional book just before getting laid off in an economic downturn. She made a career change – committing her time to writing and helping others along the path of publication.

She took a hiatus from writing to care for her terminally ill mother and deal with a long series of losses. Born of the pain and sorrow of her grief, and combined with her education background, she wrote *Honest Grief* as a way to help others facing the hurt of deep losses. The additional pain inflicted by those around her who didn't understand grief or the deep gaping wounds of one who grieves inspired her to write a companion book, *Supporting Honest Grief.* It is written specifically for people who have a grieving friend.

Along with writing, art and photography, Serenity is a dog lover and enjoyed the sunny disposition of golden retrievers for over thirty years. Currently, she lives with one sweet goldie that loves to play hide and seek, ball chase, and of course, swimming. In the summer months, Serenity and her dog can be found on the water and under the sun.

You can follow Serenity using the links below.

She looks forward to hearing from you.

Connect with Serenity:

Website: www.www.serenitymclean.com

Pinterest: www.pinterest.com/mclean3963/

Facebook: www.facebook.com/Serenityauthor

YouTube: www.youtube.com/channel/
UCt82lzlc7NDixFAHfuFZXfg